ALPHA CENTAURI:
FIRST LANDING

a novel of early T-Space™

Alastair Mayer

Mabash Books

Alpha Centauri: First Landing

This is a work of fiction. Names, characters, places, and incidents are either the product of the author's imagination or are used fictitiously, and any resemblance to real people or incidents is purely coincidental.

Copyright © 2016 by Alastair Mayer

All rights reserved. No part of this book may be reproduced, scanned or distributed in any printed, electronic, or other form without permission. E-book editions of this book are available wherever fine e-books are sold.

Cover © 2016 by Mabash Books
Image credits:
  High altitude view of the Earth in space. © marcel - Fotolia.com
  Anderson Class Ship © Alastair Mayer
Images used by permission.

T-Space is a trademark of Alastair Mayer

For announcements about other T-Space books and special offers, sign up for Alastair Mayer's mailing list at
    http://www.alastairmayer.net/

A Mabash Books original.

Second printing, minor corrections, May 2017
First printing, October 2016

Mabash Books, Centennial, Colorado

ISBN-13: 978-153-913229-5
ISBN-10: 153-913229-3

*For Robert A. Heinlein, 1907-1988,
and Poul Anderson, 1926-2001.*

They gave me many hours of enjoyable reading, a few hours of great conversations...and helped save civilization.

Contents

Part I: Preparations
1: A Change of Plans — 3
2: The Moon — 6
3: Geologists — 11
4: Field Trip — 14
5: Departure — 16
6: Approaching Centauri — 25
7: Into the Centauri System — 34

Part II: Landings
8: Planetfall — 41
9: First Landing — 46
10: Post-Landing — 53
11: Suspicion — 64
12: Exploration — 70
13: The Smeerp Problem — 87
14: Second Down — 99
15: Underground — 106

Part III: Survival
16: Doing Geology — 111
17: A Murder of Crows — 115
18: Mayday Received — 120
19: No Walk in the Park — 122
20: Weather Forecast — 134
21: A Night Out — 135
22: Day After Crash — 142
23: Continuing Adventures of Fred and Ulrika — 147
24: The Storm — 156
25: Singing in the Rain — 161
26: The Return — 177

Part IV: Departure
27: Leaving — 186
28: Discussing the Findings — 195

29: Preparations	211
30: Goodbyes	217
31: Landing	221
32: Home Again	224
Epilog	227
Glossary	229
Acknowledgments	232
Preview: *Alpha Centauri: Sawyer's World*	233

ALPHA CENTAURI:
FIRST LANDING

Part I: Preparations

Chapter 1: A Change of Plans

Commodore Drake's office, Centauri Mission HQ, Earth

"No, I do *not* want that man on the mission!" Elizabeth Sawyer all but shouted. "He's an egotistical, sloppy, stubborn, irreverent . . . jerk!" Then, obviously remembering she was talking to her commanding officer, added: "Sir."

Commodore Franklin Drake took a deep breath and let it out slowly. "Look, Elizabeth, I know he's your ex. I know you guys had some, uh, interesting screaming matches. But with Doctor Grainger out of commission, we need a well-qualified exobiologist. George Darwin has the expertise and space experience. I know you're both intelligent enough to be able to get along. It's not like you ever came to blows."

Sawyer's smile tightened. "I'd have kicked his butt if it had."

Drake had no doubt of that. Commander Elizabeth Sawyer was a powerfully-built woman, with years of field geology under her belt before her astronaut training.

"What about Wallace?" Sawyer continued. "Can we get him back? And who let Grainger's backup go this close to the Centauri mission launch anyway?"

Drake shook his head. "Politics. When Wallace heard about possible lifeforms under the ice on Enceladus, there was no holding him back. He pulled strings to get on the next mission. I'm sure he'd much rather go to Alpha Centauri but it didn't look like that was going to happen. Our international partners had no problem with it, of course—"

Sawyer snorted. "Not if they had a chance for one of their own to do the first footstep if something happened to Grainger." She paused a moment. "It *was* an accident, right?"

The thought startled Drake. There *had* been plenty of political bickering over who would be first to set foot on an extrasolar planet, but it was the United States who had developed a workable warp drive. It had also been an American robotic probe which returned from Alpha Centauri with images of not one, but *two* Earth-like planets in that system, apparently complete with life forms. The partners had agreed to let an American take the first footstep on whichever of those they landed. It was also agreed that should be an exobiologist. But now Grainger's backup was on his way to Saturn, and the next most qualified exobiologist was either European or Chinese. There might be some motive to arrange an accident. Still, Drake couldn't bring himself to believe anyone with access would stoop to that.

"Yeah, almost certainly. Of course it's being investigated, just like any other on the job accident. Anyway, George Darwin has been designated as second backup all along."

"But he's in charge of the Lunar Quarantine Lab. People who don't know George like I do might think he'd prefer that to doing the first footsteps. He's had his fame and glory, and he's the boss of the facility that will be first to get its hands on whatever alien specimens the Centauri mission brings back. I can just imagine some Eurocrat thinking that's a preferred position to being stuck in a tin can for up to six months." Sawyer shook her head again. "Gods, I don't want to be cooped up with that man for that long."

"You know you won't be. A week to Alpha Centauri, a couple of weeks of preliminary survey, then he'll be down planet-side until it's time to return. Everyone's going to be busy." Drake could tell that she wasn't convinced. He knew they could handle it; they had on the Mars mission, which had been longer. Under any other circumstances, Elizabeth Sawyer was one of the most even-tempered people he knew. But there was one other point.

"Sawyer," he said, "it's out of my hands. The higher ups insist on Darwin. If you don't think you can handle it . . . well, you have a backup too."

Her eyes flared, and she slammed her palm on his desk. "No!

I will not be bumped from the mission because of that man." She settled back in her seat. "We'll be fine, on our best behavior." She muttered something else, which Drake didn't quite catch, but it might have been "or I'll break his arm."

"All right. I'm counting on both of you not to let me down." Drake made some notations on his computer. He should break this to Darwin in person, to make sure he got the whole message too. He would have to review his task list, to see what else could he get done while on Luna. But first. . . .

"Speaking of crew assignments," he said, "how are we coming on plans to redistribute the European contingent amongst the remaining ships?"

"So we're not waiting on the *Jules Verne*? I can't say I'm sorry."

The European ship, the *Jules Verne*, had run into problems during its interplanetary shakedown testing. Waiting for repairs would push the mission back several months.

"No. Our taxpayers don't want to wait, and the Chinese, Russians and Indians aren't willing to either. Their ships are ready. The *Verne* is to be held in reserve. Maybe they'll send it out if we're not back in six months, but some of the crew comes with us."

"Okay. At least they didn't name it the *Perry Rhodan*."

Drake snorted. For a while, that had looked like a real possibility, because of a popular campaign. Just as *his* ship had almost been named the *USS Enterprise* instead of the *USS Robert A. Heinlein*.

Chapter 2: The Moon

Interstellar Quarantine Facility, on the Moon

Drake finished suiting up for the walk from the lander to the base itself. At any other base on the Moon, there would be a docking tunnel or some other convenient way of getting from the ship to the buildings without going outside. Here, though, the short trip outside was part of the quarantine protocol. If something got loose in the lab, it would be that much harder for it to get back to Earth.

It was also a pain in the ass.

He exited the airlock and bounced along the surface to the lab. At least they'd hardened it—"paved" wasn't quite the word, it had been sintered using focused sunlight—so he wasn't kicking up dust at every step like the first time he'd set foot on the Moon. How many years ago had that been? Too many.

He was expected, of course, and some minor assistant was there to help him out of his suit as he cleared the lab entrance.

"Welcome to the Moon. We weren't given details of your visit, just that you were arriving. What can we do for you?"

"Later I'll want a tour of the facility, I expect to be spending some time here when we get back from our mission."

"Of course, sir. Um, you said later? Was there something first?"

"I want to pay a visit to an old friend. Where's Darwin's office? I'll find my own way."

"Uh, Director Darwin is a busy man—"

"So am I, and I outrank him. I also want to surprise him. Now, which way?" Drake felt a little bad about taking that tone, but what was the point of having rank if you couldn't pull it once in a while? The aide gave him the directions and he set off down the high-ceilinged corridor.

∞ ∞ ∞

Darwin's office

"You've gained weight since Mars, George." Drake said.

Darwin looked up from his desk, scowling. Then he recognized the unexpected visitor at his door and smiled. "Captain Drake! I didn't know you'd arrived, I'll have to talk to someone about that. Come in. What brings you here?"

Drake entered the office and seated himself in the chair across the desk from Darwin. "It's Commodore Drake now, actually. Commanding a fleet and all that, if a small one." He paused a moment, glancing around the high-ceilinged office, taking in the spider plants hanging in the corner, the pictures on the wall. Most were scenes from Earth, of Darwin in unusual environments. Hot springs, a glacier. He recognized one, a bleak rocky landscape in shades of red with a pinkish sky. Two space-suited figures posed for the picture; Darwin and himself. "You have *that* picture on your wall? I get tired of seeing it."

Darwin glanced over his shoulder at it. "That's why it's behind me. It's to impress visitors, my glory days."

"Don't say that, it makes you sound like an old man, and where does that leave me?"

"In my office trying to avoid telling me why you're here when I thought you had a starship to make ready."

"You're right," Drake said. "Neither of us was ever much for small talk. How would you like to go to Alpha Centauri?"

The look on Darwin's face was almost worth the trip in itself. It managed to combine deer-in-the-headlights with complete disbelief with a kid seeing the presents under the tree on Christmas morning.

"What? In what capacity? You've got an exobiologist."

Drake shook his head. "Actually we don't. Grainger managed to fall off the descent ladder in a rehearsal exercise. He broke some bones and punctured his spleen. He's not going."

"Is he all right? No, stupid question."

"He's fixable, but waiting for him would push back the schedule, and our international partners don't want to wait. China and the European Union have already offered replacement exobiologists."

"Hah, no way that's going to happen." The first ship to land would be the Indian vessel *Subrahmanyan Chandrasekhar*, but the privilege of first footstep would go to the mission's lead exobiologist. "But what about Grainger's backup?"

"Wallace? Last month the Enceladus exploration team found signs of life under the ice. Since it looked like he wouldn't be needed on the Centauri mission he lit out for Saturn as soon as he could get authorization. We could get him back—Saturn is at least on the same side of the Sun as we're going, although we're headed out of the ecliptic—but I decided to offer the slot to you first. I know it's a bit of a demotion, but—"

"No, no. I mean, sure, I'd have to give up the glamour and excitement of running the Interstellar Quarantine Lab, but I'm willing to sacrifice to help out an old friend."

Drake snorted. "Right. The opportunity to investigate two planets' worth of alien lifeforms first hand has nothing to do with it."

Darwin smiled. "Well, maybe a little." He sat forward on his seat, sobering. "Okay, how long do I have to transfer operation of this lab, and what's my training schedule going to be?"

Drake wasn't surprised at how quickly Darwin had gotten down to business. It was one of the things he liked about him. He pulled a data chip from his pocket and placed it on the desk in front of Darwin. "The details are all in there. You already have plenty of space experience, and you're one of the best exobiologists in the business, so your focus will be the detailed mission plan—"

"Okay, I know some of that from how it ties into the LQL requirements for when you, or we, get back. And I developed the mission biology protocols."

"I know. The only other thing is general starship systems, although aside from the warp drive it's not much different from what we went to Mars in."

"Oh, and about that," Darwin said.

"Yes?"

"The gravity is lower here. I've *lost* weight since Mars."

Drake laughed and shook his head. "All right. Read through the briefing on the chip and contact me later today." He turned to leave, then stopped and turned back. "There is one other thing."

"What's that?"

"Elizabeth Sawyer is on the mission team. Will that be a problem?"

The deer-in-the-headlights look came back, this time without being combined with the kid on Christmas morning. So much for being happy to see her again, Drake thought.

"In what capacity?"

"My second in command, and geologist. Look, I know you two can get along in public. And for all the screaming matches, it never got physical, right?"

A wry grin crept onto Darwin's face, like he was remembering something. "Well, not in *that* sense. She'd have broken my arm."

Drake remembered something he'd once heard about makeup sex being the best kind. Fortunately his dark skin didn't show a blush. "I don't need to know any other details. So, no problem?"

Darwin's expression sobered. He looked a little like he'd swallowed a bug, but said: "No, no problem at all."

∞ ∞ ∞

One problem down, a dozen to go, Drake mused as he left the quarantine lab. The planned six-ship fleet was already down to five, after the problems with the European craft *Jules Verne*, leaving him to rearrange the crew to ensure a European presence, and ever since the robotic probe, Nessus, had returned with pictures of not just one, but two Earth like planets in the Centauri system, the taxpayers were anxious to see a mission get out there and "boldly go where no-one had gone before".

More importantly, at least to the United States government, was the concern that China and perhaps other nations were close to discovering the secret to creating a stable warp field. Without warp technology to bargain with, the Chinese-designed compact tokamak fusion reactors necessary for a manned warp ship might suddenly become unavailable, giving China a monopoly on interstellar flight. The fission reactors that powered the Nessus put out too much radiation to be used within the limited confines of a warp bubble with humans present, and their relatively limited power reduced both the size of that bubble and the available speed. Not a problem for a robotic probe, but unworkable for sending a crew beyond the solar system.

Politics. Drake hadn't gotten where he was by ignoring it, but that didn't mean he liked it.

Chapter 3: Geologists

Centauri Mission Headquarters, Earth

Sawyer's omniphone beeped at her. She glanced at the screen on her wrist, it was reminding her of a meeting with Fred Tyrell, another of the geology crew. *Already ahead of you*, she thought, as she entered Tyrell's office.

"So, Fred, anything new?" The man before her had the characteristic leathery skin of someone who had spent more time in the field than in the classroom or laboratory.

"I've been going over the geology manifest. With the extra crew member our mass allotment has been cut by over a hundred kilos. That seems excessive, especially considering that the biology team has been similarly cut."

"It's not just the mass of the crew member. We're adding a couch and life support reserves. I know it sucks, but it's what we've got."

Fred sighed. "Yeah, I realize that. At least we're not totally eliminating any of the experiment packages, just reducing the redundancy somewhat. For example, we're only taking half the geophones and seismic charges you wanted to."

That would cut into their ability to do detailed subsurface profiling, and who knew what interesting clues to the planetary history. "That's unfortunate. What about the ANT gear?" That would give them a gross picture of the planetary interiors, but nothing fine grained.

"No change there. The neutrino detectors are built into the ship. Even if we wanted to take them out it would delay things too much. As long as we have a working reactor to generate anti-neutrinos, we're good."

"And if we don't, we have bigger problems," Sawyer said. "What else?"

"What do you think of cutting the equipment on the fliers? There's a lot of sensor gear there. If we cut out either the multispectral scanner or the ground imaging radar that's a good percent of our weight right there."

Sawyer considered this. The fliers were electric ultralight aircraft, powered by photovoltaic film in the wings, and modified from a commercially available model to fold up for storage in the lander. She hated to lose any of the sensor gear. "If we take out one of those, could we rig the flier for an extra passenger? Might come in handy."

Fred's brow furrowed as he thought about it. "It'd be heavier with three people, but it might be workable. We want to make sure we have margin. The radar is heavier, and the biologists will care more about the multispectral anyway."

Personally Sawyer cared more about the ground radar. Overlying vegetation, which the radar could see through, often hid interesting geophysical details. But the multispectral scanner could also reveal things about surface chemistry. And it didn't hurt to keep the biologists happy—she winced as she remembered who the new lead biologist was—it was the fact that there were clear signs of life in the Alpha Centauri system that was driving the mission, after all. "Okay," she said, "let's do the biologists a favor."

"Speaking of biologists, I have a training session with them tomorrow. We're going on a field trip."

"You're teaching them geology?"

"Yes and no. Surprisingly, there's not a paleontologist in the bunch."

"But I thought—"

"Oh, sure, they know some, especially in their own specialties, but no field paleontologists. They want me to show them what to look for in terms of possible fossil-bearing formations. Actually, I think they wanted you, but you've got your hands full."

"Tell me about it. So what did you have in mind?"

"A couple of ten- or fifteen-kilometer hikes through some

interesting formations. I'm limiting it to what's most likely to be in range of the landing areas, so nothing too arctic." Orbital mechanics meant keeping the landings away from the poles to maximize their payload.

"Okay. By the way, I don't know when he's due Earth-side, he may already be back, but George Darwin is now leading the biology team. He's Grainger's replacement. If he's back he'll be joining your field trips, he needs time with his team."

"Darwin?" Tyrell's expression suggested that he wanted to add some comment but wasn't sure if he should. He settled for saying: "He's been on the Moon for what, several months now? He won't have his Earth legs back yet. I'll go easy on him."

"Don't." At Tyrell's startled look, she realized that had sounded more mean-spirited than she'd intended. "The planets we're going to are Earth sized, and we'll be spending two weeks or so in zero gee before we get there. He's going to need to rebuild his muscles before that. He'd tell you the same thing." Knowing Darwin's stubborn pride, she had no doubt of that.

Tyrell still seemed skeptical, but nodded. "All right. I hope for his sake he's been keeping up his exercise program."

"He was a fanatic about it on the way to Mars. The man's a born overachiever."

"And you're not?" Fred said, then looked down and mumbled "Sorry".

Sawyer wasn't offended. "Yes, I guess I am. That's probably why we got along so well," she with a wry smile.

Chapter 4: Field Trip

Geology Field Training Site 1, Earth

Fred Tyrell surveyed his troupe of biologists, who stood looking expectantly at him in the morning sun. He waited as the rotor throb of their helicopter faded in the distance. He'd met all of them before at various training and orientation sessions, of course, but except for the American crew, he didn't know any of them well.

There was Dr. Jennifer Singh—they all had at least doctorates in one field or another—the botanist, part of the Indian contingent. George Darwin, of course, who didn't seem in the least perturbed standing there in gravity six times what he'd been living in for the last few months. *We'll see how long that lasts*, thought Fred. Xiaojing Wu, the Chinese microbiologist. Then there was Dr. Ulrika Klaar, whose picture could be in the dictionary beside the definition of "Nordic beauty". Tall, with long, straight, almost platinum blonde hair which normally hung loose to her waist but now was done up in a more sensible braid. Fred wondered if she'd get it cut before the mission left, long hair could be a hassle in zero gee.

It hadn't occurred to Fred before, but looking out over the team he realized the disproportionate representation of females in the biology team. He shrugged. Nothing wrong with that.

"All right people, listen up," he said. "We're going to head north for about eight kilometers to where the chopper will be waiting to take us to the next site. It's not a race but it would be nice to be there in time for lunch. We'll be traversing a mix of rock types, from sedimentary to igneous—" Dr. Singh coughed and raised her hand.

"Yes?"

"Why igneous? Surely there would not be any fossils in igneous rocks?"

"In general you'd be correct." At least somebody was paying attention. "We certainly wouldn't find fossils in granites or basalts, although it helps to know what isn't biologically of interest too. However a lava flow or volcanic ash-fall can preserve larger structures like trees, or footprints, and I'm sure George or Xiaojing could tell you all about microfossils near hot springs."

"Of course, thank you."

"No worries. If anyone has questions, just call them out, let's keep this informal."

He checked the map on his omniphone, looked up at the sun as though to confirm his sense of direction, and gestured toward a low hill a few hundred meters away. "All right, let's head out that way." He began lecturing as they hiked. "What we're walking on is shale, where it shows between the vegetation. It's a layered stone, made from mud and clay, with a lot more silicate than your limestone, and where it does show fossils they can show a lot of fine detail . . ." Fred had given lectures like this often enough that he could probably do them in his sleep. It occurred to him that they wouldn't be relying on their omniphones much on the planets of Alpha Centauri. They'd have satellite photos and some location information from the ships that remained in orbit, but nothing like the network of navigation satellites which girdled Earth. Perhaps he should throw in a lesson on reading a compass. At least the planets they were going to had magnetic fields.

Chapter 5: Departure

Interstellar Quarantine Facility, on the Moon

"Director Darwin, I wasn't sure we'd be seeing you before you returned from Alpha Centauri."

"That's ex-Director now, Doctor Kemmerer is the Director."

"Of course. It was a courtesy title. So, one last look around before heading off into deep space?"

"Something like that. Does Charles know I'm here?"

"He does. He had planned to meet you here himself but got called away at the last moment. He said he'd be back as soon as he could."

Darwin sighed. "I know how that goes."

At that moment Charles Kemmerer came in through the hatchway leading to the rest of the base. "George, welcome back. Sorry about not being here in person," he said, shaking Darwin's hand.

"No worries. And I'm not here to jog your elbow. Mostly just give the place a once-over, and to congratulate you."

"Congratulate me? On what?"

"You're no longer Acting Director, you're confirmed as the full Director of this place. I can't have two jobs at once, so my resignation as Director here has been accepted, I'm now the 'Director of Field Exobiology for the Alpha Centauri Expedition'."

"Well, thank you, and congratulations to you too. And you're welcome to it. This is about as far as I want to get from Earth," Kemmerer said.

"Ha! Fair enough. So, shall we go say hello to a few folks? And if you have any questions, now's your last chance to ask them."

With that, the two left the reception area and headed down a hallway in an easy low-gravity loping walk. Darwin had to watch his step. His month on Earth had altered his muscles and reflexes, but the method came back to him, like riding a bicycle.

Kemmerer picked up the conversation. "I was your deputy for six months, I probably know where more bodies are buried than you do," he said, and grinned. "But how long do you have? When we heard you were coming, some of the gang wanted to throw you a bon voyage party."

Darwin smiled at that. "I'll be back here in a couple of months, albeit as an inmate rather than Director—"

"Guest," Kemmerer interrupted, "or perhaps at worst patient. Inmate sounds a bit . . . depressing."

"Guest, then. I need to leave tomorrow to rendezvous with the *Heinlein* and the rest of the fleet, but sure, I'm up for something informal this evening."

∞ ∞ ∞

The going away party was indeed small and informal, as Darwin had hoped. The staffing level at the facility would rise when the Centauri crew was due to return, and many of the technicians involved in the construction had already departed, so what was left was a small maintenance crew of technicians and biologists to maintain the samples they'd be testing for exposure to anything brought back from Alpha Centauri. It was similar to what had been done for the first few Apollo Moon landings a century ago.

Toward the end of the party, Kemmerer produced a small gift-wrapped package and handed it to Darwin.

"What's this?" Darwin asked, taking the package.

"Go ahead and open it. It's too late for your Mars trip, not that you needed it, and we hope you don't need it at Alpha Centauri either."

Puzzled, Darwin shook the package gently. It didn't rattle or make any noise, and whatever was inside felt moderately dense. He had no idea. He tore the wrapping off and opened the small specimen box inside, then laughed.

"A *potato?*"

"Yes, *Solanum tuberosum*. We had extras."

Darwin grinned and held it up for the others to see. "Thank you all. I may have briefly been a Martian, but I'm no Mark Watney. Let's hope I don't need this."

That drew a round of applause and congratulations.

A short while later Darwin bid everyone his goodbyes and retired to his room. He'd be leaving first thing in the morning.

∞ ∞ ∞

Aboard USS Heinlein, approaching the fleet

Darwin had rendezvoused with the *Heinlein* in orbit above the Moon several hours ago, now they were approaching the area beyond Luna where the rest of the fleet, and a handful of support vessels, were gathering. He watched through a viewscreen as they drew closer.

The interstellar ships were all similar, a cylindrical midsection with a rounded, conical forebody and widening aft to a curved heat shield with engine nozzles around the periphery, very similar to a popular class of commercial single-stage-to-orbit vehicle used in Earth-to-orbit operations. Three of them were designated as landing vehicles, with over half the volume taken up by the chemical fuel tanks for landing and take-off, the deep space plasma thrusters not having sufficient force to lift a vehicle from an Earth-sized planet, and the warp drives only being useful well away from atmosphere.

The landing vehicles—*Chandrasekhar*, *Krechet* and possibly the *Anderson*—were each fitted with a large fat cylinder which completely circled the ship and held the warp drive units and a tokamak-based fusion engine to power them. Officially this was the IPM, or Interstellar Propulsion Module, but everyone referred to them as warp collars, or donuts. A ship would undock from its warp donut and leave it in orbit during its time on-planet, to save weight for the return launch. Darwin chuckled to himself as the comparison came to him, of an ice-cream-cone rammed through a donut, although that really wasn't a fair comparison. The ships were wider and shorter.

The design of the *Heinlein*, and of the Chinese ship *Xīng Huā*, was subtly different. Never intended to land (except on the Moon after they'd returned), the warp and fusion systems were built into the structure, and the space which would have been taken up by chemical fuel tanks became additional cargo space.

∞ ∞ ∞

The fleet, beyond Lunar orbit.

Drake looked over at Darwin, who was watching the viewscreen. It would be nice to have some idle time like that. The previous month had been a blur of final shakedown flights, crew re-integration, supply loading, fueling, and countless reports. There had also been far too many bureaucratic meetings for Drake's comfort. Finally here they were, a million kilometers from Earth.

As the support ships retired to a safe distance from the Centauri expedition fleet, Drake left the cockpit—*bridge*, he told himself, *we're using nautical terms now*—to inspect the *USS Heinlein*'s interior one last time. She looked good.

He drifted back into the bridge area and strapped himself into the center couch. His second in command, Elizabeth Sawyer, had already strapped in and was reviewing the checklist on one of her screens. "Darwin, straps?"

"Right." Darwin had been wearing them loosely, at this reminder he pulled them tight.

Drake scanned his display console. One screen showed his ships own displays, an other showed telemetry summaries from the other ships. They showed everything in readiness. The center screen was set to a fleet-wide teleconference, giving him views of the ships' captains.

Given the status displays, verbal confirmation was a formality, but a socially necessary one. "Commander Sawyer, is the *Heinlein* good to go?"

"That's affirmative, Sir. All systems go."

"Thank you." Drake unmuted his microphone. "All ships, this is Commodore Drake. Please stand by to report status. *Xīng Huā?*"

"*This is Lee on the* Xīng Huā. *We are go.*"

"Thank you. *Krechet?*" The Russian ship.

"*Da,* Krechet *is go.*"

"*Chandrasekhar?*"

"*Affirmative, we are prepared.*"

"*Anderson?*" The second US ship, a backup lander, captained by his old friend, Geoff Tracey.

"*The* Poul Anderson *is go.*"

"Stand by, Fleet." Drake muted his microphone and said in an aside to Darwin, sitting on his left: "I've wanted to say this for years." He tapped the mute button again. "All ships, prepare for warp!"

The four other ships of the fleet were positioned at the corners of a square three kilometers on a side, with the *Heinlein* in the center, like the five-side spots on a six-sided die. "Take your aim point precisely at Alpha Centauri B." The two stars were a few seconds of arc apart, amounting to hundreds of millions of kilometers. Drake wanted everyone going in the same direction. "Our first hop will be a short one. We've all calibrated our systems individually; let's see if our calibrations agree. At ten second intervals from my mark, engage warp for exactly one thousand milliseconds." That would take them some seventy million kilometers, or about four light-minutes. "We'll coordinate at the second rendezvous."

The calibration flights had fine-tuned the ships' alignment scopes, their warp module mounts, and the warp fields themselves. But there was no way to see or steer while in warp, so maintaining formation was impossible.

How much they spread out in this first jump would give Drake some idea of what to expect on the longer hops..

"Okay, at ten seconds from my mark, *Heinlein* will warp first. At ten second intervals after that, the *Xīng Huā,* then *Krechet,* then *Chandra.* The *Anderson* will take up the rear." Drake paused, watching the countdown timer on the control panel. His next word was redundant; the other ships would have already synched up to the clock on the *Heinlein*. As the last digit flipped back to zero, he said it anyway: "Mark!"

∞ ∞ ∞

Elizabeth Sawyer sat with her finger on the warp button. That was as redundant as Drake's speech had been—the sequence was programmed in to all the ships—but there was something fundamentally satisfying about a manual override button, even if that button was itself connected to the computers. She watched as the timer counted down from Drake's mark. As it reached five, she counted aloud: "Warp in four, three, two, one, now!" Even as her finger mashed down on the button she felt a strange tingling jerk, like being mildly startled. *Probably just adrenaline*, she thought. The counter ticked over the next second and she lifted her finger. She looked over at Drake. "Secured from warp."

Darwin piped up from the other seat. "Are we there yet?"

Jerk, she thought. *What did I ever see in him?*

∞ ∞ ∞

To the other ships of the fleet, it was as if the *Heinlein* had just disappeared. One moment it was there and then, without a sound, without weird stretching effects, without even a flashy light display, it was gone. It left just a faint glowing trail from solar wind particles kicked to higher energies by the edge of the warp field. The trail faded almost immediately. At the specified ten-second intervals, they too each in turn disappeared in a faint violet flicker.

∞ ∞ ∞

Darwin watched the aft "window" view-screen. The sun, a glaring disk behind them, disappeared and then reappeared, perhaps a third smaller. They'd certainly moved. But where to?

"I want a navigation fix," Drake said, voicing Darwin's thought. "I want to know exactly how far we jumped and in which direction. At the ten second mark start hailing the *Xīng Huá*."

"Roger that." Elizabeth's voice, smoothly competent. That was part of what had attracted him to her in the first place. Darwin would have been tempted to add "hailing frequencies open" just to lighten the mood, but he suspected it would have the opposite effect with these two, if they even got the reference.

∞ ∞ ∞

Sawyer scanned the navigation data. The ship's sensors quickly identified distant reference stars. Alpha Centauri hadn't moved at all, and Sirius and Canopus were within a fraction of an arc-second of their previous positions. The Sun was still too big a target for an accurate fix, but it gave a ballpark which was refined by locating Earth, Jupiter and Saturn. She tapped out a sequence on her keypad.

"Got the fix, sir. We went 71,501,000 kilometers, that puts our speed at 238.5 cee."

"Thank you. Less than optimal but within tolerance. How's our angle?"

"Dead on, as best I can tell. No more than a twentieth of an arc-second off, perhaps less."

"Excellent."

An indicator on her panel lit up and she heard another voice on her headphones. "The hail from *Xīng Huā* is coming in now."

"Okay, get their position and stand by for *Krechet*."

∞ ∞ ∞

All ships completed the first jump without a hitch, confirming the results of the shake down flights. A one percent speed difference between the fastest and slowest ships would mean a ninety minute difference over the trip's six-and-a-half days in warp, but they wouldn't be doing it in a single leap. After tweaking the navigation and control systems to compensate for differences, they'd enter warp for a few hours and then regroup. Drake knew they would end up spending hours travelling on the plasma thrusters at the rendezvous points, to join up after each hop in warp, but that was better than ending up at the Centauri system spread over a distance equivalent to that from Earth to

Venus.

Drake led the fleet in progressively longer jumps. A light-hour, taking them further from the Sun than Jupiter, in fifteen seconds. Ten light-hours, over twice as far from the sun as Neptune and well outside the "edge" of the Solar System, took two-and-a-half minutes. The longer jumps also gave them a feel for travelling while in warp. The windows and viewscreens showed nothing at all but for the occasional sparkle of energy as a dust grain disintegrated under the tidal stress at the edge of the warp bubble. There would be some minor radiation exposure from that, but not as bad as what they'd get from cosmic rays in normal space. It would take something big to cause a problem, and their path took them well away from the asteroid belt or any cometary debris streams. In short, warp travel was boring, which is just how Drake and the other ships' captains wanted it.

A twenty-minute jump took them a hundred light-hours, further than the old Voyager probes, and now that the robotic Alpha Centauri probe was back in Earth orbit, further out than anything made by man.

Finally....

"All right," Drake announced. "We've spent enough time paddling in the shallows. At this rate we'll run out of life support before we get there." That was an exaggeration. "Next jump is one quarter light-year; four hours and twenty minutes. We'll rendezvous again for a full systems check. If everything is in order, we'll take the rest of the trip in half light-year hops. I like to look out the window and actually see something once in a while."

That got a polite chuckle. But there was also a practical reason: the ships couldn't communicate with each other in warp. Even if a radio signal could penetrate the warp bubble without being scrambled to mere noise, it would be like the pilots of two supersonic jets trying to shout at each other.

The stops would also let them recalibrate their aim points. Alpha Centauri A and B were in almost eighty-year elliptical orbits around each other; in the four-and-a-quarter years it took light from them to reach Earth, they would have moved over twenty degrees around their orbits.

They would likely be giving Alpha Centauri C, better known as Proxima Centauri, a miss on this trip. While a tenth light-year closer to Earth, it was at a considerable distance from the more interesting, apparently life-bearing worlds orbiting A and B. Proxima did have a planet, but it orbited so close to its red-dwarf primary that life was unlikely. Certainly none had been detected. It was considered a "target of opportunity" in the mission profile if they had time and consumables to spare before returning to Earth.

Chapter 6: Approaching Centauri

Interstellar Space, aboard the USS Heinlein

"All ships," Drake broadcast, "This is the last big jump into the Alpha Centauri system. We want to arrive one AU from the system center of gravity, toward B, then we'll take it from there." One AU, astronomical unit, was the average distance from the Sun to Earth, about 500 light-seconds. The system center of gravity was, at this point in their mutual orbit, about nineteen AU from B and sixteen AU from the slightly more massive A. The planned jump would place them in a clear middle ground, too far from either star for objects to be in a stable orbit around one or the other, and close enough to the system center to be clear of anything orbiting both.

Drake gave the specific coordinates and then waited the several minutes for all ships to confirm their alignment on the target. "Usual jump sequence, starting thirty seconds from my mark. . ... Mark."

Again, at ten second intervals, the five ships winked out.

∞ ∞ ∞

Drake checked the clock on his screen. Sawyer had secured from warp a full two minutes ago, everyone should have checked in by now. They'd heard from two of the other ships, but were still waiting to hear from the *Anderson* and *Xīng Huā*. A slight variation in the warp direction or timing could make a difference of a million kilometers or more, but even the *Anderson*, last ship to jump, was a full twenty seconds late calling in. *Xīng Huā* should have checked in already, it was first in the sequence after *Heinlein* itself.

The communicator chirped and Drake looked at the speaker. "Calling *Heinlein*, this is the *Anderson* checking in." Twenty seconds late, they were almost six million kilometers away if that was all radio lag. Where the hell was the *Xīng Huā*?

"Sawyer, acknowledge that and broadcast this to all ships. Please close up formation on the *Heinlein*, and if anyone has had contact with the *Xīng Huā*, let me know at once."

"Yes, sir," she said and began relaying the messages.

The remaining ships cruised to close with the *Heinlein*. The *Anderson* was not as far away as their radio delay had indicated, it had just been a minor delay in making their jump, nothing serious. They'd rendezvous in an hour.

Drake considered the alternatives. The *Xīng Huā* had entered warp, the other ships in sequence had seen her go. Did they miss-time the jump and end up several light minutes short or long? If so, it might take them a while to determine their position and then warp again to the rendezvous. That was unlikely, the *Xīng Huā*'s crew knew what they were doing, but that was more probable than anything else. However: "I want all sensors aft and periodic scans in a full sphere," he said. "If the *Xīng Huā* makes a peep I want to hear it. And keep an eye out for anything unusual."

∞ ∞ ∞

It was the gamma ray pulse, three hours later, which let them locate the *Xīng Huā*, or rather, what was left of her. Each ship detected a short spike of radiation, and by correlating the times at which the ships detected the pulse, they triangulated back to a spot some twenty AU behind them. A review of the logs of the aft-pointing telescopes—normally locked onto the Sun—revealed a short, intense bright flash at the same time as the gamma pulse, followed a moment later by a slower and dimmer flash and a glowing dot that quickly faded. It was too far away to get clear details, but it was enough.

∞ ∞ ∞

This is a lousy way to start the mission, Frank Drake thought. *Four crew missing and almost certainly dead, their ship missing and presumed destroyed. Damn.* Drake opened the conference circuit to the other ships.

"As you all know by now, the *Xīng Huā* has not reported in and we've detected a probable explosion on her course. At this point we must assume the worst. The loss of the *Xīng Huā*'s crew, of our friends and team-mates, is of course tragic, but my continued responsibility is the safety of the other ships and crew on this mission. To that end, we need to establish precisely what happened, at least well enough to determine if there is an ongoing threat to ourselves, or if this was an isolated incident." He looked at the screens relaying images from the rest of the small fleet. The crew were subdued and somber, understandable given the circumstances.

"So," Drake said, "what happened? Any ideas?"

One of the *Poul Anderson*'s crew signaled for attention.

"Yes, go ahead."

"This is Vukovich on the *Anderson*." The primary astrophysicist. "Our best guess is that the *Xīng Huā* encountered a large chunk of rock or ice while still in warp. The flash originated inside the radius of Alpha Centauri's Kuiper belt, if in fact it has one—"

"If?"

"This is a multiple-star system, so orbits are either close-in or further out. The gravity of the two main stars would interfere with anything like our Solar System's Kuiper belt. Besides, we're well away from the plane of rotation. There should be almost nothing in the way of cometary debris on this track, but it only takes one piece in the wrong place at the wrong time."

Drake waved his hand in negation; head-shaking wasn't something you wanted to do much in zero gee. "What are the odds on that? They must be infinitesimal."

"Yes, very small. A ship in warp passes through a given volume of space in picoseconds. The odds of anything bigger than a grain of sand being in the path, out here away from the main Oort cloud, are vanishingly small." Vukovich shrugged. "However, it fits the facts. From the pattern of flashes the ship clearly dropped out of warp before exploding. We—the physics team—think the explosion pattern would have been different if it had been the explosion itself that collapsed the warp field."

"So it wasn't an internal problem, some flaw in the ship design or construction, then."

"We can't know for sure, but I doubt it. An internal explosion would have had a different signature."

"Explain." Drake thought he understood, but this was also for the benefit of everyone else.

"Well, if the ship, or rather the warp field, had hit something fist-sized or larger, the energy release would have been intense. The tide at the edge of the warp bubble would tear the atoms apart and the energy release would be like a small fission bomb. That would explain the gamma pulse we saw, and that first flash."

"Excuse me," said Dmitri Tsibliev, commander and pilot of the *Krechet*, "but we hit matter all time in warp. We get sparkles and little bit of radiation, but is not shutting down warp field."

"Yes, but that's from tiny dust particles, pretty mild stuff. In this case the radiation surge would have been big enough to damage the circuits and *that* would collapse the warp field. Between the energy surging through the electronics, and through the deuterium tanks, the fusion reactors would overload and the tanks rupture. If the hull or the life-support oxygen tanks were breached you'd get a chemical explosion. That was most likely what caused the second flash."

"And the crew?" asked Drake.

"Already dead from the prompt radiation of the initial impact. Even if not, they wouldn't have survived the secondary explosion or the damage to the ship. That was hours ago, there was never anything we could have done. It was just incredibly bad luck."

"How bad? What was the probability?" asked Sawyer.

"Ballpark is a quadrillion to one. About the same as being hit by lightning the same day your lottery ticket won the jackpot."

Drake thought on that. "I don't like it. Shit does happen but the odds are off-scale."

"If there'd been an internal problem, the explosion signature would be different," said Vukovich. "I think it hit something. No other explanation fits."

Sawyer turned her head to look at Drake. "If that was the cause there's no risk to the other ships."

"No, probably not. Wait one." Drake muted the audio pick-up and froze the video. He wanted to discuss this with his own team for a moment.

"Damn it," he said, "this causes all kinds of problems. The mission plan was based on five ships and twenty crew members, and that's after cutting back because the *Verne* wasn't ready. The Chinese will have a fit. They might accuse us of sabotage."

"That's ridiculous!" said Sawyer. "Anyway, we have the sensor data."

"There is that. But we may have to abort the mission."

"You can't do that," said Darwin. "We just got here!"

"And we're already down four crew members, one ship and all the gear it carried." Drake reviewed the possibilities. They still had two good landers—three counting the *Anderson*—and most of the other gear was duplicated or could be substituted for. The loss of the *Xīng Huā*'s crew was tragic, but their tasks could be covered by the remaining crew. On the other hand, the safest course might well be to return immediately. That would also minimize any political repercussions with the Chinese. He couldn't just bump the question back to mission control and get an answer within minutes. He was riding in the fastest way to get a message back to Earth. He felt a sudden kinship with the pre-radio, age-of-sail sea captains of old. Out here, *he* was mission control.

He turned the audio and video feed back on.

"All right, team," he said, "we're down four crew, one ship and its gear. We could scrub the mission and return to Earth immediately, although remaining here doesn't seem to impose any additional dangers beyond what we already expected. However, we still have landers and equipment with which to fulfill at least part of the mission." Drake had been watching the monitors for the reactions of the crew. They seemed to favor the latter.

"I propose we adjourn for a half-hour. I want each team to

evaluate the impact on their individual mission objectives and the mission plan overall. Consider both the exploration mission and the return voyage. We're low on the profile for fuel consumption with our extended maneuvering here. When we reconvene I want a go or no-go recommendation on continuing the mission, and a list of mission plan amendments if it's a go. Either way the final decision will be mine. Any questions?"

"Are we going to try to retrieve the bodies?"

Drake had hoped that question wouldn't come. "No." He held up his hand to still the murmuring. "For one, there wouldn't be much left after the double explosion. Two, it's too far away to travel in normal space. It would take days to get there at maximum thrust, and we don't have the fuel to spare."

"We could warp there."

"Not into an expanding debris field. We don't want to warp anywhere near it or we might end up like they did. If we had a precise fix—but we don't—we might warp to a few million kilometers away and move in with the plasma drive, but there are too many variables both in their position and the accuracy of our warp navigation, and again, we don't have the fuel to do that and complete the mission. If the consensus is that the mission is a no-go, I'll re-evaluate, but the concerns about warp accuracy still hold. So no, much as it pains me, we're not going to try to retrieve anything. We'll note the location and orbital parameters as best we can; hopefully somebody else can retrieve them at some time in the future.

"Any other questions?" There were none. "All right, reconvene in thirty minutes. Carry on."

∞ ∞ ∞

"Okay, so what did we lose on the *Xīng Huā*?" Darwin asked. As head of the biology team he was getting a consensus on the go or no-go decision.

"You mean, besides four colleagues?" Xiaojing Wu asked bitterly. She would have been on the *Xīng Huā* if it hadn't been for the late crew shuffle because of the *Verne*.

"I'm sorry, Xiaojing, I know this must be hard on you. But

yes. I think we would honor their memory best by proceeding, but we need to be sure we have the equipment to do our jobs."

Wu nodded. "You're right. This is just such a shock." She brought up the *Xīng Huá*'s manifest on her computer screen and studied it. "A lot of this gear is duplicated; we were planning on parallel landings on the two planets." She kept scanning the list. "Damn, the DNA sequencer. We were only bringing one of those; we don't even know if Alpha Centauri life is based on DNA. That's gone."

"Okay, that would be a nice-to-have but not essential. And as you say, it's moot if the life isn't DNA based." Personally Darwin thought it most likely that it was; the conditions for early biogenesis almost certainly favored ribose and nucleic acids similar to Earth's, with perhaps some specific variation in the nucleotides. Since early in the century, biochemists had managed to create synthetic RNA and DNA strands using different nucleotides, and the DNA analyzer aboard *Xīng Huá* had been modified to work with the entire range. Whether or not the specific enzymes it used would work on alien DNA was another question, and didn't matter now. Besides, now wasn't the time to bring up old arguments.

"Didn't I hear that you built a DNA sequencer for a high-school science project?" Ulrika Klaar asked Darwin.

"I did. But I used a lot of off-the-shelf components and enzymes from lab supply companies. If we decide we need one I can see what we might cobble together by cannibalizing other equipment, but that was pretty crude. Anyway," Darwin said, bringing the meeting back on point, "that's irrelevant. We don't need a DNA analyzer to continue the mission. What else might be a show stopper?"

"The *Xīng Huá* carried one of the refueling modules. They weren't designed to return to space after they landed. Now we've just got one left, so that means only one landing."

"Damn, that's right." Technically that was something the flight team would address, but it affected everyone. "So we'll have to choose which planet we're landing on."

"But we could take both landers down to the same planet,"

said Klaar. "Maybe we could load the refueling module back aboard one of the landers, and still do both planets?"

"No, the thing masses several tons. I don't think there's any way to get it to fit even if the *Krechet* or *Chandra* could handle the mass. Nice idea though."

"We could cover more ground if the landers land in different areas, pick two biologically different landing sites." That was Wu again. Good, focusing on the problem at hand was taking her mind off the fate of the *Xīng Huá*'s crew.

"But the refueling pod would only be at one site, we're back to the same problem with landing on two planets." Darwin said.

"The crew of one could rendezvous with the other, we have the ultralights. I don't know about you or Xiaojing, but I'd be willing to do that," Klaar said.

"If something went wrong with the aircraft one of the crews would be stranded."

"So, we don't send the second lander down until everything has checked out with the first. And we could always hike, if the air's breathable."

"Let's table that for later discussion, we're getting sidetracked again. We've settled that we can only do a landing on one planet, although possibly in two locations if they're not far apart," said Darwin. He looked at the clock. "We only have a few minutes left before we reconvene. What else?"

They continued their review of the *Xīng Huá*'s manifest and what impact it might have to the biology mission. They could still proceed. The other teams would be going through the same process, and Darwin hoped they'd reach similar conclusions.

∞ ∞ ∞

"All right," said Drake, bringing the meeting to order. "Has everyone reviewed the options?" There were nods and murmurs of assent. "Okay. Understanding that we'll have to make changes to the mission plan if we go on, I want the inputs from the team leads. Just a 'go' or 'no go', then we can get into the details. Engineering?"

"We can go on."

"Biology?"
"We're go."
"Geology?"
"Go."
"Astronomy?"
"Was there ever a doubt? Go."

"Thank you. As mission commander, the final decision is mine. Proceeding at this point is a risk." He paused, looking at each of his team members in turn. Some looked eager to go on, but he thought he saw hints of doubt on other faces. Peer pressure? They were hanging on his next words. "But we knew that when we started. We go."

He heard a collective sigh of held breaths being released.

Chapter 7: Into the Centauri System

The reduced fleet continued deeper into the Alpha Centauri system in short hops. They had basic data on the positions of the planets both from the telescopic observation from Sol, and from the data returned by the Nessus robotic probe. They refined that data by imaging everything each time they moved in warp, then comparing the pictures. Anything within the system—anything big enough to be seen—would be apparent by its shift in position compared to the background of distant stars.

Aboard the Heinlein, Drake, Sawyer and Darwin were discussing landing options.

"We have photo-maps of all the planets from the Nessus probe," Drake said, "but the resolution isn't high and there are gaps in the coverage."

"Gaps?" asked Darwin. "What did it miss?"

"It was under a time constraint to return the data, as well as a storage constraint. There are parts of both habitable planets that happened to be cloud-covered each time Nessus made a pass over them. Nothing sinister, the overall weather patterns weren't the same each time, it's just that some places are naturally cloudier, or dustier, or it was nighttime, and so on. In places we do have some excellent photographs."

In part it had been some of those higher resolution pictures from orbit which had prompted the speed up in the mission schedule. They had shown vegetation and, in places, what might be herds of large animals. Just as significantly, they had detected no signs of civilization—Earth wasn't ready for a first contact. The planets and their life had been there for millions or billions of years and would be for a while yet, but the people footing the tax bills wanted to know *now*.

"Anyway," he continued, "my point is that we need to scan both in more detail to decide on our landing, especially now that we're limited to landing on one planet."

"Actually sir," said Sawyer, "we're limited to taking off again from one planet. Technically we could still land on both."

Drake eyed her curiously. That was true; they had two landers, plus the backup *Anderson*, but now only one refueling system, with no way to return it to space once it had landed. Meaning that anyone landing on the second planet—whichever they chose as second—would be stranded. "Are you suggesting we strand somebody on one of the planets? Maroon them?"

She paused, then shook her head. A short, slow movement, they were still in freefall. "I'm not proposing it, although I imagine we could find volunteers to do just that. It wouldn't even be for very long, we could return to Earth and bring another refueling platform in a matter of a few weeks, a few months at the most if they don't already have them in production."

"Months, cut off from Earth and no way to get out in an emergency. I don't think so."

"No worse than any early explorer. But no, I wasn't proposing it, just making the point that we still have multiple landers."

Drake wondered about that, but didn't press the point. "Be that as it may, we still need to decide where we're going to land. We need to prioritize targets, and that includes deciding whether to land on Able or Baker. My choice for mission safety reasons would be the smaller planet, with the lowest escape velocity. That will make it easier for the lander, both in landing and returning to orbit. That assumes there's a suitable landing site."

"There should be plenty of potential landing sites, we picked out dozens from the Nessus data," said Sawyer.

"Right, I'm not too worried, we just need to properly evaluate them. And perhaps we could use two landers, but both on the same planet—if we can find two landing areas close enough."

"And how do they get off again, they'd have to be close enough to refuel," asked Darwin.

"We could use the plane to ferry the crew to the first lander," said Drake. "You look surprised."

"That sounds like more of a risk than I thought you'd be willing to take."

"I didn't say we'd do it. It's a hypothetical we can evaluate. We would have to adjust the mission rules to minimize risk. Besides, I'd probably have a mutiny on my hands with a shipload of scientists that I wouldn't allow down to a planet."

Sawyer chuckled dryly. "Yeah, you might at that." She looked pointedly at Darwin, who pretended to ignore her.

"Let's just keep that hypothetical to ourselves for now, All right? I don't want anyone expecting something we can't do, and it's a long shot."

"Agreed," said Sawyer. "We're closer to Alpha Centauri A than B at the moment, so let's do a pre-landing survey at A first. We can also set up for the anti-neutrino tomography."

Simply put, the anti-neutrino tomography, or ANT, was like a planet-sized CAT scan. Two ships would orbit on opposite sides of the planet, one equipped with a neutrino detector and the other with a nuclear reactor optimized to emit anti-neutrinos. Differences in composition and density within the planet would, ever so slightly, affect the anti-neutrino flow differently. Most such particles would pass through the planet, and the detector, without even noticing, but slight differences could be built up into a crude virtual image of the planet's interior in the same way a medical CAT scan's x-rays did of a patients. The technology had spun off from instruments designed to help enforce nuclear non-proliferation treaties, for all the good those had done, but it was revolutionizing planetology.

"Can we do an ANT scan without the *Xīng Huā*?" asked Drake

"We still have our own reactor and the detector is on the *Anderson*, so yes."

"Okay, I'll have everyone set course for Planet A."

∞ ∞ ∞

The expedition spent the next two weeks doing detailed

analyses of the two Earth-like planets in the combined Alpha Centauri system. They established orbit around Planet A, or Able, and examined it by remote sensors, ANT scan and unmanned probes while doing a detail telescopic analysis of the other bodies in the system, but especially of Baker, the planet orbiting Alpha Centauri B. The latter was nearing its furthest distance from A, about as far as Neptune from Earth. They could cover that distance in about a minute in warp, but that would mean undocking all the ships and collapsing the inflatable docking hub. Since they were now limited to one landing, the undocking would wait until they'd decided where.

Both Able and Baker turned out to have large moons, roughly similar in size to Earth's Moon, but Baker also had a smaller satellite, much further out, about one-eighth the Moon's size.

If warranted, one of the unused landers, the *Poul Anderson*, would do close-up investigation of any other interesting bodies in the system during the *Chandrasekhar*'s stay on the surface of whichever planet it landed on, while the others would remain in orbit around the planet as a base of operations.

∞ ∞ ∞

Daily status teleconference, orbiting Able

"Physical parameters." Greg Vukovich, the astrophysicist reviewed the data for the assembled team. "Able rotates more slowly than Earth, so the day is longer. It's twenty-five hours, forty-four minutes and seventeen seconds long."

"Is that a sidereal day or a solar day?" asked Sawyer.

"Well, given that Sol is 4.3 light-years away, a solar day *is* a sidereal day, but—"

"Come on, you know what I meant."

Frank Drake thought he'd heard her mutter "as bad as George" under her breath, but he ignored it.

"As I was about to say, but I assume you mean a local Centauran day," continued Vukovich. "The time I gave you was local noon to local noon. The sidereal day is—"

"Never mind, that's close enough," said Drake. "Just shy of

twenty-six hours. Just the thing for people who complain there aren't enough hours in a day."

"How do we set the time?" Sawyer asked. "Would we just jump from 25:44:17 to 00:00:01 at local midnight, or make the hours sixty four minutes long?"

"That would give you an error of about eight minutes each day," pointed out Vukovich.

"Roll that into a leap hour each weekend."

"Or you could do a week of five twenty-six hour days with the weekend days twenty-five hours," Darwin said. "Hmm, Then use the left-over quarter-hour to give an extra hour every fourth weekend."

"What? You are wanting shorter days on the weekend? Are you a workaholic?" asked Jennifer Singh.

Drake rolled his eyes. *Scientists*. The by-play was amusing but it was sidetracking the meeting. Drake raised his voice: "All right, folks. You can do the clock and calendar reform on your own time. Let's get this back on topic. Just the numbers, please."

"Yes sir. Alpha, diameter is 13,390 kilometers, a bit larger than Earth, but density is only 5.23, a bit less. The surface gravity is 9.682 meters per second squared, about 98.6 percent of Earth's. The escape velocity is 11.42 km per second, higher than Earth's."

"Higher? But it has lower gravity."

"Yes, but the larger radius means it falls off slower," Vukovich said. "Anyway, the rotation rate at the equator is 0.45 km per second, so we can subtract that from delta-vee to orbit. It has one moon, 2876 km diameter, with surface gravity 1.322 meters per second squared, about 80% of Luna's."

"Thank you. What about Baker"

"Baker is a bit smaller and denser, 12,680 kilometers diameter and density of 5.76, so smaller but denser than Earth, giving a surface gravity of 1.028 gees. The escape velocity is only 11.35 kilometers a second, with a 0.48 km/sec rotational boost at the equator. There are two moons, the larger and closer is very similar to Luna, 3300 km diameter, gravity 1.6 m/sec-squared, or 98% of Luna's. The outer moon is a bit smaller than the asteroid

Pallas at 460 km, with about 12% of Luna's gravity. Not quite low enough to just jump to orbit, but it'll take you a while to come back down."

"Okay, I think we'll give Pallas Junior a miss. What are the mission implications?"

"The slower rotation of Able means we don't get as much of a boost when launching. That narrows the latitudinal limits for our landing area. On the other hand, Able's gravity is a little lower, so that helps. On the *other* other hand, the gripping hand, the lower density of the planet overall means a larger radius so by the inverse square law, the gravity doesn't fall off as quickly on Able as it does on Baker. The escape velocity is higher."

Drake wanted a bottom line. "So what's the net of that?"

"We'll know more after the close survey, but Planet Baker gives us approximately 130 meters per second more delta-vee to play with. For what it's worth, A's light in the night sky of Baker will be brighter than B's light on Able, although both are way brighter than the full moon on Earth. Fortunately we picked the right time of their years to get here." It hadn't entirely been good luck, the Nessus probe had returned enough data on the orbits so that the timing was a driver in the overall mission schedule. "Anyway, I'd suggest Alpha Centauri B II."

"Good. If the biology and geology teams have learned all they can from orbit here, let's pack up and head for Baker."

Part II: Landings

Chapter 8: Planetfall

Centauri Station

The ships orbited above Alpha Centauri B II, also known as Planet Baker, all now docked together to form what they called *Centauri Station*.

"All right, choice of landing site." Commodore Drake had the combined crew assembled in the docking hub, the largest clear volume on the now-linked ships.

"Wasn't that decided before we left Earth?" asked Darwin. He'd been more focused on the quarantine requirements of the return until he'd been pulled in as the replacement lead exobiologist.

"Not exactly. There were recommendations based on the pictures and imagery returned by the Nessus probe, but that was a list of some dozen possibilities and subject to change depending on what we found when we got here. Conditions change, weather changes, the planet is in a different season than when those pictures were taken, and so on." Drake flashed a list up on a large monitor screen. "Sawyer's the planetologist, I'll turn this briefing over to her."

"Thank you. Here are the absolute criteria. Any landing site has to satisfy these simply to meet operational limits and mission safety requirements. One, local geography. We need reasonably flat terrain. No hills, cliffs, rock outcrops, ravines, etc, etc. A dry lake bed would be ideal—"

"But there would be nothing to see there!" Jennifer Singh exclaimed. "What would be the point?"

Sawyer held up her hand. "Relax, let me finish. Obviously we're going to land somewhere more interesting, I'm just going over the requirements; I want you all to be aware of the constraints and what's optimal.

"Now, as I was saying, a dry lake bed would be ideal from a mission safety perspective but, as Dr. Singh suggests, boring, and we'd miss one of the operational requirements to make as broad a survey as possible. Which brings me to the other geographic requirement. It must be near a broad mix of terrain types, including both land and ocean. However, we don't want to land on soft ground or somewhere we'd have to worry about high tides or rogue waves." Drake brought up a display on a second screen, a Mercator projection map of the planet below them. "Now, we're not landing in the polar regions because of launch constraints, we need to take advantage of the planet's rotation to get the most lift back to orbit, same as launching from Earth."

At the planet's rotation rate, the equator was moving nearly a half-kilometer per second compared to its north and south poles. That speed was automatically added to any vehicle launching from the equator, which could make a significant difference in the payload a rocket could carry to orbit. Since the return craft would have none of the usual ground support of an Earth launch, it would be at operating at the limits of its performance to return to space. The further north or south of the equator they launched from, the less payload they could carry back, until further than sixty degrees north or south, depending on other conditions, they couldn't make orbit without leaving something significant behind, even with the assist of the planet's rotation.

"So, that said, we've reduced our choices as follows." Sawyer clicked another key and the top and bottom of the map display were overlaid with red, as were the oceans, inland areas, and mountain ranges. "River delta areas might be a great place to site possible future settlements but until we evaluate flooding risk and surface stability, they're ruled out. We don't want to land in a swamp." Several areas on the map, where major rivers met the sea, were overlaid with orange.

"That still leaves two dozen possibilities, everything from coastal desert to jungle. Jungle's obviously out because we need a cleared area to land." More of the map turned red. "We have three survey drones to check out potential landing sites."

"What's the range on the drones, can we check out more than one site with each?"

"They're solar-electric—"

"Don't you mean Alpha Centauran electric?" Darwin piped up from the back.

Sawyer scowled. "All right, smart ass, they're photovoltaic. The point is they have indefinite range but they're not fast and they could run into bad weather or whatever. If there are two potential sites within a couple of hundred kilometers of each other we might be able to cover them with a single drone, but we need to prioritize. I want recommendations back from both your biology and my geology teams for the top five sites. If we're lucky we might even agree on a couple." '

∞ ∞ ∞

Ultimately they chose a landing area on a broad flat river valley, about five kilometers wide and sixteen long, with only low vegetation. Low tree-covered hills surrounded it, with the range higher to north. Beyond that was denser forest. The small river bisecting the valley wound through a gap in the hills to the ocean fifteen kilometers further downstream. They had a small inflatable boat, electric powered, virtually identical to several commercially available models on Earth, but the initial forays would be on foot or by air. Their plane—big brother to the drone, with room for a pilot and passenger—could follow the river to the coast, and orbital inspection suggested they could land on the beach. The one concern was that the valley might be subject to flooding if the river rose, in the spring perhaps, but the nature of the vegetation implied that it wasn't likely, and since it was late-spring in this hemisphere and they weren't far from the equator, meltwater floods wouldn't be a concern until months after they'd left.

The river was also a source of fresh water, when suitably filtered. They had desalinators for the ocean water should they need them, but this would be one less variable. They'd also need water to electrolyze, to break down into hydrogen and oxygen to replenish their fuel supply for the launch back to orbit.

∞ ∞ ∞

Sawyer and Patel were doing a final site inspection by remotely piloted drone, to avoid surprises on landing.

Over their shoulders, Singh watched the on-screen view. Sawyer piloted the drone across the broad valley a hundred meters above the ground, its radar penetrating the low, grass-like vegetation to track for potholes or small boulders that might cause trouble for the lander. There were a few scattered trees, but it wasn't until the drone reached the end of the valley and banked over the hillside that Singh got a closer look at what was growing on the slopes.

"Are those *pine* trees?" she exclaimed.

"They sure look like pines," said Sawyer, "but isn't this area a little warm for that? No snow."

"True pines, yes, but related species grow in warm climates on Earth. Hawaii has Cook pines, *Araucaria columnaris*, although they are not native. But on an alien planet?"

"Sure, why not? What's it called, parallel evolution?"

"Convergent evolution, but yes. It's very surprising."

"If it is anything like pine, that could be handy for building materials."

"What do you mean, like a log cabin?" Singh shuddered. "No thank you."

"Hey, it's a step up from a sod house, but I was thinking more as feedstock for composites," Sawyer said. "Throw some cellulose pulp into a large-size fabber and have it build whatever you want. Okay, it may not be cellulose, being alien and all, but it has to have similar properties, or it wouldn't be a tree."

"Trees without cellulose. Now that *is* an alien concept." Singh said and grinned.

Patel brought them back to the task at hand. "We are not going to land in the trees. Let us go back up the valley."

"Right," said Sawyer, and continued the turn back to the general landing area. They surveyed the valley until they had identified a clear area about a kilometer in diameter, then commanded the drone to drop a homing beacon near its center. The package landed and unfolded itself, then extended a telescoping mast upward. The top of the mast contained sensors for wind speed and direction, which the beacon would transmit to the refueling package as it descended.

The refueling package was a small unmanned lander all its own, about a third the size of the crewed landers. The non-landing ships, *Heinlein* and the late *Xīng Huā*, had each stored one in an area taken up by fuel tankage on the other landers. The package contained a small nuclear power supply, pumps, electrolysis gear and cryogenic systems, everything needed to create the liquid hydrogen and oxygen propellants that the personnel lander would need to take off again. The *Chandrasekhar* would not descend until they were certain that the refueling gear was operational. The refueling package also contained a more sophisticated instrument package, which together with the original beacon would guide the *Chandra* to a pinpoint landing.

Chapter 9: First Landing

When the fleet was being designed and built, the political considerations had been almost as difficult to overcome as the technical problems.

The warp engine technology was American, although India, Japan and China were probably close to developing their own. The compact fusion engines that would provide the enormous power that the warp drives needed were Chinese, based on the toroidal tokamak concept. Other nations had fusion prototypes but nothing as compact or power-dense as the Chinese systems, and size was a key design constraint. Neither the Chinese nor the Americans were eager to give up their respective technology monopolies, but they were willing to work out a limited mutual sharing agreement and retain a duopoly on the core technologies for interstellar travel.

All the involved nations had manned space capability, with certain components or subsystems being the particular skill of one nation or group or another. Electronic systems were largely Japanese, reentry technology was split between the Russians and Americans, the Russians also contributed to life support. India and Europe contributed software with Europe also contributing general systems design, The docking hatches were based on a standard that traced back to the original International Space Station.

The five ships fell into two design classes. All had a docking mechanism at the forward end. The command ship, the *Robert Heinlein*, also had a central hub in its forward area with four additional docking ports arranged equidistantly around it, and another on the far forward end. The other ships could all dock to it in a cross or plus formation, providing a continuous pressurized volume connecting the ships, much like the early space stations. The *Xīng Huá* had also followed this configuration with the docking ports. In both the *Heinlein* and *Xīng Huá*, the fusion generators and warp drives were integrated into the ship.

This contrasted with the design for the *Chandrasekhar*, *Krechet*, and *Anderson*. None of the ships had the capacity to carry separate landing craft to take the explorers down to the surface of the planets and bring them back again; the requirements of launching from an Earth-like planet were too great. Instead, these starships were designed as landing—or rather shuttle—craft first, and the necessary fusion and warp systems were built into a separate ring-shaped module, the "warp donut," that could detach and reattach to the landers. This design had the added advantage, to Chinese and American eyes, of keeping the details of fusion and warp technology limited to China and America.

The baseline mission plan only called for two landers, with the third held in reserve as a rescue vehicle should that prove necessary. With two operational refueling stations, they could land one on each planet and conduct the exploration in parallel, reducing overall stay time in the Centauri system.

The landing shuttles themselves were based on the "plug nozzle" or aerospike designs first proposed as long ago as the 1960s by Phil Bono, and periodically dusted off, refined, and even flown by early private aerospace pioneers. On reentry—or rather entry—the broad curved base of the ship would act as an aerobrake and heat shield, much like the old Apollo, Soyuz and Dragon space capsules. Liquid hydrogen was pumped through cooling tubes on the back of this heat shield, and the resulting hydrogen gas vented through the circumferential engines to protect them. The engines would power up just before landing to control the final descent to the surface.

To return to space, the heat shield or "plug", surrounded by the ring of thrusters would act as an inside-out rocket nozzle, and aerodynamic forces acting on the exhaust would provide additional thrust. That the overall design of the landers, with their attached interstellar modules above the base, made an efficient fit to the teardrop shape of the warp bubble was a happy plus.

∞ ∞ ∞

"*Centauri Station* this is *Chandrasekhar* ready for undocking." The five-person exploration crew were in their seats, the forward hatch at the docking station was secure.

"*Roger* Chandra, *we're all buttoned up too. You are clear for undocking.*"

Ganesh Patel, captain and pilot of the *Chandrasekhar*, reached over to his control panel and flipped the "Arm" toggle. A bright red border lit up around the edge of his screen to warn that the controls were now live. He touched an icon on that screen and heard a ripple of "clank" sounds as the docking latches retracted, and felt a small nudge as the mechanism's shock absorbers pushed the *Chandrasekhar* back. He let that small impulse drift the ship back three meters and then gently tugged the hand controller to give an additional burst of speed. "*Chandrasekhar* is clear, we are moving to separation position."

The ship glided back until it was five hundred meters from *Heinlein* and the others, then Patel pushed the controller forward briefly to stop the motion. One of the control displays showed a schematic of the connections between the Interstellar Propulsion Module and *Chandrasekhar* proper.

"Initiating the separation sequence now." He pressed a button and felt a series of thumps and vibrations as valves closed, cable connectors detached, and clamps released. He followed the activity on the screen, and released a breath he hadn't realized he was holding when everything went green. If there'd been a hangup at this point, the *Chandrasekhar* wouldn't have been landing.

"Everything is clear," he said. "I am passing control of the IPM to you *Heinlein*, on your mark."

"*Thank you* Chandra. *Mark.*"

Patel pressed another button, directing the computer aboard the IPM to take commands from the *Heinlein* until further notice. It would hold here in orbit until *Chandrasekhar* returned.

"All right, I am clear of the IPM, how I am looking?"

Cameras on the Propulsion Module focused on the heat shield/plug nozzle of the *Chandrasekhar*, doing a last inspection before reentry. Patel could see the image on his screens just as well as anyone on the station could on theirs, but it didn't hurt to get a second opinion.

"*You're looking good,* Chandra," came the response. "*Continue retreating to safe distance and let us know when you're ready for deorbit burn.*"

"Affirmative." Patel adjusted the controls and glided the *Chandra* further away from base. It had to be clear enough to avoid any chance of damage to the other ships from its main thrusters, and as a safety margin in the unlikely case something blew up. So far it was as routine as undocking from a space station.

∞ ∞ ∞

Forty-five minutes later, *Chandrasekhar* had reached its designated orbit some kilometers below and ahead of *Centauri Station*.

"Chandra, Centauri Station *here, your orbit looks good and you're coming up on your burn window in twelve minutes. We'll confirm your state vector at t-minus ten, coming up in ninety seconds from the mark. Mark.*" The state vector was the collection of orbital parameters, altitudes and angles that would line the *Chandrasekhar* up for an optimum burn, placing them as close on track to the landing site as possible.

"Roger that."

A few minutes later, the radio sounded again. "*Okay* Chandra, *everything looks good. You are GO for entry burn.*"

Patel's face widened into a huge grin. He looked around, the others were smiling too. This was it. "Thank you very much. *Chandra* is GO for entry burn."

He toggled the switch which authorized the computer to initiate atmospheric entry, and poised his finger over the manual engine fire button.

"In five. Four. Three. Two. One. Fire."

Even as he pushed the button, he felt the whine of the turbo-pumps on the retro engines spool up and the growing vibration and roar as they fired. The force pushed them all back into their seats, but gently. The ship slowed in its orbit and began to drop toward the surface of the planet.

The engines throttled back to idle as the ship continued its descent, and as the air grew thicker the ship started to tremble and buffet. Through the view ports the dark black of the sky began to lighten, taking on an orange pink tinge as the air heated to incandescence by their passage. As the orange light grew brighter he felt himself pushed back further into his seat, the gee force rising.

He scanned the instruments. "On track and on target; entry is nominal."

They continued their plunge toward the alien planet below. The vibration became stronger as they encountered thicker atmosphere, and with it turbulence. The guidance computer started to throttle up the engines. The gee force increased.

Out the window the orange glow started to fade and flicker, with a deep blue behind it. As the ship continued to slow and sink into the atmosphere, the orange faded completely to be replaced by a deep blue.

"The sky is blue," one of the landing team, Darwin, remarked.

"Of course it is, Rayleigh scattering," said Sawyer. "The sky's always blue on an Earth-like planet."

"That sounds boring. And just how many Earth-like planets have you visited?"

The dark blue began to pale, and wisps of cloud could occasionally be glimpsed. Patel scanned the panel again.

"Ten thousand meters, we're looking good."

"*You're GO for landing,* Chandra," the call came over the radio. Which was good, since they didn't have the fuel to make it back to orbit.

"Roger. We have the beacon. Landing radar is good. Locked in." In a pinch, Patel could fly the landing manually. It would be tricky, but possible. As it was, with the landing radar and the beacon and weather info from the ground, the computers could do it all just fine.

After a few minutes, the gee force faded; they were at their optimum velocity for approach. "Five thousand meters, throttling up," said Patel. "Sawyer, please call the numbers."

"Roger that," she acknowledged. She would read the numeric displays so that he could concentrate on the landing area.

The engine noise got louder and there was a brief gee surge as the ship slowed.

"Three thousand, range five kilometers," Sawyer said, They were still coming in at an angle, which should straighten up soon.

"Coming down, two thousand, range one point five kilometers."

"Fifteen hundred, one kilometer," Sawyer continued the call out.

"One thousand meters, right over the target."

The ship was now in a vertical descent directly above the chosen landing spot. "Okay, coming down," Sawyer confirmed. "Seven hundred meters, four hundred."

The trick was not to slow down too much too soon, or you'd run out of fuel before running out of altitude, which would be regrettable.

"Two hundred. One fifty."

He throttled the engines up. Below them the exhaust started to scorch the ground.

"One hundred. Fifty. Thirty. Fifteen."

The engine noise rose to a loud roar and through the window all he could see was dust, smoke and steam. They must be close now.

"Five, three. Contact!" The enthusiasm in Sawyer's voice at the last contrasted with her earlier deadpan updates.

He felt a bump as the landing pads touched the ground, a little unevenly, then a brief surge as the ship threatened to lift again. He reached the ENGINES OFF switch just as the engine valves shut under computer control, and the ship dropped back to the ground with a thump. Somewhere below he heard a crash as of some inadequately stowed equipment jarring loose and hitting something. The motion stopped. The engines were quiet.

Patel heard the muted tick and ping of cooling metal.

"*Centauri Station, Chandrasekhar* has landed," he called over the radio.

Around him the cabin rang with whoops and cheers.

Chapter 10: Post-Landing

Chandrasekhar landing site

The atmosphere had been extensively scanned and examined from orbit via spectrograph, sniffed and analyzed and chromatographed and tasted by remote landers, and deemed breathable. There was one more test before any crew members ventured outside without breathing gear.

"The tests all look good," said Darwin. "Let's deploy the canary."

It wasn't really a canary, that traditional bird coal-miners had used as a warning against the buildup of toxic or explosive gases in mines, but rather a specially bred white lab mouse. It was genetically just as sensitive, perhaps more so, than a canary and closer in physiology to humans because it was a mammal. There wasn't—to the limits of their instruments, which were enormously sensitive—anything in the atmosphere which would kill humans any faster than the usual trace brew of natural toxins and industrial pollutants in Earth's atmosphere, or even in the air they breathed aboard ship, but there was something psychologically reassuring about seeing the caged white mouse, exposed to the outside air, happily running in its exercise wheel and otherwise acting like a healthy critter. That it didn't suddenly turn green and sprout alien fungus from inhaling some exotic spore was a great relief.

"I officially pronounce the mouse still alive and healthy," Darwin said some hours later. "Mission biology chief gives a GO for EVA."

Of course, they would have to wear their purple Biological Isolation Garments, BIGs, for the first few days. They would take enough samples and run enough tests and culture enough specimens to be confident that nothing fast-acting was going to infect them. In theory, biomedical science was advanced enough that anything slow-acting could be isolated, analyzed and neutralized before much serious damage was done. Before setting foot back on Earth, they'd be confined to the Lunar Quarantine Facility for an extended period, but it was larger and more comfortable than the sealed trailer the returning Apollo Moon astronauts had been restricted to. The concern was an alien biology that might be just alien enough to evade easy detection by sensors designed to look for Earth-biochemistry life-forms, or to evade treatment by techniques developed for Earth organisms, but yet not so alien that Earth biochemistry wasn't something it could feed on.

∞ ∞ ∞

"Remind me again," Sawyer said, struggling with the bright pink suit she was donning. "The air tested out, the mouse didn't die, so *why* do we have to wear these stupid quarantine suits?"

The official name for them was BIG, Biological Isolation Garment, an echo of the same-named suits worn by returning Apollo astronauts to ensure that any germs they'd picked up on the Moon didn't contaminate Earth. They were plasticized fabric, a bright fuchsia color for visibility, with self-contained breathing gear. One advantage they had over the old Level-A biosafety suits that they resembled was that large panels of the fabric were a smart material, with nanopores just big enough to let individual water molecules through but block anything else. At least the wearers wouldn't dissolve in their own sweat.

"Just because the mouse didn't die right away," Darwin said as he fastened his boots, "it doesn't mean it hasn't picked up some disease that will kill it horribly in a week."

Sawyer paused with her seal half closed. "Do you really think that's possible?"

"I'd be extremely surprised, but I can't rule it out. We also don't want to expose the Centauri life to us until we have a better idea of how it will react. It would be a shame if our common cold virus goes through the native life like the Black Death. Of course, that's unlikely too."

Sawyer finished fastening her torso seal and reached up to flip down the hood. "At least it's not space suits."

Darwin and Sawyer finished sealing themselves up and inspected each other's suits.

"Okay, let's do it," Sawyer said. "One small step for a person and all that."

Darwin shook his head, a motion barely visible through the hood of his suit. "You had to bring that up, didn't you. I still have no clue what my famous first words should be."

"Just don't claim the place in the name of Queen Isabella."

"Thanks."

They opened the outer hatch and Darwin turned to descend the ladder, Sawyer helping him to find his footing in the bulky quarantine suit. "I wish they'd chosen some other color for these suits."

"It's for the visibility."

"I know, but there's a 'famous first footstep' coming up, and I'm going to be recorded forever in that picture looking like some kind of purple dinosaur."

"It's more pink than purple. But come on back, I'll go first." Sawyer smiled when she said that, she didn't really care.

"Never mind. Okay, I'm at the bottom of the ladder now. The ground cover near the base of the lander is scorched, of course. There don't seem to be any insects, but again, our landing exhaust probably took care of that. We'll see what we find farther out.

"Okay, I'm going to step off the ladder now." He reached down and out with his foot, and stepped down. "And so life from Earth takes its first step out into the galaxy."

∞ ∞ ∞

"'Life from Earth?' Well, it's no 'giant leap for mankind'," Sawyer said after she'd joined Darwin on the surface.

"Give me a break. I was going to say 'mankind' or 'people from Earth' but I was there on the bottom of the ladder, looking out at the stuff growing in the landing field, and remembering what we'd just discussed about cold viruses, and it just came out. You know, it's not like the video feed is going back to Earth live, we *could* edit it out and do over."

"No, no. It was great. Here, let me give you a hand with that."

They had begun unloading gear from one of the external equipment lockers. The first order of business was to sample everything in the vicinity and analyze it for toxicity and biological activity. One key test would be growing—or trying to grow—whatever passed for the native equivalent of bacteria in culture dishes, and then see if they could *stop* it from growing using common antibiotics. That would give them some confidence that if they did pick up a local infection, they could stop it.

Working in the BIGs turned out to be easier than Darwin had thought it might be. The suits were thicker and heavier than the biosafety garments he'd worn when called in to help inspect a suspected biohazard site. That had been rather gruesome. A road crew had uncovered a mass grave which appeared to date from the war. Everybody had worried about biological warfare agents, since there was no record of a nuclear detonation in that area. It had turned out to be the aftermath of a nasty chemical spill, a too-hasty cleanup and misfiled data rather than a biological agent, but there were a couple of tense days before it had been sorted out.

Heavier though the suits were, the thicker fabric with tougher gloves and built-in knee pads meant that he didn't have to worry about tearing the suit on a sharp rock every time he knelt down, or about puncturing a glove, and perhaps himself, on a thorn while taking plant samples.

With the preliminary samples gathered and returned to the airlock to be disinfected and conveyed to Doctors Singh and Finley—Singh had won out over Xiaojing Wu for the extra biology slot since the *Chandrasekhar* was an Indian ship—for further analysis, Sawyer and Darwin began the next phase of the landing; connecting up the refueling system.

∞ ∞ ∞

They had landed half a kilometer away from the refueling package. From orbit they had been no sign of large animals on the plain, but they kept a wary eye out. Chances were that the noise and exhaust from their landing had scared off everything that could move.

"Hiking on a planet around another sun," Sawyer said. "Did you ever think you'd see the day?"

"It is pretty amazing. But you know, it just doesn't feel alien enough. Mars felt more different. Here we've got a blue sky, a yellow sun . . ." Darwin said. "I know mentally that it's bigger and brighter than Sol but it just doesn't look much different."

"It's orange, and smaller. You're thinking of Alpha Centauri A. It looks the same size because we're a little closer to balance the temperature, and it's so bright you couldn't tell the difference with the naked eye anyway."

"Oh, right. See, it looks so similar I forgot the difference. Anyway the gravity doesn't feel much different, especially after two weeks in microgravity, and while this field we're walking through isn't grass or any plant I recognize, it could still be an Earth plant. It's got green leaves, not blue or pink."

Sawyer found herself agreeing. The ground cover they were walking through wasn't anything like grass. Most of the plants were ankle to knee-high, a single main stem, greenish-brown, with leaves in opposing pairs projecting horizontally every centimeter or so. In fact it reminded her of some ornamental plant she'd seen in flower arrangements on Earth, but had never learned the name of.

The refueler was just a few meters ahead of them now, the surrounding vegetation flattened and charred from the lander's exhaust. It stood comfortably on its four landing legs, a squat platform with odd geometric shapes of the machinery housings upon it, a mast extending upward with various sensors.

She checked her computer pad and tapped out a command. On the lander, a panel dropped open to reveal a screen and some controls. She walked over to it and entered a sequence, putting the lander through a diagnostic routine. Theoretically that was redundant. The lander had been thoroughly checked out from orbit; had been anything wrong, their landing would have been scrubbed. Still, it was good to know that nothing had changed between then and now.

"Okay, it looks like we're good to go," she said. "Now we just walk it back to the lander."

She meant that quite literally. One of the thorny issues of the mission plan was the fact that the refueling system had to be reasonably close to the lander so that it could pump liquefied hydrogen into the lander's tanks without running inordinately long lengths of cryogenic hoses, and yet the refueling lander had to be far enough away when the *Chandra* or *Krechet* landed that it would neither pose a hazard to the lander nor be damaged by the lander's exhaust. The solution was rather clever. The landing legs were mounted with joints and pivots, and several key struts made of a shape-memory alloy. The motors which had deployed the landing gear could also—with a minor gear change that Sawyer and Darwin were now performing—be used to manipulate the main leg joints in a different direction. Reconfiguration complete, Sawyer stood to one side and tapped another command on her computer pad.

The lander flexed all four legs, lowering itself slightly, then straightened them. Then it raised each leg in sequence, lifting it up, pivoting it, setting it back down.

"Can you make it dance, too?" Darwin asked.

"Sorry, this thing has two left feet," Sawyer replied. "Fortunately it also has two right feet. Okay, off we go."

Slowly, with stiff jerky motions more reminiscent of a twentieth century child's toy than the fluid motion one normally saw in robots, the lander began lurching off with its peculiar four-legged gait toward the *Chandrasekhar*.

∞ ∞ ∞

They set up the refueling module twenty meters from the *Chandra*. Sawyer and Darwin laboriously unrolled the water hoses from their spools and dragged them the seventy five meters to the river.

"Wouldn't it have been easier to walk the pod down to the river first and have it unroll the hoses as it walked back to the lander?" Darwin asked.

"The soil might be softer near the river, we couldn't risk the module getting mired down or having a leg slip out and it taking a spill."

"Come on, we'd already checked out the river, the banks are solid. And we could have at least had it come a lot closer. Dragging these hoses is a real pain. Admit it, you just didn't think of it."

"I didn't hear you making any suggestions." Sawyer said. She was angry enough at herself for not thinking of it, Darwin didn't have to make an issue of it. He was right, though, dragging the hoses was a pain in the butt, especially in their pink suits.

They reached the edge of the waterway and paused.

"Now what?"

"Now we need to extend the intake hose out from the shore and keep it up off the bottom so that it doesn't suck too much mud."

"That's what the float is for, right?"

"Right, but we don't want the hose to float downstream. We'll need to rig up a mooring line of some kind, maybe anchor it with some poles."

They assembled the end of the intake hose to the self-inflating float mechanism, fastening screens over the opening to keep out anything too big for the downstream filters to handle.

Sawyer looked over the setup. It seemed a bit ad hoc. "We really need to anchor some of these poles further out, or run a rope across the river."

"We're not going wading in there until we've checked out the local wildlife."

"No, we'll do something temporary for now. But we want to get the water flowing so we can bring more power on line." The refueling pod had a nuclear reactor to power the electrolysis units, pumps, and cryogenic refrigeration gear. It also had surplus power that the *Chandrasekhar* could tap into. However, the reactor couldn't be fully powered up until sufficient water flowed through the cooling system. The water was also the raw material for *Chandrasekhar*'s propellants.

"Speaking of wildlife, I think we should set up a camera to keep an eye on the hoses and this section of the river while we're back at the ship," Darwin said.

"Good idea. We have plenty. Let's rig them with motion sensors too."

A few minutes later the camera and motion sensor were rigged, and the water platform ready to test.

Sawyer hailed the *Chandrasekhar*.

"*Chandra* this is Sawyer."

"*Go ahead*," Patel responded over the radio.

"We're done here. We've also set up a camera." She read a number off the housing. "Number one three seven. Please tap in and make sure you're getting it."

"*Roger, wait one.*" Then, a moment later: "*Very good, we have a picture. A couple of bipeds in purple suits near a river with some hoses. Looks like something out of a cheesy sci-fi vid.*"

Sawyer raised a middle finger at the camera.

"*Hey, be nice.*"

"That's the Alpha Centauran gesture for 'we come in peace'," she said.

"*Of course it is.*"

"Are you ready to run the pumps?"

"*Let me switch the power.*" They would power the pumps from the *Chandrasekhar* until they were sure the water was flowing properly, then start up the reactor/generator system and switch the power source back to it. "*Okay, we are go.*"

Sawyer gave the system a last look-over, and looked over to Darwin who gave a thumbs-up. "Okay, let her rip."

After a moment the intake hose began to twitch and vibrate, and Sawyer heard a muffled splashing and gurgling from within it. "Seems like it's flowing at this end," she said.

"*Nothing here yet,*" Patel came back on the radio. "*Wait, okay, we are seeing a flow now. It should be returning back down the discharge tube.*"

The twitching of the inlet hose smoothed out, and the outlet hose started doing a little wormy dance of its own. The river surged with bubbles at the hose outlet, then smoothed out again. Sawyer knelt down and put a hand on each hose in turn. They felt cool, and they both vibrated gently with the flow of water in them.

"We have water from end to end. Thanks *Chandra*, I'll be back there in a minute."

Sawyer turned to Darwin. "Okay, I'm going to follow the hoses back to the refueler and check for leaks, then I'll start up the reactor. Stay here and keep an eye on things until I give you a shout."

"Will do."

The hike back to the refueling pod only took a few minutes. As she got closer, Sawyer saw that the ground under the hose looked damp, and on closer inspection the surface of the hose was wet. *Damn, is it leaking?* She knelt down and ran her hand along the hose surface. It was covered with fine water droplets. *They gave us a hose that isn't waterproof?* Then she realized her mistake. The hose was cold, pulling in cool river water from below the surface. Did rivers have thermoclines? What she was looking at was condensation.

She arrived at the refueling pod and accessed the console. Everything checked out.

"Okay. Ganesh, I'm going to start up the reactor. Everything set?"

"*Affirmative, you are good to start reactor.*"

She pushed a series of controls that retracted the safety interlocks from the fuel rods, then activated the motor that slid the rods into the reactor assembly. She confirmed their positioning and then activated another sequence that began withdrawing the control rods, allowing the nuclear reaction to start building. The core temperature started to rise.

"Reactor is live, *Chandra*, how are your readings?"

The *Chandrasekhar* had a full set of controls for the reactor hard-wired via the umbilical they'd connected earlier. "*It is looking good, please ramp it up.*"

She adjusted the controls to crank up the reactor power and

switched on the generator, hearing the whine as it spooled up over the low thrum of the pumps. She gave it a minute to make sure that everything was stable.

"Okay *Chandra*, we have power, go ahead and take the batteries off line."

"*Roger that, Sawyer.*" There was a short pause, then: "*We are good to go.*"

The *Chandrasekhar* now ran on external power, and their stay time was no longer limited to the life of the on-board batteries. The next step was to process enough fuel so the whole ship could return to space.

Sawyer didn't want to start that in earnest until they had done a better job of securing the water hoses. Besides, even with the cryogenic refrigeration system and the super-insulated propellant tanks on the *Chandrasekhar*, there was no point filling the tanks just to have the propellant sitting there boiling off. However, she did need to at least run a check that the cryogenic gear and electrolytic separator was working, so that they would have time to fix anything if they needed to.

She checked the intake water filter system, then routed power to the electrolysis unit. After a minute the gauges for H_2 and O_2 production showed a build up of gas. So far, so good. She flipped a switch to turn on the ultra-Peltier pre-chiller as the compressor began cycling to squeeze the gas into the storage cylinders. With gas now to work on, Sawyer started the refrigeration pumps to ensure that they worked. The storage Dewars in the refueling pod quickly began to cool down.

"How do the tank temperatures look?" she asked Patel. The system had its own gauges, but she wanted to confirm the data relay to the Chandrasekhar.

"*They are dropping as expected. Everything is nominal.*"

Sawyer strode around the pod and opened a panel on that side, revealing a nest of plumbing. The test valve on this side ended in a simple spigot on a narrow insulated pipe. She activated the valve then turned the spigot, resulting in a thin stream of pale blue liquid which left a cloudy trail of condensing water vapor as it went. Good, the oxygen feed was working.

She shut that off and moved to another panel, with another snake's nest of tubing. Here there was no manual spigot at all, just a more complicated sequence of push-buttons to control the valve electrically. She pushed one briefly and a small jet of vapor-sheathed liquid squirted from an opening beneath the panel. Excellent, the cryogenic gear was working just as the instruments said it was.

She checked the tank readouts to confirm pressure and temperature were holding, confirmed those readings with Patel, and then shut the fueling system down and closed the panels.

"I've buttoned up the fueling system. Is external power still good?"

"*External power is good,*" Patel responded. "*I think we are go for an extended stay.*"

Sawyer smiled. Darwin, standing nearby, gave her a thumbs up. "Roger that," she said.

Chapter 11: Suspicion

Centauri Station, in orbit

"Commodore Drake, this is Greg Vukovich aboard the Poul Anderson.*"*

"Vukovich?" The astrophysicist. "What can I do for you?"

"I've been going over some data and I found something you should be aware of." He sounded nervous, almost furtive.

"Is this urgent, is there some danger?" Drake wondered what the astronomical data might turn up that was so worrisome.

"I'm not certain. I can explain it better in person, may I come over?"

Except for the *Chandrasekhar*, all the ships were currently docked to the central hub module, so that wouldn't be a problem. Drake checked his schedule for the next few hours. There was nothing critical scheduled. "Sure, I can give you a few minutes now."

With the ships docked, they had increased their living space with an off-the-shelf inflatable habitation module. Drake now had a cabin area to himself. When Vukovich arrived there a few moments later, Drake waved him to a set of foot loops. In the freefall conditions aboard the station, desks and chairs didn't make a lot of sense, instead there were soft loops on the floors and walls, for hand or foot holds, at places convenient for somebody working with the computer console.

"So what's this about?" asked Drake.

"I've been reviewing the data from the *Xīng Huá* explosion. The astronomical instruments on the *Anderson* were automatically recording whenever we were out of warp."

"The *Xīng Huá?*" Drake had been expecting something completely different, an impending stellar flare, or a too-close approach to the debris stream from a comet. "What about it?"

"I was trying to get a better idea of what could have happened. I analyzed what we have on the radiation pulse and the secondary explosion. I've also examined the spectra of stars in line with where it took place."

"Stars? What for?"

"Oh. By comparing the spectra that we see now, through the debris field, with spectrographs on record for the stars as seen from near Earth, we can see how the absorption lines change. That gives me some idea of the composition and density of any gas cloud from the explosion," Vukovich said.

"Very clever."

"Of course that doesn't account for any solid debris."

"No, of course not." Drake didn't quite get the point yet, but checking that way hadn't occurred to him. "So what did you find?"

"Well, not as much as I was expecting. I ran several simulations of a ship hitting a large object while in warp. The results of course depend on what it hit and how big, but. . . ." Vukovich's voice trailed off, as though he were unsure how to continue.

"But?" Drake prompted.

"Well, for one thing the model puts a lower bound on the size of whatever it hit to cause an explosion. On the upper end we have a maximum size constraint by what we could have observed before entering the system, and from the Nessus data. Since we didn't see anything there before, whatever it was had to be smaller than what we could detect."

"Okay, fair enough," Drake said, "but that could be pretty large."

"Right. So they had to hit something smaller than that, but bigger than about twenty kilograms." Vukovich gestured with his hands not quite shoulder-width apart to give an approximate size. "Now, assuming a normal distribution of sizes—"

"Slow down. What?" Drake was losing the direction of this discussion.

"There tend to be more small rocks or chunks of ice than big ones, and how many of each depends on size. And I just meant a usual distribution, not a 'normal distribution' in the statistical sense. It would actually be log—"

"Okay," Drake said, raising a hand and trying to get Vukovich to re-focus. "I get you. Go on."

"Well, from that we can calculate what size object the *Xīng Huá* most likely hit. The thing is, the debris cloud is too small. If it hit an object big enough to destroy the *Xīng Huá*, the object would be big enough to contaminate the debris field. But it doesn't. It would have to be at the lower end of the size scale to account for what we see."

"Okay, so it was a small chunk of rock or ice. I don't see your point." Drake wondered if Vukovich even had one.

"My point is, there's not even enough debris to account for the *Xīng Huá*."

"*What?*" That couldn't be possible.

"Between the life support reserves, the propellant tanks, and the fusion fuel tanks, I should be seeing a lot more oxygen, nitrogen, hydrogen, water and deuterium than I'm seeing. The emission spectrum from the initial gamma pulse didn't match my computer simulation for an object torn apart by a warp bubble. I ran the sim with ice, rock, a mixture of ice and rock, anything we're likely to run into out here." Vukovich suddenly paled. "Oh, sorry, that was in bad taste. The pun was unintentional."

"Don't worry about it." The pun didn't concern Drake, but the implication that the Chinese starship *hadn't* exploded did. "So, before I leap to conclusions here, are you suggesting what I think you're suggesting?"

"I don't think the *Xīng Huá* hit an iceberg, sir."

"Then what. . . ." Drake stopped himself, changing his mind about what he was going to say. "Could the gamma flash be faked?"

Vukovich nodded. "With access to nuclear material, pretty easily. Less easily but still possible with high current particle accelerator."

And the builders of *Xīng Huá* had all kinds of access to nuclear material and particle accelerators. "Could you tell the difference between a fake and a real warp impact?"

"With more data on this and real warp impacts, yes, but we weren't looking for the pulse so what we recorded doesn't have enough detail to say for sure." Vukovich shrugged. "But it doesn't match my simulations."

It occurred to Drake that with FTL travel, they could outrun the wavefront of that pulse and measure it again—except by now it was a couple of light weeks away and so too faint to detect. He dismissed the thought.

"So it's possible that the *Xīng Huā* faked the explosion?" asked Drake, then added "Hypothetically speaking, of course."

"Yes. I can't rule it out, and it would explain some anomalies."

"Damn. Those wily sons of. . . ." Drake muttered to himself.

"Commodore? If they did—hypothetically—fake it, why would they do that? Why jeopardize the whole mission?"

"They'd know we had enough redundancy to go ahead if we chose to—which is what we're doing after all. As to why—perhaps to give them leisurely access to a working warp drive. The Chinese have been trying to develop one ever since those first papers on induced space bending. As has almost everybody else, we just happened to get to it first, thanks to Brenke. But they were running close second."

"Can they figure it out from a working unit? I understand that there's pretty complex nanostructure involved." Vukovich would know the theory, of course, but not the implementation.

"There is." Franklin was privy to more engineering detail than the rest of the crew, although most of the theory was lost on him. Heck, Dr. Algernon Brenke was probably the only person who really understood both. "However, I'm sure they have labs capable of reverse engineering a warp module. It won't tell them how to build it, but they're probably close to that already, they may just need a few hints on how we solved the stability problems. And then they'll have the warp drive *and* the fusion reactor to power it."

"So, what do we do about it, Sir?"

"Do? You keep this quiet, for starters. This is all hypothetical, we have no real proof, and we don't need peoples' emotions flying off in all directions. As far as we all know, the *Xīng Huā* was destroyed and her crew all killed. People are used to that idea now, let's let it rest."

"But—"

"Oh, I'll report the possibility. Somebody will probably want to question you about it when we get back to Earth. But there's not really much we can do about it in the meantime, is there?"

"No. I see your point."

"I want to thank you for bringing this to me, Greg. That was some clever analysis. What made you think of it?"

"I'm not really sure, I was just following the data. I did wonder a bit at the unlikeliness of it all, since our paths were well off the ecliptic and the space is pretty empty. It could have been an accident, of course, but it just felt too, well, random."

"Ah. Well, let's not say any more about it for now. Thanks again, Vukovich." Drake gestured toward the door. As Vukovich unhooked from the foot loops and turned to leave, Drake stopped him. "Oh, and Greg?"

"Yes?"

"Would you make a secure backup of those files for me and restrict access to that data for now? I don't imagine anyone else is likely to be accessing it anyway, but just to be sure."

"Uh, of course. Can do."

After Vukovich left, Drake considered the situation. What he'd told Vukovich had been the truth, raising these suspicions now would be rough on the crew, either because of the level of mistrust it would raise, or the hope—possibly false—that their colleagues on the *Xīng Huā* were still alive. That would be mixed with disgust at the *Xīng Huā*'s crew for taking a lot of essential gear with them, including the second refueling pod and the DNA sequencer.

Drake shook his head. From the list of equipment that people complained had been lost with the *Xīng Huā*, that ship must have been a lot bigger on the inside than it was on the outside. Perhaps it should have been painted police box blue.

The other thing he'd told Vukovich was also true. There wasn't anything they could do about it now. They'd be back home years before any radio or laser signal they sent could get there, and the *Xīng Huā* itself, if it really had faked its own destruction, had nearly two weeks head start. By now it could have landed at the Chinese base on the Moon, or perhaps rendezvoused at some deep space location Drake was unaware of. The best he could do was to transmit an encrypted data dump as soon as they were back in the Solar system. He didn't see any particular need to let other members of the coalition know about it, he'd leave that decision to the higher-ups.

Chapter 12: Exploration

Chandrasekhar landing site

"Frank, I want to get the plane set up. We've sampled everything withing walking distance of the lander." Darwin said over the radio to Commander Drake.

"*Everything? Why do I doubt that? You're not even cleared to go out without the BIGs yet.*"

"I don't want to go far, just see which directions might be worth taking a longer hike to." Well, that and he was getting bored. The local life so far just didn't seem very alien, although mostly they'd just seen plants, Jennifer Singh's specialty. Any large animals must have been scared off by their landing, and while he'd collected a few insect specimens, entomology was never his strong suit. Even on Earth, one bug looked as alien to him as any other.

"*Admit it, you're just getting bored silly watching bacteria grow.*"

Ouch. "They'll grow fine, or not, without me watching them. We're wasting exploration time down here."

"*No, George,*" Drake said, "*you can't go flying off until the next stage of the protocol. You know that, you helped put the exploration protocol together.*"

"That's right, damn it, and now I'm saying the protocol is too conservative. I didn't know what to expect then, we've had plenty of time to investigate hazards now."

"*But if you're forced down, if your BIG rips. . . .*"

"So what? We're going to take them off in a day or two anyway. It's alien life, even if there are similarities." Darwin was sitting under the tarp of the portable lab they'd set up some meters from the ship, talking via relay through the ship's comms.

He looked around at their landing field. Nope, nothing obviously hostile. "It doesn't seem to want to eat Earth biochemistry." Not at a high level, anyway. It didn't object to basic sugars and starches. Singh was still investigating.

"Sorry George. Anyway you don't have a second pilot; I need Sawyer there at the landing site for at least one more day working on the fueling setup, and then a good part of another day to assemble the aircraft."

"I can assemble it, or Ganesh can finish the fueling setup. And I can fly it, Sawyer doesn't need to come along."

"No, that's right out, no solo forays until we know more about the planet. Come on Doctor, patience."

"What about Ganesh?" Even as he said it, Darwin knew the objections.

"He's needed at the landing site no less than Sawyer. You know that."

Darwin kicked at a clod of dirt. "Yes. All right, two more days."

"Nice try. At least three by my calculations. And Darwin?"

Not George. Uh oh. "Yes?"

"Sawyer's still first pilot for the plane. Got it?"

Darwin bit back his first thought. He sighed and said "Roger that."

∞ ∞ ∞

Three days later, Chandra landing site

Sawyer finished her assembly work and stepped back to look the vehicle over. The aircraft resembled its original commercial brethren, a fixed-wing ultralight with an electric propeller drive and solar film on the wings to provide power and keep the reserve battery charged. The flight control software had been modified so it could be tailored to the exact gravity and atmosphere of the new planet, and the navigation system had been replaced. No GPS here, but the landing craft and the ships in orbit would triangulate on the plane's tracking beacon and relay the position to them.

The plane had an open cockpit, with the two seats side by side, and big balloon tires to make it easy to land or take off from unpaved fields. In a pinch, it was light enough that the two crew could foot launch it, but the scramble to climb aboard at flying speed would make for an exciting ride. Besides, any terrain too rough for the wheels would be difficult to run on. Sawyer wondered whether such an aircraft could be fitted with robotic legs like the refueler, but decided that it would make the thing's takeoff, um, run make it look like a gooney bird, or perhaps some kind of crazed stork. No, the wheels would do.

The plane had of course been disassembled and repacked into the smallest possible volume for the voyage to Alpha Centauri, but the reassembly went quickly. Many of the joints and connectors were smart materials, the connectors self-aligned and then linked with each other at a microscopic scale to form a bond as strong as if they'd been expertly welded.

Sawyer, and for that matter Darwin, as he'd pointed out earlier, was well checked out on the little electroplane, having flown over fifty hours on it from various rough fields back on Earth, in different weather conditions. They'd also practiced in simulator mode back on the *Heinlein*.

The vegetation in the *Chandrasekhar*'s landing area was short and sparse enough that they hadn't needed to cut or clear it for a runway. Sawyer had rigged a windsock from the sleeve of a biological isolation garment, and the electroplane's flight system also received weather data from the *Chandra*'s sensors.

She noted the direction of the windsock, which mostly hung limp, and paced out the hundred or so meters of "runway," checking the ground for any hidden rocks, potholes, branches or animal warrens that might snag a wheel on her takeoff or landing roll. It was all clear.

She walked back to the plane and strapped herself into the lightweight seat. This was a test flight, not a foray. She would keep the landing area in sight at all times, so the "no solo" rule didn't come into play. Sawyer flipped on the master switch and reviewed the computerized checklist on the panel. Everything looked good, and the instruments had been reconfigured for the local gravity and air density. She slipped her headset on and keyed the mike. "This is Sawyer, comm check."

"Loud and clear. Whenever you're ready."

Sawyer slid the power control forward and the propeller spun to life with a whine. She eased off the toe brakes and the plane started to roll out, bumping gently over the occasional plant or irregularity in the ground. "Okay, rolling."

After taxiing the plane from one end of her runway to the other, she satisfied herself that the plane would hold together and could handle the take-off and landing rolls.

Sawyer pushed the power lever all the way forward and felt the plane surge in response. The vibration from the bumpy ground grew faster and more violent, then lessened as she came up to flight speed and the wings started to take the weight. She gave it plenty of take-off roll, bringing the speed up high to compensate for the higher gravity on this planet, then pulled back on the stick. The nose lifted as the aircraft rotated, then the main wheels left the ground. She was flying. She climbed out straight forward, reaching an altitude of a hundred meters before she was a kilometer from her starting point. She waggled the stick and rudder pedals experimentally. The plane responded well.

By now she was level with the tops of the hills surrounding the valley they'd landed in. She pulled up higher. At two hundred meters she had a clear view over the hills. To the west their little river snaked through a notch, the line of hills paralleling the coast north and south as far as she could see. To the west . . . ah, to the west, beyond a thin strip of what looked like sandy beach and the whitecaps of low rolling breakers, lay the ocean, the light of Alpha Centauri B glistening off the deep blue water.

Sawyer was tempted to turn and fly out there now, it would only take five minutes, but no, it wasn't part of the mission plan. Reluctantly she banked the plane back toward the *Chandrasekhar*.

The wind sock was still hanging limp and as she passed the ship she set up for her turn to final. She glided in to a smooth landing, bumping just a bit on the roll out, then braked to a stop and killed the master switch. She unbuckled and hopped out, a huge grin on her face.

"So, how does it fly?" asked Darwin, who'd been waiting on the ground.

"*Fantastic!* And the view is tremendous. We'll need to fly over to be sure, but it looks like there's plenty of beach to land on, and it extends as far as I could see. Perhaps we can fly an extended foray and follow the coast."

"Whoa, slow down. I thought I was the anxious one," said Darwin. That's great. But first let's you and me do a few circuits to get comfortable with the plane."

"Okay. Get your gear while I do a post-flight to make sure it's all still in one piece."

∞ ∞ ∞

They cruised westward at three hundred meters above the valley where the *Chandra* had landed. Darwin enjoyed the feel of the wind in his face, the whine of the motor. They'd flown a half dozen touch-and-goes and he was happy with the way the plane handled. "I see what you mean about the beach, from here it looks wonderful." They were high enough to see the beach in the distance, some twelve kilometers away. "Let's head toward it, but I want to follow the river valley," he said. The broad shallow valley where *Chandrasekhar* had landed narrowed to the west and curved south, becoming a narrow "V" that the river had channeled through the hills.

"Fine with me," said Sawyer. "Shall we take her down?"

"Yeah, I want to get a better look. Just keep it out of the trees."

"Always." Sawyer eased back the throttle and nudged the stick forward, gently diving toward the point were the river channeled into the surrounding hills. Strictly speaking, flying higher was safer, it gave you more time to react to a problem and, if you had to, more gliding range to find somewhere to set down. On the other hand, you just couldn't see as much detail from a higher altitude, and it felt like you were crawling along. It was more fun to follow the river valley, level with or even below the ridges on either side, but she stayed well clear of the treetops. The river was wider here than where the ship had landed, and the valley was wide enough for a tight turn if it came to that, but she could as easily just pull up and fly over the valley walls.

"Aren't we flying a little low?" asked Darwin. "I mean, I appreciate the view and I get a better feel for the terrain from down here, but don't we want more altitude in case of engine trouble or something?"

"That's the way you were taught, right? Higher altitude gives you more options."

"Of course."

"That's true as far as it goes," she said. "But 'engine trouble' is a holdover from combustion engines. Electrics don't get engine trouble, barring some random mechanical failure. But these are low time motors which have been thoroughly inspected."

"So you're saying 'don't worry about it'?"

"Pretty much, yes."

"I was hoping you'd say that," Darwin said. "Let's go lower. Tree top level."

Sawyer turned her head to look at him. He grinned back.

She sighed. He'd done it again. He had a knack for getting her to do things that made it seem like it was her idea. She loved and hated him for it. "You just suckered me, didn't you?"

"Let's just say I didn't think you'd do it if I just came out and asked cold."

"You're probably right. All right, down it is." Sawyer eased back the throttle some more and angled the plane into a gentle dive toward the tree-tops.

∞ ∞ ∞

The river here was well over thirty meters wide, closer to fifty or sixty. Darwin looked down at the dark blue water. It was hard to say how deep it was, but there were no obvious sandbanks, and the slow-moving river wasn't muddy. *At least three meters deep, maybe five.* He thought about putting pontoons on the aircraft. The river looked smooth enough for a landing but he wasn't sure they'd have enough straightaway for takeoff. It would be a convenient way to check out the river fauna otherwise. He mentioned the possibility to Sawyer.

"We could do that. But don't you want to be sure there are no alligator or hippopotamus equivalents in the river first? It'd be embarrassing to hit one on landing or get eaten by gators trying to take off."

Darwin hadn't considered that. Stupid. "You're right. Hell even a sunken log could ruin our day. Okay, we'll come back later in the boat and check it out."

"Oh we can probably do some low and slow a few meters off the water, it's not that bad."

They followed the curves of the river valley toward the ocean. Every so often Sawyer lifted the plane to climb above the ridge-line so they could see how close they were getting to the river's mouth. At last they rounded a curve in the valley and saw the ocean spread out ahead as the hills on either side tapered off. Beyond the banks of the river, a broad sandy beach ran up and down the coast as far as they could see. A line of breakers was rolling in.

"Look at the size of those waves!" It had taken Darwin a moment to realize the scale. They were probably eight or ten meters high. "I don't think we're going to be taking the boat out in those."

"Wow. No, but a gal could do some serious surfing here."

"Did you bring a board?" It wouldn't have surprised him. Even with the limited volume she might have squeezed something in, and he knew she'd done some competition surfing in her high school days. He certainly would have gone for the opportunity to do something like be the first human to surf an alien ocean.

"Hah, no. Who brings a surfboard on a starship?"

Or perhaps not, Darwin thought.

"But give me a bit of time and the right kind of tree and I could make one," she finished.

"Are you serious? Those waves look like killers."

"They're a challenge, but I've surfed waves like that before. Hawaii. This place reminds me a bit of that. Oh, a few more of those Cook pines or whatever they are, and few palm trees, but still."

She still has the upper body strength for surfing. But: "Hold off on that, we need to check for whatever passes for the local equivalent of shark first."

"Absolutely."

They were off shore now, having flown out from the beach above the waves. There wasn't much to be seen through the water, apparently the beach shoaled off gently for some distance. Further west there was nothing but ocean, they'd seen that from orbit, and the size of the waves confirmed it.

Sawyer banked the plane and turned back toward shore. "Have you seen enough or do want to explore a bit more?" she said.

Darwin pulled up the satellite photographs on one of the dashboard display screens. "If we're at the mouth of the river then we're a bit south of west of the landing field. Let's fly north up the beach a ways and then turn east over the hills."

"Roger that." Sawyer banked the little plane to the left, bringing it into an easy turn that straightened out over the beach, level with ridge of low hills a few hundred meters further inland.

Above the tide line the beach was scattered with the usual beach litter: bits of driftwood, small sticks and leaves, strands of something that might be a kind of seaweed. In the distance Darwin thought he could see some flying animals, occasionally they'd swoop down to the water and zoom back up, or land on the sand and walk around a bit. At this distance they could easily be birds, but they were far enough away that Darwin couldn't be sure.

The birds, or whatever they were, kept retreating from the airplane, or flying out to sea and circling around behind it. Either the prop-noise, or perhaps more likely the silhouette, was scaring them off. *We must resemble some large predator species*, thought Darwin, *I sure hope it isn't something that might decide we're prey.* The electroplane was small as planes went. He hoped it was big enough to discourage any local raptor equivalents.

"Can we land? The damp sand above the waterline should be smooth and firm enough."

Sawyer banked the plane, cross-controlling the rudder and putting the plane into a gentle side-slip so she could get a better look at the ground beneath. She nodded. "Yeah, looks like we can."

"Then let's do it."

"Let me do an inspection pass first to check. Look for wind indicators." Sawyer wanted some reference—vegetation blowing in the wind, flying creatures floating on a headwind, something to give her a feel for the wind direction at landing.

"It will probably be on-shore, but I'll give you a wind indicator." So saying, Darwin pulled a small object, like an orange golf ball, from a pocket, pulled a tab off it, and tossed it over the side. It trailed a stream of orange smoke to the ground, bounced and rolled a few meters, and came to a stop, still smoking. The orange smoke drifted back away from the waterline and slightly northward up the beach. "I'd say the wind is out of the west southwest at eight kph."

Sawyer grinned. "Sly dog, I didn't know you had any of those with you." She turned the aircraft again, turning south, and glided to a landing roll about five meters up the beach from where the waves *ssshhd* over the sand.

"Okay, we're here," she said after switching off the motor. "Now what?"

∞ ∞ ∞

Aboard Krechet, *part of* Centauri Station

"Captain Tsibliev, may I have a word?"

"*Da*, of course, Ulrika, or is it Doctor Klaar if we are being formal?"

"Probably this should be informal, Dmitri. The *Chandrasekhar* has been on the surface for nearly a week now."

"*Da*, we are all knowing this." Dmitri suspected where she might be going with this, but wanted to hear her words. "What is your point?"

"I'm a biologist. I didn't come four light-years to sit in a can in orbit 250 kilometers above all the interesting lifeforms." She softened that with a grin. "Present company excepted, of course."

"But without the *Xīng Huā* . . ."

"We could still land near the *Chandrasekhar* and refuel from their system. It wouldn't be as interesting as landing elsewhere of course, but Commodore Drake might be willing. Besides, they don't have a proper zoologist down there."

"I would certainly like to land on the planet myself, but I think that Commodore Drake will not think the risk is worth the relatively minor scientific reward from landing in the same area."

"But. . .."

Dmitri raised a hand to cut her off. "No, let me think on this a while, there may be some other arrangement to be made. If you are serious, you can do the same, but meanwhile work with the ground team as best you can."

"I . . . *da*, Captain. Thank you for your time." She turned and left, the swirl of her platinum hair emphasizing the chill Dmitri felt as she went.

He didn't want her to get her hopes up, much less did he want her saying anything to anyone else which might be taken as grumblings of mutiny. But Klaar wasn't the only one of the originally scheduled second landing crew to make such comments to him. He just needed a proposal that would win Drake over on the first approach, since he wouldn't likely get a second chance. He had a duty to present a good option to the Commodore if changing circumstances deserved, but Drake would not take kindly to being pestered about it.

∞ ∞ ∞

Centauri Beach

"Let's head north up the beach a bit. I want to see if I can get closer to those flying things."

"The birds?"

"The alien birds, or whatever they are. They do look a lot like birds from here, but that's probably because there's only so many ways a flying animal would work—look at the similarity between birds, pteranodons, and bats, for example."

"Right. Wasn't there a four-winged bird on Earth, same time as the dinosaurs?"

"You're probably thinking of *Microraptor*. Yes it had flight feathers on its legs, although they may not have been true wings. There's some debate as to how they were used."

As they walked north along the shore it was surprisingly easy to imagine that they were on a beach on Earth. There was the same smell of salt in the air, the same waves lapping at the beach and the same roar of the huge waves just offshore. Nothing really screamed *alien* about the place. Darwin was almost disappointed. No green sky or purple ocean or blue sand. Intellectually he knew that none of those made sense, the physics and chemistry that caused the sky to be blue would hold for any planet with an Earth-like atmosphere, just as similar forces would hold for the ocean and rocks. But the lifeforms, now *there* was the possibility of the truly weird.

He'd been keeping an eye on the beach at the water's edge as he walked, and up ahead in the damp sand there was what looked like a jellyfish, a gelatinous mass, fist-sized, which had just washed up. From the mass, a dozen or so brilliant fluorescent green tentacles sprawled over the sand, and opposite those what looked like a small plastic bag grew out of the mass, partly filled with air. He crouched down to get a better look, Sawyer squatted down too.

"Careful," he said, "if this is like terrestrial jellyfish those tentacles could pack a powerful sting, and who knows what effect it might have on us."

"What is it?"

"An alien."

"Gee, thanks professor. Can't you ever give a straight answer?"

"Okay, it looks a bit like a Portuguese man-o'-war, except they have purple tentacles and just the one sail. The air chamber lets them float at the surface, the wind blows the sail around, and the tentacles trail beneath, stinging potential prey."

"Charming." Sawyer stood up, and looked out to sea, scanning the surface. "Are there likely to be more of those, do they travel in packs, or schools, or flocks, or whatever you'd call it for jellyfish?"

"A smack."

"Really? A smack of jellyfish? So they do travel in groups?"

"Some species do. Obviously I have no idea if this does."

"Guess I won't be going surfing for a while yet."

"You could wear your BIG."

She gave him a dirty look. "That kind of defeats the whole purpose of getting wet."

"And it doesn't do a thing for sharkoids, or whatever fills that niche, either." He pulled a transparent plastic specimen bag from a pocket and opened it up. From another pocket he pulled a handful of plastic gloves, and handed a pair to Sawyer. "Here, put these on and help me get this critter in the bag. No telling when we might find more."

They scooped and slithered the jelly into the bag, together with some of the beach sand that adhered to its tentacles. The tentacles proved surprisingly long, given the small size of the rest of the jelly, but they managed to get them stuffed into the specimen bag without getting anything on themselves, except for the gloves. Darwin pulled another bag out of his pocket.

"Hold out your hands," he said.

Sawyer did so. Darwin deftly stripped the gloves off, inside out, and placed them in the bag. Then he stripped his own, careful not to touch the outside of the gloves with his bare skin, and sealed them into the bag too.

"Playing it quite safe, aren't you?"

"There could still be nematocysts—if this thing has them—on the gloves, or even just whatever toxin it might used on its prey," Darwin explained. "Ever been stung by a jellyfish?"

"Actually yes." She winced. "Not something I'm likely to forget. Okay, you make a fair point." She eyed the bagged jelly, and the bagged gloves, warily.

"Okay, let's keep moving on. Those bird things don't seem spooked by us, we can get closer."

They continued further up the beach. Sawyer had borrowed another pair of disposable gloves, just to be safe, and would occasionally reach down and pick up a smooth stone. She'd examine it briefly, then pitch it side-hand out over the water, putting a spin on it so that it would skip when it hit.

Occasionally one of the flying creatures, attracted by the series of splashes as the stone skipped over the water before sinking, would swoop down and investigate.

Sawyer watched as one swooped close to shore, then beat its wings to gain altitude and turned away from them. "George, is it just me, or does that thing *really* look like a seagull?"

He had been watching the creature too, with a growing unease. "I'm no ornithologist, but if we were on Earth, I'd say no. There are detail differences from any seagull species I know. But damned if it doesn't look a lot like one. And it looks far to much like a bird to make me happy."

"Why not, you said yourself that flying animals only take a few forms."

"I did. And part of that is that Earth fliers ultimately all descended from four-limbed vertebrates, not counting the insects. But these things have feathers, or what looks like feathers from here. I'd love to get those things under a microscope."

"What's wrong with feathers?"

"On Earth they're unique to birds. Pteranodons and bats have stretched-skin wings, totally different origins yet convergent evolution. Only birds and dinosaurs had feathers on Earth, they're a unique adaptation of scales."

"Wait, weren't pteranodons dinosaurs?"

"No, they were a side branch. Actually they might have had downy feathers in infancy, I'd have to check the literature, but not flight feathers."

"Oh. But so, convergent evolution again, right?"

"Up to a point. There's too much of it. Things are just too close to Earth life."

"Similar planets, similar conditions, similar geological age. Why wouldn't that produce similar life forms? Especially if its DNA-based, similar biochemistry. That's going to constrain the variation, isn't it?"

She had a point, but Darwin wasn't convinced. "Not if you go back to when complex animals started to evolve, back in the Precambrian. It was mostly invertebrates, and they came in all kinds of shapes and sizes and, more particularly, body plans. Five-eyed *Opabinia regalis*, for example, with a claw on the end of something like a trunk. Even stranger stuff before that. We're so used to bilateral symmetry that we think it's inevitable, but—"

"Maybe it is. Nice and simple, maybe the embryology of DNA-based creatures prefers bilateral symmetry."

"Except that it wasn't ubiquitous originally, and isn't even now. We've got five-fold radial symmetry in starfish and sea urchins, and the Precambrian had other weird shapes. It was probably the development of light sensors, of eyes, that gave just a couple of body plans a huge advantage and they out-competed everything else. But why would that happen here? Couldn't something with tri-fold symmetry have developed eyes first?"

"I guess that's something you'll help figure out. Maybe it's just coincidence, maybe there are some fundamental laws of evolution, that it's not as random chance as you might think. Emergent properties and all that."

Darwin sighed. There might be something to that, but the answers would be so much easier to find if there were clearer differences. But this was only the first extra-Solar planet that they'd explored. It looked like there were many more out there, many with life, a nice big sample size to hang a theory on. His partial namesake, Charles Darwin, hadn't come up with his theories after looking at just one island, after all.

"Yeah, you may be right. I was just hoping for something more, you know, alien. Too much science fiction when I was growing up. Where are the flatcats, the tribbles, the jotok, the sandworms?"

"It's too wet here for sandworms, I should think. Unless you mean the little critters crawling around in this stuff." Sawyer gestured at the damp sand at their feet. There were little holes, about the diameter of soda straws, scattered about. Small mounds of fine sand, in some places looking like mud squeezed from a toothpaste tube, were heaped beside some of the holes. A soft looking, wormlike creature poked up through the sand, slithered along the surface for a few centimeters, then plunged back down.

"Oh!" Darwin squatted down for a better look. He pulled out another sample bag and waited. When next worm poked its head —or whatever body part that was—out of the sand, he quickly scooped it up, along with some surrounding sand and a bit of seawater. "Got you!"

Sawyer had been staring out to sea again, watching the breakers. She turned and looked up and down the beach. Darwin followed her gaze. They'd walked further than he'd thought, they must be a kilometer or so from the where they'd left the plane. But something looked odd.

"Wouldn't it have made sense to park it further up from the water line?" he asked.

"I thought I did. That's odd." A wave surged in and the water lapped over their feet. Sawyer must have realized the problem at the same time he did. She cursed. "Damn it, the tide's coming in!" She started running back down the beach toward the plane. "Come on, before it floats away!"

Darwin was right behind her. In the distance ahead, he could make out that the glistening patch of freshly-wet sand was nearly at the plane's landing gear. As the waves surged in and receded, every third or fourth wave would come a little higher up the beach. Soon the water was starting to splash against the starboard wheel, the one nearest the ocean.

"Will that damage anything?" Darwin called between panting breaths. They were running as hard as they could, staying to the damp sand where the footing was firmer, but it was still tough going. They hadn't quite got their full strength back after nearly two weeks in weightlessness, and this planet's gravity *was* about three percent higher than Earth's.

"Depends. A little water won't hurt the wheels, but if they get soaked we'll need to rinse the salt out or we'll get corrosion. But the plane's light, if the water gets deeper the wave surge could start pushing the plane around, or undermine the wheels." She slowed a bit to catch her breath. "And I really don't want salt water into the electrics."

They were closer now, about a hundred meters. The advancing waves reached up under the plane to lap at the wheel furthest from the sea. The water was now up to the hub of the port wheel; even when the waves receded there was still water around it. The side glistened from splash.

Sawyer reached the plane, splashed out into the incoming surge, and started tugging on the right wing strut. "Help me get it up above the water, this wheel is stuck."

Darwin rushed over to join her, and they struggled to pull and lift on the wing strut together, the water washing around their shins.

"This isn't working," said Sawyer, "go around to the other side, pull down on the left wing. That will pivot this wheel up and I'll push it out."

"Okay." Darwin moved to around the plane. The port wing extended out over still-dry sand. He reached up to the wing tip, heaved down. "Okay, push!"

The right wheel pulled loose from the wet sand with a squelch, and Sawyer pushed and lifted to pivot the plane around, getting all the wheels up onto dry sand, the tail still extending out over the water. "Okay, let's check it over and get out of here!" So saying, she did a quick walk—more of a jog—around the plane, checking the wheels and making sure no water had gotten into the battery or electronics areas. "Okay, we're good, get in."

They both climbed into the cockpit and Sawyer started the motor, the prop coming up to speed with a whine. Darwin buckled in. "Let's roll."

Sawyer pushed the throttle all the way in and the plane surged ahead, bumping over the sand. It got up to a fast walking pace and kept bumping along. "Damn it, the sand's too soft, we can't get up to speed."

"Should I get out and push?"

"Don't laugh, it may come to that." Sawyer pivoted the plane around, aiming back toward the water.

"Where are you going?"

"The damp sand is firmer, we can get a better roll."

"But the tide is coming in, most of the damp sand is underwater."

Sawyer turned her head to him and grinned. "Yep."

She pivoted the plane again as they reached the water's edge, the nose wheel just at the midpoint of the waves' back and forth surge, the left wheel now high and mostly dry, the right wheel raising a rooster tail of water as they accelerated down the beach.

"How come I get the wet side?" Darwin asked, shaking splash from his sleeve.

"Wind direction. Not my fault."

They rolled faster now. Darwin watched as Sawyer struggled with the controls to keep a straight path, between the constant drag of the water on the right wheel and the irregular drag of patches of wet and dry sand on the left. But they were gaining speed.

He felt the vibration smooth and then the plane tilted up, surging forward a little faster as the nose-wheel lifted from the water, then the splashing stopped and the whole plane lifted clear. Sawyer lowered the nose just a bit to build more speed in ground effect, then angled it up to its best climb rate.

"Whoo ha. Let's not do that again!" she said as they climbed out above the ridge line.

Darwin shook his head. "You've got that right. First thing we do when we get back is have somebody work up some tide tables."

Chapter 13: The Smeerp Problem

Centauri Station, in orbit

Drake was in the hub of Centauri Station when Dmitri Tsibliev, commander and pilot of the *Krechet*, drifted over to him.

"Commodore Drake, I would like to talk with you," he said in a low voice.

"Certainly Dmitri. Go ahead."

"I would prefer this private for now." He gestured toward a hatchway. "Shall we go to different deck?"

"Fair enough." Drake pushed away from the panel toward the panel above the hatchway in the floor, grabbed a hand-hold, pivoted, and glided through the hatchway feet first. Tsibliev followed, diving headfirst through the hatch.

"What's on your mind, Dmitri?"

"We have been in orbit nearly two weeks. The *Chandra* landing party shows that it is safe. The boat and aeroplane are operational."

"This is all true." Drake had a feeling he that he knew where this was going.

"I would like to take *Krechet* down too. We can do more science."

"But in the same place as the *Chandra*. What would be the point?"

"No, elsewhere. We have several landing spots picked out."

"'We'?"

"The biologist and geologist on my team have already been looking at this. I have made no commitment."

"And have you figured out how you're going to get home without access to a refueling pod?"

"*Da*, we have. We can use the planes to transport personnel to *Chandra* when research at second landing site is complete. They will return to orbit in *Chandra*."

"And abandon the *Krechet* on the planet?"

"The mission plan is to leave a lander in Centauri system anyway, is it not?" They both knew that it was. Quarantine was one reason, in case the landers had picked up something unnoticed. The other was to reduce overall fuel requirements on the return trip—the ships left behind would transfer fuel to those returning.

"It is, but in orbit, or a controlled reentry, not on the surface. And you want to bring ten people up in the *Chandra*? The landers aren't designed to carry that many people."

"Respectfully, that is not completely correct. They are designed to carry more people in an emergency."

"Three people, yes, not a full landing party in addition to their own full landing party."

"That limit would hold for the planet at Centauri A, it is larger and has higher escape velocity. Here at Planet Baker it would work."

"Even at *Chandra*'s latitude?" *Chandrasekhar* had landed significantly north of the equator, although still a long way from its theoretical limits. Still, those limits were calculated with a standard lift-off weight, not carrying extra passengers.

Tsibliev looked away.

"It won't, will it?" Drake pressed.

Tsibliev looked back at him. "It will. It is on edge of limit, but within parameters. So long as nobody gets too fat while we are down there. There is mass we can strip out for margin."

Drake didn't like the idea. There was the risk factor of having the two landing parties separated by a significant distance, the risk of not being able to ferry the *Krechet*'s personnel to the *Chandra*—if there were an accident with the planes, for example—and the risk of launching *Chandra* back into space with almost no safety margin in the payload. On the other hand, the second landing team was not doing much up here but using up consumables. He was already hearing some grumbling about taking part in the landing. There wasn't likely to be an outright mutiny, but he'd have a lot of explaining to do when they returned as to why he didn't let the science crew do their science.

"I don't know if you appreciate the risk."

"We know what are the risks. Every member of team is willing to accept these risks for landing opportunity."

Drake considered all this. It could also be politically advantageous to let the Russian ship land, helping to make the best of the bad situation of the loss of the *Xīng Huā*, but only if the *Krechet*'s landing team returned safely. It could also be a huge disaster.

"Could you reduce your landing party to four? And, could one of those be Xiaojing Wu?"

Dmitri narrowed his eyes and wrinkled his nose, then looked back at Drake resignedly. "It will be difficult. The mission would not be as effective. Perhaps Roger Dejois can continue his ecology studies from orbit. But if that is what makes the difference. . . ."

"I'll tell you what, Dmitri. Write it up as a formal request and include your preferred landing area. I'll make a decision based on that."

Tsibliev paused, as if considering, then nodded. "*Spasibo*, Commodore. Thank you."

∞ ∞ ∞

Biology Lab, Chandrasekhar, on the surface

Darwin had a small furry creature in a cage trap.

"What's that?" Jennifer Singh asked.

"A runny babbit," he replied.

"You mean bunny rabbit?"

"No, a runny babbit."

At Singh's questioning look, he continued: "It's about the size and shape of a rabbit, has the long ears, and probably fills a similar ecological niche. But the hind legs are different, it runs rather than hops. Hence runny babbit."

"If you don't want to call it a rabbit, then why not just make up a name? Call it a smeerp."

"A smeerp?"

"Whatever, why not?."

"That sounds more like you're describing road-kill; a smear with a lump at the end. No, it's a runny babbit. I'll let Doctor Klaar come up with a Latin name when we have a better feel for how it fits in to the overall picture."

Singh just rolled her eyes and shook her head.

"You know," Darwin continued, "this is pretty exciting. We get to name all the new species—new families and orders and kingdoms (oh my!)—and we can do it methodically, in a way that makes sense, instead of the hodge-podge of species names of terrestrial biology."

"That's a pretty tall order, and we have to describe everything we name. You might just have to settle for naming the families and a few select species. But new kingdoms? We haven't seen anything to suggest there's anything but the basic three or five here." She knew as well as Darwin did that the exact number depended on whose classification system you were using, but general agreement oscillated around those.

"True so far, but we've only begun looking," he said. "We may yet find microbes that don't fit into the bacteria or archaea families, or something larger that's neither plant, animal or fungi."

"Perhaps. I would be more convinced if what we'd found was not DNA based, then everything could be separately classified. But the plants here aren't merely DNA based. We don't have the sequencer, but we can tell that much using basic chemistry, and so far as we can tell they even use the same four nucleotides. Where's the fun in that?"

Darwin was inclined to agree. Native Earth life DNA was based on four basic nucleic acids: guanine, adenine, thiamine and cytosine. There were many more potential nucleic acids, but most of them were too big or too oddly shaped to fit into the DNA helical structure, or didn't have a corresponding base to pair up with to form part of the double helix. Experimental biochemists had, however, found or managed to synthesize some base pairs that would fit as new letters into the DNA helix, or team with other pairs to create DNA helices of a different size or twist. It had been widely expected that extraterrestrial life could as easily have started with a different combination of nucleic acids, and that their genetics and general biochemistry, while similar in principal, would be wildly different from Earth life as humans knew it.

That it wasn't—at least, what they'd found here on Alpha Centauri B II, or Baker—was a disappointment for some of the biologists. It meant that Earth life's particular DNA sequence was less likely a chance occurrence—why GATC rather than some other set of code letters?—and more likely due to some specific selection mechanism at work in the prebiotic oceans and tidal pools where life had arisen. But what was the mechanism? The biologists were both intrigued at the thought that there was a mechanism there to find, and concerned that when the news leaked out, it would trigger yet another round of "intelligent design" creationist nonsense.

Perhaps the life on the planet orbiting Centauri A would be different, but there was little expectation of that. The astronomers and planetologists had pointed out that the two systems were easily close enough to have cross-contaminated each other with fragments kicked off by giant meteor impacts. The exobiologists reluctantly agreed that hardy lifeforms could survive just beneath the surface of such rocks for the few hundred or even thousands of years it took a wandering piece of impact splash from A-II, Able, to intersect B-II, Baker, or vice versa. *We need to come up with some better names for these planets*, thought Darwin, momentarily side-tracked. And if the DNA did match, it might be impossible to tell on which planet life arose first.

The same argument had been raised when the first bacteria-like structures had been found in the Martian meteorite back in the 1990s. If they were "nanofossils" (it was later decided that they probably weren't), was it life that had independently evolved on Mars? Had life evolved on Mars first (it would have cooled before Earth, after the planets formed) and then traveled to Earth in the same way that meteorite had? Or could an impact on

Earth—something like the Sudbury impact of two billion years ago, perhaps—kicked off a piece of Earth with enough velocity to travel through interplanetary space and reach Mars? And if it could, could it have carried primitive lifeforms that survived the trip, and found Mars habitable? Analysis suggested that the answers to all these questions was "yes, but...." The "but" being that it would be extremely unlikely. In either case, the primitive organisms which Darwin had discovered on Mars had the same genetic biochemistry as Earth life, so the question was still open.

Darwin realized that Singh was still looking at him expectantly. "Well," he said, "maybe these planets were contaminated by something that got kicked off of Earth. It's only four light years."

Singh rolled her eyes. "Not likely. I do not think there are enough zeros to express how infinitesimal the chances of *that* are. Perhaps Fred Hoyle was right."

Hoyle was a 20th century astronomer who had become a strong advocate of the theory of panspermia. The theory held that life originated far too quickly after Earth cooled to be explained by the random assemblage of primitive biochemicals into DNA and proteins, so early life must have originated in space, on comets where it might have had billions of years more to develop before encountering the early Earth, and that such life-bearing comets could just as easily seed (or infect) planets in other star systems. While it was true that organic precursors such as amino acids had been found not just in comets but in interstellar gas clouds, most exobiologists felt that it required something warmer and more energetic than a wandering comet's surface to actually develop life.

Darwin just snorted. "Anyway, I'm going to examine my little babbit friend here and see what makes it tick. I'll send my data up to Ulrika so she can examine it too. She's been itching to get a look at the local fauna. This thing is surprisingly mammalian—fur, warm blooded, endo-skeleton—so it'll be interesting to see what the differences are at the detail level."

Hours later, Darwin and Klaar were still looking for those differences.

∞ ∞ ∞

Centauri Station, in orbit

Doctor Ulrika Klaar examined the image on one screen and then again at the notes Darwin had sent up. This didn't make sense, why would he do this? She opened a comm circuit to him.

"Darwin, this is Klaar. Are you making a joke? It is not very funny."

"No joke, Ulrika. I thought it was strange, but you're the zoologist. Dr. Singh is here, she'll tell you it's real."

"It is." Jennifer Singh's voice came over the comm. Darwin must have it in speaker mode.

"Damn. I would almost rather it be a joke. I don't understand how, but this is a mammal."

Singh's voice came again. *"Darwin did say it was fur-bearing and warm blooded. Does it give milk?"*

"That I don't know. This one is male. I don't even know if it lays eggs or is placental. But the skeletal structure is all wrong for an alien!"

"And you know what is the right skeletal structure for an alien?" asked Singh.

"No, no. It's wrong for an alien because it is exactly right for a terrestrial mammal. Bring up your screen, I'll show you." Klaar touched a control to conference her screen to theirs. "Look at this." She brought up an image of the animal's skeleton, as determined from the CT scan Darwin had performed. "See here." She moved the cursor to point at parts of the image in turn. "Skull, spine made up of vertebra, shoulder blades, ribs, pelvis, the limb bones—the anatomy screams 'terrestrial vertebrate'."

"Convergent evolution?" Singh said, but her tone of voice suggested that she didn't really believe it.

"At this level of detail? But it gets worse." She pointed at the hip joint. "Look, ball and socket, and that's clearly a femur. Below that, two bones, fibula and tibia. Ankle bones. Five toes."

"I only see four." Darwin said.

"Look closer, see that small bone?" she zoomed the screen, expanding the view. "Vestigial fifth toe. The front paws are similar."

"*Okay, that is weird.*"

"You could say that. I am not finished. Count the cervical vertebrae." She panned the image to the animal's neck area, focusing on the region between the skull and the first vertebra with attached ribs.

She heard Singh counting, then a gasp. "*Seven.*"

"Seven indeed. Every terrestrial mammal from a mouse to a giraffe, with only rare exceptions, has seven cervical vertebrae."

"*I know, but that's. . ..*"

"Impossible, yes. Which is why I was hoping for a joke."

"*Have you checked the ears?*" Darwin asked. Part of the very definition of Mammalia was based on the specific structure of the jaw joint and bones of the middle ear.

"The scan doesn't resolve enough detail, but there was nothing to rule mammals out. I'd have to dissect to be sure. *Damn* I want to get down there." Tsibliev had mentioned that might be possible, but arrangements were not yet final.

"And look at this." Klaar stabbed at another computer key and the skeleton's thoracic cavity filled in with organs: a pair of lungs, a heart nestled between them, a liver tucked up under the lungs on the right, stomach sitting under and to the left of that, intestines, a pair of kidneys. . . .. "The *forbannet* internal organs could be that of any terrestrial vertebrate." Klaar's frustration began to color her language. "How the *frack* does a terrestrial *mammal* get four light years from home?"

"*Uh, a stowaway?*" suggested Singh tentatively. That would break all kinds of quarantine regulations and cause a furor if true. They had some lab animals, like the mouse used as a "canary", but they were carefully managed.

Klaar was about to reply when her omni chirped. It was Captain Tsibliev. "*Da?*" she said.

"*Crew meeting in five minutes. I have some news.*"

"I'll be there." Klaar felt her heart beat rise, would she be landing after all? She turned her attention back to her link to the surface. "I have to go, let me know if you find any more mammals."

"*Roger that,*" said Darwin.

∞ ∞ ∞

Biology Lab, on the surface

Singh turned to Darwin. "*Could* it be a stowaway?"

Darwin scowled at her. "I only wish it were. But if it is, it's a previously undiscovered species. Ulrika says it doesn't match *any* terrestrial mammal—placental, marsupial or monotreme for that matter—alive or extinct. For that matter it doesn't match any known reptile, amphibian or dinosaur. She knows; she checked the database." He paused, staring a little wild-eyed. "It does, however, *resemble* many terrestrial placental mammals, marsupials and monotremes in the way that terrestrial placental mammals, marsupials and monotremes resemble each other. If this were found on Earth it would be classified as a new species of mammal, or perhaps marsupial."

Singh pointed at the screen. "Not a marsupial; no epipubic bone. That thing's a placental."

Darwin pressed a key to make the internal organs disappear, and looked at the pelvis again. She was right, non-placental Mammalia, the marsupials and egg-laying monotremes, had additional bones in the pelvis that would interfere with development and birth in a placental mammal. Klaar hadn't mentioned it, perhaps that wasn't definitive, but he hadn't asked. "Huh, I missed that."

"You're a male."

"And so is this guy. I don't know what would disturb me more when we find a female: evidence that it was placental or that it laid eggs."

"Heh. Or something completely different." She paused. "By the way, what I came here to ask in the first place, what is the status of the protein sequencer?"

With the loss of the DNA sequencer on the *Xīng Huā*, the team had investigated possible substitutes. It turned out they could, in theory, adapt a mass-spectrometer to the job of sequencing the amino acids in proteins—assuming the local proteins were made from amino acids, which had proved to be the case—it just required a proper supply of reagents, a lot of software modifications, and some custom parts. "The new parts are in the fab queue. It'll be another day before the parts are fabbed and the modified system assembled. And it will take another day, at least, to calibrate it and modify the peptide database for the new calibration. We won't be able to look at this silly babbit's proteins for a couple of days." The results might not be quite as interesting as a DNA comparison, but he could at least find out if proteins which performed a given function in the babbit, or other Alpha Centauran life, were at all similar to proteins performing the same function in Earth life.

She sighed. "That means I can't sequence my plant specimens until then either. We are building up a backlog."

"Don't I know it. Any surprises so far?"

"No terrestrial carrots to go with your runny babbit, if that's what you mean, but there are some parallels with terrestrial species. There is sufficient variety in Earth plants that a few parallels wouldn't surprise me, but now you have me wondering. I'd been focusing on gross morphology and the ecological relationships, but I think I'll start taking a closer look at the cellular level. I'm just so used to green plants having chloroplasts that it had not quite occurred to me that green plants here might *not* have them. But now that you've brought it up, why *don't* they use some other mechanism for photosynthesis? Why similar organelles?"

"Why does a babbit have two kidneys and seven cervical vertebra? I think that's got to be the question of our mission. Not 'how does alien life differ?', but 'why are there so many detailed similarities?' That's a more fundamental question about the origin of life. Differences are going to be important for settlers, but it's the similarities that get to the fundamental question."

"You make a point," Singh said. "But, 'settlers'?"

"We're just over a week from Earth, that's far less time than it took the post-Columbian colonists to cross the Atlantic. It's about what a steamship took, and look at the immigration wave *they* set off. The air's breathable, and even if the local life isn't edible we can expect that Earth life will grow here. There'll be settlers here in no time."

"But the cost?"

"Three or so weeks for the round trip, operating cost for one of our starships? Not a lot. Sure, they cost billions to build, but they're the prototypes, the first ones. Ramp up a production line and the unit price will come down. I don't know how hard it is to build a warp module or a fusion reactor, but it's got to be comparable with any other complicated piece of equipment. Once the production engineers put their minds to it, the prices come down. You can bet the Chinese started planning settlement expeditions when the first results came back that there might be habitable planets."

"But they don't have warp technology, the United States provided the warp drives."

"And you think that situation will hold for long? If they can't just outright buy the technology they'll find a way to get it. Look at history. And they've got practical fusion reactors, we're still working on it. Do you think the U.S. government wouldn't do a trade? Cheap power for the folks at home is more important to politicians than Chinese exploring the galaxy."

"That is rather short-sighted."

"Politicians, hello? Their event horizon is the next election."

Singh sighed. "You are right. I had hoped that finding all this," she waved her arms to indicate the planet as a whole, "would encourage more global thinking, that we could all work together."

"You are an idealist." Darwin was a little surprised at her naivete. He saw her shoulders slump, the expression of frustration on her face. "But it's possible," he continued, trying to cheer her up. "I've read that the first pictures of Earth taken from the Moon helped inspire environmental awareness and more international cooperation."

"And yet they still had the Unholy War." She shook her head, then seemed to brighten. "At least now we know there are places we could live should that happen again." Then she slumped. "Of course, that might make it even more likely that it does. Humans are such idiots." She turned, to leave, turned back. "Present company excepted."

"No offense taken." Darwin grinned.

Singh smiled back. "I am returning to my plants. I will see you later."

As she left, the comm link chimed again. Darwin activated it. "This is *Chandrasekhar*, Darwin here. What's up?"

"*This is Klaar. Good news, Commodore Drake has authorized a second landing. I'll be coming down on the* Krechet."

Chapter 14: Second Down

Chandrasekhar, on the surface

"Word from *Centauri Station*, the *Krechet* is scheduled to land tomorrow morning," Ganesh Patel said. "They would greatly appreciate for somebody to fly the plane down to the designated landing area for a detailed check out and to set a beacon. I need to stay with the *Chandrasekhar*. Commander Sawyer, Doctor Darwin, can you do the needful?"

Darwin leaped at the chance. "Sure, I've been looking forward to doing an aerial survey between here and there."

"I'm okay with it too," said Sawyer. "Let me get the plane checked out tonight, we'll leave at first light. George, it's a long flight, we'll want to take survival gear."

"Okay, I'll pull the kit together."

∞ ∞ ∞

Alpha Centauri B was still just a red-orange glow over the hills to the east as Sawyer and Darwin began their take-off roll. Sawyer had put a full charge on the batteries overnight. They could fly almost the full three hundred kilometers to Second Landing on that alone, but in another hour Centauri B would be high enough in the sky to start recharging the batteries with the photovoltaic film.

She lifted the plane up over the hills and banked south, keeping the rising sun on her left. The moon had dropped below the horizon and the ocean was a broad dark patch to her right. Below them, the tips of the higher hills were just catching the morning light.

"Any preferences on the flight plan? If it were me I'd just

follow the beach" Sawyer asked.

"That's kind of boring, we won't see anything new that way."

"But it's easier to set down there than in the hills."

"Anyway, we have to cut across the peninsula," said Darwin, "unless you were planning on taking the long way around."

"No, and I didn't think you'd want to keep to the beach." Sawyer touched a control and a satellite view opened on one of the dashboard screens. A yellow line traced a slightly zig-zag path over it. A small red airplane symbol marked their current location and heading, at least as best the navigation systems could determine it. "There, that's the route I planned. It covers as many different-looking terrains as I could easily fit along the way. And I fitted belly and side cams that are relaying data back to the *Chandra*."

"That's fantastic. Remind me to tip you."

"Thanks. Tell you what, you can take over the flying for a bit, I'm going to take a snooze. I was up late."

"Okay." Darwin grasped the control stick at his knees and rested his feet on the rudder pedals. "Okay, I have control."

"You have control." Sawyer released her own grip on the controls. "Wake me up if you see anything interesting. The nav system will beep at you if you get too far off the path, but keep an eye on it anyway."

"What about the autopilot?"

"I don't trust it that much. If we had GPS and a good digital terrain model maybe, but surprisingly I trust even your flying more than an autopilot designed for another planet." She knew its software had been modified to take differences in gravity and air density into account, but that didn't mean she trusted it.

"Gee, thanks."

∞ ∞ ∞

Darwin had been flying for almost an hour when he noticed a dark smudge in the sky to the east. *Smoke from a fire?* he wondered. If so, it had to be a big fire, the cloud was kilometers away. It was moving, but it didn't seem smoke-like. *Birds?*

"Elizabeth, wake up," he said, nudging her.

She was instantly awake. "What?"

"I see something interesting. Look to the east."

She turned to look. "That dark cloud? What is it?"

"Good question. Take the controls while I grab binoculars."

She took the stick. "I have control."

Darwin reached down behind the seats and rummaged in the backpack. He pulled out a pair of binoculars and leaned forward to peer around Sawyer at the cloud. It was still so distant that he couldn't make out much detail, but it was definitely made up of many small dark objects, flying in generally the same direction but with random individual shifts, like a large school of fish, or yes, a flock of birds.

"Looks like birds, but there must be thousands of them, or more. The flock is huge."

"Let's give them a wide berth."

"Sure, but they're not headed this way. Nothing to worry about," Darwin said. "I'd like to come out this way again to check them out." He settled back in his seat. "Want me to take over flying again?"

"No, I've got it. We'll be there in another half-hour."

∞ ∞ ∞

Alpha Centauri B was well above the horizon when they reached the broad plateau which had been picked out as the second landing site.

Sawyer could pick out tell-tale signs of an ancient volcanic outflow. The edges of the plateau had the characteristic columnar structure of flood basalt, below which broad talus slopes led down to the surrounding forest. At the western edge the cliffs dropped abruptly to the sea, which hammered at them with a pounding they could hear even over the whine of the propeller.

She flew a lazy pattern over the plateau, several kilometers across. It was old enough that the surface was warn smooth and had collected a thin layer of topsoil, but the vegetation was thin. It would make an ideal landing site for the *Krechet*.

Landing the plane might be more problematic. The *Krechet* would be coming straight down, landing vertically, so minor irregularities in the terrain wouldn't bother it. The plane needed a relatively smooth area. In a pinch and with a modest headwind, the plane could be flared into an almost vertical landing itself, but it needed some runway for a takeoff roll. A fresh lava field—and here "fresh" could mean anything less than ten thousand years or so—was, depending on the lava type, a ropey or cindery mass of uneven rock and potential potholes.

She pulled an orange sphere from a pocket. "I'm going to drop smoke to mark a landing area for us." Keeping one hand on the stick, she held out the smoke pellet for Darwin to pull the tab off, then tossed it over the side, watching which direction the smoke blew. She brought the plane down to thirty meters off the ground and started to circle the area. "Keep your eyes peeled for uneven ground."

"Looks good so far."

"Okay, one more pass." She brought the plane down to five meters, just in ground effect, and slowed it down further. There were hints of worn rock poking through the dirt, but it was mostly thin ground-cover plants with the occasional scrubby bush or wildflower. "Perfect."

She climbed out and came around again, this time setting up the approach for a proper landing. As she neared the ground a third of the way down her imaginary runway, she killed the motor, pulled back into a flare, and gently stalled out just as the main wheels touched the ground. They rolled about five meters.

"Nice one," Darwin said.

"Anything you can walk away from," Sawyer said deprecatingly, but she had a grin on her face. "Let's get the beacon set up and give *Krechet* a call. She glanced at the omni on her wrist. "They're going to want to do their deorbit burn in forty-five minutes."

∞ ∞ ∞

An hour later, Sawyer and Darwin flew their plane to a safe distance to watch the entry and landing of the *Krechet*. It came in like a slow meteor, leaving a condensation trail behind it. Its engines throttled up at ten thousand meters, slowing the descent, and as it came down into the thicker air, engines firing, they could hear the roar even over their prop noise.

"Looks good from here, *Krechet*. I've got a spot marked for you about a kilometer from the cliff."

"*Da, I see it.*"

Tsibliev brought the *Krechet* in high, coming to a hover about five hundred meters directly above the designated landing spot. He throttled back and the ship dropped quickly, leaving a trail of cloud above it. It slowed abruptly about thirty meters above the ground and descended the rest of the way at a more sedate pace, the exhaust plume searing the ground beneath. Dust, smoke and steam kicked up around it and for a moment the *Krechet* was lost in the cloud, then the roar of the engines stopped. The cloud drifted away on the slight breeze, to reveal the *Krechet* sitting solidly on its landing gear. It was down.

"Nice job. I'll bring the plane in now."

Sawyer landed the plane and then taxied it to within twenty meters of the lander. A few small plants were still smoldering but the ground around the lander was clear, and had already cooled enough to walk on. As Sawyer and Darwin approached, the side hatch opened and a ladder dropped down. A figure started climbing down it.

Darwin remembered the accident which had made him the mission's lead exobiologist. "Why a ladder anyway?" he asked. "Why isn't the side of the ship made of smart materials that can just extrude a ladder?"

"Actually they were going to make more use of smart materials," Sawyer said, "but the hull of the ship is a high radiation environment. Even in normal space there's cosmic rays, and when the warp is turned on we get a constant stream of radiation from matter intersecting the warp bubble."

"Yeah but that's pretty mild, it doesn't bother us."

"And you a biologist." There was a hint of good-natured derision in her voice. "Our living cells can generally repair what damage it does cause. The nanocells in the smart material aren't self-repairing, just redundant. Damage enough of them and they'll stop doing what you need them to do."

They reached the foot of the ladder just as Dmitri stepped off.

"Welcome to Kakuloa," Darwin said, extending a hand to shake. "Did you bring the required landing fee?"

"Forgive me, I could not find anyone to exchange rubles for Centauri currency. I will have to owe you."

"That's okay, we'll take it in vodka."

"Ah, now that, that I can do. *Strasvoytye!*" And with that he stepped over and grabbed Darwin in a bear hug, then turned and did the same to Sawyer. "It is good to be in open air, even if does smell like someone is burning leaves." He looked around at the barren plateau. "You know, you could have marked closer to trees. I am doing precision landing, not looking for place to build shopping center." He grinned again and slapped Sawyer on the shoulder. "Come, let us get everyone else off ship."

Dmitri turned back to the *Krechet*, stopped, and turned back to Darwin. "By the way, what is Kakuloa?"

"Ah, it's my working name for this planet. I got tired of calling it Baker or Alpha Centauri B II. Elizabeth said the waves near Landing Site One reminded her of Hawaii, so I picked something Hawaiian."

"You do know that there's no such word as kakuloa in Hawaiian, right?" Sawyer said pointedly to Darwin. "And the beach at Ka*ha*kuloa"—she emphasized the extra syllable—"looks nothing like the one at the landing site. I looked it up."

"So you keep insisting. And yet here we are standing on a lava flow by the beach. Sounds like Hawaii."

Sawyer rolled her eyes. "Flood basalt, not lava flow," she muttered. She turned to Dmitri. "Anyway, let's help you all get unloaded. At least you don't have to spend the next few days in BIGs."

∞ ∞ ∞

The crew set up a base camp about fifty meters from the ship, to give them room to spread their gear and more living space. Much of the gear was stowed in externally accessible compartments, and they were midway through unloading it, when they all heard a sharp, loud, *crack!* followed by a muffled rumble.

"What was that?" asked Klaar of nobody in particular.

"Was that earthquake?" said Dmitri. "It felt like ground shook."

"That was damned odd," said Sawyer. "Everybody spread out, stay clear of the lander." Contrary to her own advice, she herself started back toward the lander, scanning the ground intently like she was looking for something.

"What is it? What are you looking for?" Darwin called over to her.

"Something I hope I don't find." She checked out the ground around one landing pad and walked over to the other, still scanning the ground. She looked back at Darwin. "This plain is flood basalt, there shouldn't be any—"

CRACK!

"*Shit!*" Sawyer managed to yell as the ground fell away beneath her.

Chapter 15: Underground

Krechet *landing site*

Her voice faded as Sawyer disappeared from view. The lander lurched and tilted sideways, the leg that Sawyer had been standing near seeming to drop into the ground. Again Drake heard a rumbling, less muffled this time, as of rocks falling.

"*Elizabeth!*" Darwin and Tsibliev began to run toward where they'd last seen her.

"*Stay back!*" Sawyer's voice came, sounding distant and echoey. "I'm okay, but stay back!"

"Where are you?"

"In a lava cave, hanging on to the landing pad. Roof broke through. I don't know how stable it is. Keep your distance!"

"We've got to get you out of there."

"That would be nice, but right now I'm hanging above the cave floor, I don't know how deep this is. I don't want you stomping around and breaking the rest of the roof."

"All right, let me get ropes." Darwin turned and called back to Tsibliev and the others. "Somebody get rope from the gear we've unloaded. Stay clear of the ship. Dmitri, how stable is it like that, will it fall?"

"Is good for now, but balance is delicate. If any more ground breaks, could tip over. We need to anchor opposite leg."

"Great, how do we do that." There wasn't much other than scrubby bushes to tie anything to, and he didn't want to risk hammering pins into the ground until they knew how solid it was.

"Sawyer, which way does the tube run?"

"It's fucking dark in here, how should I know? But my guess is more or less toward the ocean."

∞ ∞ ∞

There was light coming in the hole around the landing gear, but Sawyer was hanging on to the leg for all she was worth, and the light was in her face. She couldn't see into the gloom beyond. The rock where they'd broken through was about twenty centimeters thick—that might have been enough to support the landing leg, had been enough for a while, but for cracks in the rock that would have been aggravated by the landing jets. They were lucky it hadn't collapsed immediately.

The part of Sawyer's brain that wasn't focused on not falling wondered about that. Lava tubes, channels where molten lava kept flowing while the edges and top solidified, were not uncommon in lava flows, but in a flood basalt where the lava has just formed a big pool, the tubes usually stayed filled until the cooling lava solidified all the way through. It was only where there was enough slope to keep the liquid lava draining after the source had stopped that you got a hollow cave like this. Flood basalts never had lava caves. At least, not on Earth. *Except*, the thought came to her, *that one place in Brazil. And near the Columbia River Basalts' terminal margins. Or the Moon. Damn it!*

She tried to pull herself up. If she could hook her leg around the foot-pad, she should be able to shift her weight and get herself up to where she was sitting on the pad, straddling the landing leg. From there she could stand up, reach up and get herself out of the hole, if no more of the ceiling collapsed. She heaved and swung her right leg. Almost. Heave, swing. Nope. The muscles in her forearms were starting to cramp from holding her weight on the landing strut, and every time she tried to haul herself up her biceps protested. Damn, she *used* to be able to do this. All that time in zero gee hadn't helped.

She called out again. "What's happening up there?" A face appeared over the edge of the hole. "Oh, hi." It was Darwin's. *Idiot.* "I told you to stay clear of the hole, what if it collapses more?"

"And I'm pleased to see you too," Darwin said. "I'm on a rope, I've got three people belaying me. Let me get some more light down there and see how we're going to get you out."

"Take your time, I'll just hang out here." Sawyer's panting breath and the strain in her voice belied the casual words.

The head disappeared for a moment, then reappeared with a hand holding a large flashlight next to it. Sawyer was momentarily blinded as Darwin flicked the light on. Then she heard laughing. Darwin was pointing the flashlight down beneath her, shaking as he laughed.

"What's so fucking funny?"

"*Ah ha, hoo.*" He caught his breath. "Sorry. Look down."

"I did, it's pitch black."

"No, look where I'm shining the light."

Sawyer twisted around so that she could look past her upraised shoulder, still keeping a death grip on the landing leg. The light beam picked up the dark gray basalt, but she still couldn't see much. She'd been staring up at the sky through the hole, her night vision was shot. Slowly the black faded and she picked out the shape of the cave walls, the small pile of rubble on the floor of the cave.

"Oh," she said, and let go of the landing leg.

The ground had been a half meter beneath her toes, the lava tube wasn't even three meters high.

She stood flexing and shaking her shoulders and arms to loosen the knotted muscles, looking around to see what she could by the light coming in from above. "Toss me the flashlight, I want to check out the cave roof."

Darwin did so and Sawyer winced at the pain in her arms as she reached to grab the light. She shone it around. Loose rock littered the floor of the cave. Shining the light up at the ceiling, she saw the inverted step pattern of broken rock layers. The hole was near the apex of the slightly curved roof, roughly centered on an irregular area where a large slab had fallen, leaving a thinner layer above it. Sawyer played the light over the rockfall on the floor. There was a layer of wet, dirty rock below the recent fall from the just-opened hole. "Just our luck, he must have landed on one of the thinnest parts of the cave roof."

She shone the light up and down the tunnel, which seemed to

peter out after a dozen meters in each direction, although it was hard to tell in the dim light. It didn't look like rockfall had closed it, which explained why they hadn't seen any indication from the surface, but rather the lava had just solidified.

"I think this is more a huge vug than tube drainage, although I don't see any crystallization. A gas pocket perhaps." She looked up at the landing leg and tried to gauge the location of the ship relative to the tunnel. "It looks like the ship is over solid ground, but the roof here is weakened, it might not take much to open it up more."

"Any suggestions?"

"If we've got something we could use as a two-and-a-half to three meter jack, we can prop the leg up off the cave floor. Other than that maybe lay something down to spread out the weight. Floor plates or tree trunks or something."

"Are we okay to drive anchors? Tie down the opposite leg?"

Sawyer looked around the cave walls and ceiling. "Yeah, this doesn't go anywhere near that. As long as there are no other vugs we should be good. Hammer on the ground to see if it sounds hollow first."

"Aren't you coming up?"

"You'd better get that tied down first. If us climbing around this hole loosens any more rock, we don't want the ship to tip any further."

"Right you are." Darwin's head disappeared, then popped back. "Don't go away."

Funny man, said Sawyer to herself, then sat down on a boulder away from the loose rock overhead to wait. She massaged her arms and shoulders. All that for a drop of one lousy foot.

Part III: Survival

Chapter 16: Doing Geology

Field Geology Site III, a week later

    Sawyer leaned into the drill, feeling it vibrate and hearing it whine as it bit its way into the sandstone at her feet. The drill reached the sixty centimeter mark and she stopped it, then flipped the motor-reverse switch and ran it again briefly to back the drill out. She paused and wiped the sweat from her brow, then heaved the drill up and out, laying it carefully down on the rock parallel to the line formed by the three holes she'd just drilled. A fourth hole, off the line, was perhaps a meter further away.

    "Hey Elizabeth, how's it going?" Fred Tyrell, thirty meters away, had finished collecting mineral specimens from the outcrop near the edge of the clearing and was strolling back.

    "Almost done here. Just need to drop in the geophones and wire them to the transmitter mast." She picked up a small plastic-wrapped package and ran a finger down one edge, unsealing it. The bag contained a small squat cylinder the size of a coffee mug. A loose coil of cable was wired internally to the cylinder at one end, with a connector at the other. She set the cylinder sideways in the hole, lining its axis north-south by comparing it with the compass rose displayed on her omni. The loop of cable trailed up out of the hole, with most of the loop lying on the ground. That done, she filled in the hole with loose dirt then squirted a binding agent from a spray can onto the dirt to mix with and solidify it.

    "Need a hand?" Tyrell asked as he walked up to where Sawyer was working.

    "Sure, take one of these," she handed him a plastic-wrapped geophone, "and put it in that hole vertically. There's a bubble level on one end. That obviously goes on top, and center the bubble. Make sure it stays centered until you get it packed in. I'll do the east-west axis."

"What about the cable?"

"I'll plug them into the transmitter mast as soon as I get it up."

At wasn't long before the seismic station was complete, with the three geophones hooked into circuitry within the mast which mounted the communications antenna. That mast was a tube resembling a fence post, ten centimeters in diameter and two-and-a-half meters long. Sawyer buried the base of this in the fourth hole and similarly fixed it in place. "All set."

"What now?"

"Now's the fun part, I get to test these." She held up a pair of blue plastic-coated cylinders.

"Ah, the seismic charges?"

"Exactly, the seismic charges. Come on, let's go for a walk."

They hiked to the other end of the clearing, a thin layer of soil over a flat bed of sandstone, with a few small scrubby bushes growing around it. Sawyer set up the drill again and bored out the hole for the charge.

"So how big a bang do these make?" Tyrell asked.

"It depends how many you screw together." The ends of each charge were threaded to permit just that. "But these guys are equivalent to a stick of dynamite. In this sandstone they'll break it up a bit and kick about fifty liters out. In softer ground they could excavate a nice hole, maybe a half-meter deep and a meter across, about 200 liters. Maybe more, depending on the soil condition. Wet ground transmits the shock better, dry sand just soaks it up."

"Yeah, I know the theory, I just haven't done this in a while."

"Oh, right." She stopped the drill and set it aside. "Okay, that's done."

She pulled a smaller plastic piece, like a bottle's screw-top with attached wires, from a package and threaded it on to the seismic explosive stick. "Okay, that's our detonator. Now we just lower it into the hole and cover it up," she said, doing just that.

"Okay, lets get to a safe distance." Sawyer picked up a spool of wire, connected one end to the detonator wires, and began walking back across the clearing, trailing the wires as she went.

"This should be more than enough," she said when they were a hundred meters away. She knelt down and began connecting the wires to the blasting box. "Fred, can you check the comms with the sensors?" She unfolded her omni and keyed in a sequence, bringing up a series of graphs on the display. She handed it to him. "Here's the app, it's already set to the right frequency."

"Sure," said Tyrell, taking it. Sawyer continued connecting the detonator wire. "It shows these are set to sensitive," he said. "Do you want me to desensitize them for the test?"

"Yeah, dial it back or we'll swamp the sensors."

"Okay, done." He handed the omniphone back to her. She finished with the blast box and checked the display. "Okay, great. We're good to go." She set the omni down and knelt beside the box. "Stand by!" she yelled to the empty field.

"Who are you yelling at?"

"Standard safety precaution. Just a habit."

Sawyer flipped open the cover and flipped a toggle switch, and turned rotary switch a quarter-turn. "Armed!" she shouted.

She turned to Tyrell. "You might want to cover your ears, this is a shallow blast." He put his hands over his ears. His eyes were bright with excitement.

"All right, in five," Sawyer said loudly. "Four. Three. Two. One. Fire in the hole! Fire in the hole! Fire in the hole!" Her thumb flipped up another clear plastic cover and mashed down on a big red button. The ground shook.

BANG! A plume of dust, gravel and smoke shot up out of the borehole and they felt the shock ripple through the ground, then everything grew silent as the echoes of the blast faded away.

Sawyer safed the blasting box and set it down, then picked up her omni and reviewed the data. "Perfect, everything looks good. Now, with the stations at the two landing sites, we have three seismic stations and can pinpoint any quakes much more reliably. Let's pack up and get out of here."

They walked back to the smoking hole where they'd placed

the charge. It was surrounded by a ring of debris, like the rays around an impact crater. In place of the borehole was a crater roughly twice as wide as it was deep. "Cool," was all Tyrell could say.

∞ ∞ ∞

They stowed their gear and samples back aboard the electroplane, EP02, and pushed it to the downwind edge of the clearing. Tyrell was about to climb into the right side of the plane when Sawyer said "Hold up, Fred. Are you up for playing taxi driver?"

"What do you mean?"

"After we get back to the *Chandra*, someone needs to take the plane down to the *Krechet* to bring Doctor Klaar back here. George wants to get all the biologists together for some kind of confab."

"Okay, sure. But EP01 is already at the *Krechet*, she could just fly up in that."

"They're going to be attaching pontoons to it to make it amphibious, so it may be unavailable for a while. And Ulrika doesn't have as many flight hours as you or some of the others, I'm not sure I'd want her doing a solo cross-country with newly attached floats. If you take EP02 here after dropping me off, floats won't be an issue. Are you okay with soloing from the *Chandra* back to the *Krechet*?"

"Sure, no problem." There was genuine enthusiasm in his voice. Sawyer wondered how much of that was the chance to do more flying versus who his passenger would be.

"Great. In that case why don't you take left seat back to *Chandra*. You can do the takeoff and landing, but I'm happy to do some of the flying once we're in the air." The plane could of course be flown from either seat, but traditionally the pilot in command sat on the left in a fixed wing, a fact reflected in the layout of the instruments and controls.

Chapter 17: A Murder of Crows

Somewhere between Krechet and Chandrasekhar

The flight down had been uneventful, and now the Fred Tyrell and Ulrika Klaar were headed back to the *Chandrasekhar*. The EP02 was cruising two hundred meters above the ground when they encountered the birds.

"Look at the size of that flock!" Klaar nudged Tyrell and pointed off a few degrees to the right. A dark cloud, so dense it was almost solid, a black mass of protoplasm, swept up from the wooded area on the hills to the north, . "There must be thousands."

The cloud kept rising. "Tens of thousands," said Tyrell.

"Can we go closer?"

"Sure, but let's get a little higher and give them some room." He increased the throttle and put the plane in a gentle climb.

"This reminds me of something I read," said Klaar.

"Oh?"

"History of American settlement, the early days. Passenger pigeons. There used to be huge numbers of them, billions. They'd form massive flocks that could block out the sun, over a kilometer wide and hundreds of kilometers long."

"Go on, pull the other one."

"No, I am serious. At least, that is what the sources said."

"Doesn't make any sense," Tyrell said. "A flock that large? What would they eat? They would be worse than locusts."

"There was food in the forests. But that was part of their downfall."

"Oh? How so?"

"As the forests were cleared for agriculture there were fewer nesting areas, and when the birds began feeding on crops they were hunted. Finally their flocking behavior made them a tempting target. Against animal predators the huge flocks were an advantage, but that made them easy to harvest by humans with nets. They were eventually harvested to near extinction, and by the time the population collapsed to the point hunting was no longer profitable, there were too few left to form a breeding population, at least with what they knew about animals in those days."

"Sounds like what happened to a lot of fish species—large schools makes taking by net easy, which depletes the breeding population drastically."

"Yes, the same idea. The ocean used to be full of fish."

They were over the trees now. Below them the birds were clearly agitated, flying back and forth in all directions with no clear purpose. Tyrell wondered if the plane was disturbing them. "What's all that about, do you suppose?" he asked.

"This is probably a nesting area, we may be making them nervous."

"Nesting area?"

"Perhaps. Can we go in a little lower?"

"Okay, I'll take it back down to two hundred meters." Tyrell backed off the throttle and began a slow descent. The forested area seemed abuzz with the birds for kilometers in all directions. He hadn't gotten a good enough look to determine what kind of birds they were, or even if it was a species he'd seen before, but there were a lot of them.

All of a sudden the whole flock, which had been flitting around within twenty or so meters of the treetops, suddenly surged higher into the air. Tyrell looked around but couldn't tell what might have set them off. *Did the plane spook them, or some larger bird?* Below them more birds were leaving the trees.

The flocks rose fast, and even as he added power to climb out himself, they overtook the small plane and kept climbing. Their flight was chaotic, birds flying in all directions, unlike the ordered motion he was used to seeing in flocks of birds in flight. They mostly stayed clear of the plane, but a few stragglers or renegades were coming closer. Tyrell eased the power back and trimmed out to lower their airspeed. It was bad enough that the cloud made it hard to see landmarks on the ground, with birds flitting back and forth across his view. "All we need now is a bird strike," he started to say, and then it happened.

The plane kicked violently to starboard when the first bird hit it, or it hit the first bird. Klaar yelled the obvious. "A bird hit the wing!"

Tyrell focused on trying to counter the loss of lift in the now-dented wing, tilting the stick and pushing the power lever forward. Klaar shouted something at him again, and he looked up to see another cluster of birds in front of the plane. He banked hard, trying to avoid them, but the panicked birds flew in all directions. The rest was inevitable.

Propeller and bird met with a loud *WHAP!* and an explosion of blood and feathers. The low windshield turned red and Tyrell felt something splash over him. He tensed, wondering if the propeller was all right, and climbed for altitude. The air was still filled with those damn birds. The prop should be okay, but—

There came another burst of feathers and blood as they hit a third bird. Tyrell reached to pull the power back but it was too late. With a loud *CRACK* the damaged prop blade flew off and the plane shuddered, the now-unbalanced motor vibrating like a love-crazed washing machine. Tyrell gripped the controls tightly and quickly slapped the switch to *OFF* before the vibration could rip the motor out of its mounts. If that had happened, the shift in balance as the motor ripped free would make the plane unflyable. The sudden silence was disturbing.

He had to find a place to set down *right now*. Even with the small plane's phenomenal glide ratio, it couldn't stay airborne for long without power. He set the trim for their best glide speed and looked for somewhere to set down, all the while also seeking to take advantage of any thermals or ridge lift that he could find. He wouldn't have long at this altitude.

Klaar, beside him, also moved quickly. She let Tyrell fly the plane but grabbed the radio. "Mayday! Mayday! Mayday! This is Echo Papa Zero Two calling mayday. We have a bird strike and have lost power." She looked over at Tyrell. He gave her a quick glance and nodded. "We are attempting an emergency landing. Over."

"*Zero two this is* Chandrasekhar, *say again?*"

"*Chandra*, we're calling a mayday. We hit birds and lost the prop. We're going down. We're a hundred fifty kilometers north of *Krechet*, on a bearing of three-five-zero."

The trees were getting closer.

"*Roger Klaar, a hundred fifty klicks from* Krechet *on three five zero. We'll get someone to you as soon as we—*"

"What was that, *Chandra*?" The transmission had cut off. They were below the level of the surrounding hills.

Tyrell searched for a spot clear of trees. If he went down in those the plane would certainly be destroyed, possibly taking him and Klaar with it. Then she elbowed him and pointed.

"There's a field!" She had spotted a clearing partway down the slope.

"Got it," said Tyrell. "That's what I'm aiming for." He nudged the stick to bank the plane around, lining up with the long axis of the field. There were no good indicators of which way the wind was blowing—and the flock of birds was still going crazy, but he was below most of them now. "Brace yourself!"

Tyrell brought the wounded aircraft in over the scattered trees at the base of the field. As they dropped below the treeline the plane dipped and wobbled in the turbulence. He wrestled it back to straight and level, feet dancing on the rudder pedals to keep the plane lined up in the slight crosswind. Damn, they were landing on the side of a hill.

Okay, focus on the horizon, not the slope in front, he told himself. *Keep the wings level until the wheels are on the ground.* As the airspeed dropped off, he raised the nose slightly to prolong the glide, bleeding off as much speed in the air as he could before the inevitable.

The trees at the far end of the clearing were too close, and getting closer. The plane wouldn't stop before reaching them.

Tyrell picked a pair tree trunks, a bit over two meters apart, and lined up on the gap between them. If he couldn't stop before that it was better to take the impact on the wings.

They were just a couple of meters above the ground now, and the stall horn started honking. Just a little further. He briefly wondered how Klaar was doing but couldn't spare a glance. "Hang on!"

The wheels hit with a bump and the plane lifted on the bounce, coming down again a fraction of a second later. Then the left wheel slammed into something and the plane pivoted wildly around, the wingtip digging into the ground on the uphill side.

Tyrell felt himself pulled violently sideways, and then something hard slammed against his head.

Chapter 18: Mayday Received

Chandrasekhar, Landing Site One

"Echo Papa Zero Two, this is *Chandrasekhar*, please respond." Ganesh Patel looked up from the radio to check the time. At his glance, Sawyer did too. It was almost two minutes since they'd received the frantic mayday call. "Klaar or Tyrell, nothing heard. Status report please."

"Maybe the radio was damaged by the hard landing, or there's a hill in the way," said Sawyer. She had been passing the bridge and caught heard the tail end of Klaar's mayday, and stayed to listen and help if she could.

"Any landing hard enough to damage the radio would have left the crew injured, or worse." Patel said.

Sawyer cursed under her breath. "Check with the *Heinlein*," she said. "Maybe they have something."

"*Centauri Station* is below the horizon. We can a signal to them using the relay, but its configuration is not suitable for the aircraft radios." Patel said. "Anyway, I am raising them now." He touched a control to change radio channels and hailed them.

"Chandrasekhar, *this is* Centauri Station. *What's up?*"

"The plane with Tyrell and Klaar is down. We got a mayday call about a bird strike and they were attempting an emergency landing." Patel touched a control to upload the recording to the orbiting station. "That was two minutes ago, we have heard nothing since. They were about a hundred fifty kilometers from *Krechet*, bearing three five zero."

"*Roger Chandra, Zero Two down one fifty at three five zero from Krechet. We won't have any contact with them until our orbit brings us around again. We'll keep you posted. Let us know if you hear anything.*"

"The other plane is at the *Krechet*, any chance they can do a pickup?"

"*We'll talk to them. Last I heard they were making a configuration change, something about putting floats on to make it amphibious. They'd have to reverse that and strip out some other gear to be able to take an extra passenger, or do two trips.*"

Sawyer heard a garbled voice in the background, somebody else was talking.

"*Ah, wait one, Chandra*"

Sawyer's mind raced. They might be all right, the mayday had faded before impact, so perhaps they were just in a radio shadow. If there was one injury, then the other plane, EP01, could keep the floats and pick up whoever it was, assuming there was somewhere nearby to land. The floats didn't replace the wheels, so it could still land on dry ground, but the floats meant it would need a longer runway. Were they near the coast? They could run the inflatable parallel to the shoreline, although that would take hours. *Damn!*

The radio sounded again. "*Okay, Chandra, we're back. Doctor Krysansky raises the point that they might need to rig a litter if there are serious injuries. Any idea?*"

"None, *Centauri*, we lost contact just before they landed. That will have to wait until you can contact them directly, or observe them from orbit."

"*Agreed. All right, let me contact* Krechet *and have them start prepping the other plane. They'll have to remove equipment to save weight anyway.*"

"Roger that."

"And don't worry, I'm sure they're fine."

Sawyer rather doubted that, and from Patel's grim look, he felt the same. They'd have to be incredibly lucky to find a good place to land, although the little electroplanes could set down with very little roll out. *If the winds were right and they'd had power.*

Chapter 19: No Walk in the Park

EP02 crash site, Kakuloa

Something poked Tyrell's right side. It wouldn't let him sleep, and that's all he wanted to do. He tried to push it away and his hands encountered graphite tubing. The memory started to come back, and with it pain. They had crashed.

He opened his eyes. Or rather, his left eye, the right one was stuck shut. He wiped it with his hand, rubbed it, then blinked it open. Dried blood covered his hand. *Ulrika? Where was Klaar?* He moved to get up, or tried to. He was still strapped in to the plane's seat, but the frame was crumpled and the wings had collapsed. It was a piece of the frame that dug into his ribs.

"Ulrika?" His voice came out as more of a croak, and the effort made his head hurt. "Dr. Klaar, you there?" *Ow*, that was enough. Time to rest again. He closed his eyes.

"Fred, don't go back to sleep on me." Klaar's voice.

"What?" He opened his eyes again. There was Klaar, leaning on the wreckage of the plane right in front of him. He could have sworn she wasn't there a moment ago.

"Here, can you drink some of this?" She held out a water bottle.

Tyrell sat up a bit further. He hadn't realized how thirsty he was. His throat hurt. He grabbed for the water bottle and drank from it greedily, chugging it down.

"Stop," she said, grabbing back the bottle. "Take it slowly, we don't have much of that, and you don't want to make yourself sick. How are you feeling, does anything hurt?"

Tyrell wondered if there was anything that *didn't* hurt, but he paused and took stock. Headache, sore throat, the pain in his side from where the fuselage had poked him. His hips hurt, probably bruised from the seat-belt. Aside from that and a general feeling of having been rolled down a flight of stairs in a cardboard box, he didn't feel too bad.

"No broken bones, if that's what you mean. How about you?"

"Shaken but not stirred. Just a few bumps and scrapes. What's my name?"

"What? Ulrika Klaar. You got amnesia?"

"No, just wondering if you do. What's your name?"

"Fred Tyrell. And my birthday's June twenty-second. And today is . . . uh, do you want Earth time or Alpha Centauri time? Why do you think I have amnesia?"

"Do you remember waking up before?"

"Uh, no, I just woke up."

"This is the third time you've woken up and we've talked. Mind, you're doing better this time. You took a nasty bump on the head, it knocked you out. You had amnesia for a little while there."

"*What?*" The thought of losing his memory was frightening.

"Don't worry," Klaar added at the look of alarm on his face, "most likely it was just short term memory. Sometimes that happens, coming around from being unconscious."

"I was awake before? Really?"

"Yes you were." She peered into his eyes and held up a finger. "Now watch my finger." She moved her arm slowly left and right, up and down. "Good, both eyes are tracking. I don't think it's anything serious."

"How long was I out?"

"Just a few minutes, I think. I don't know exactly what time we crashed. I was dazed but I don't think I was knocked out. How is your head? You're covered in blood but I don't know how much of that is yours and how much is the bird's."

Tyrell gingerly reached a hand up to his throbbing head and patted gently. The matted blood felt sticky in his hair, and—*ouch!*—there was a cut in his scalp. He felt around that cautiously. He had a nasty lump but it didn't feel like anything was cracked. He'd probably still be out cold if he'd been hit that hard. "Some of it's mine, but I'm not bleeding anymore. I hope that bird blood isn't toxic."

"It shouldn't be. We haven't found anything like that in the birds we've examined."

"Okay," he said, his self-assessment complete for now. "What now? Where are we and can we get a pick up?"

"Look around. I don't see anywhere suitable for landing the other plane."

The ground sloped, and there were small boulders in amongst the low vegetation. Klaar was right. They'd have to hike to somewhere more suitable, wherever that was.

"Have you talked to anyone at either of the ships yet?"

"No, I'm having a trouble getting a signal to either *Chandrasekhar* or *Krechet*. It's probably the terrain."

"What about *Heinlein, Centauri Station?*"

"They're on the other side of the planet at the moment, they should be over the horizon in a half hour or so."

"I knew they should have stayed synchronous." Before the landing there had been discussion, some of it heated, as to where *Centauri Station* would 'park'. The argument in favor of taking up a synchronous orbit in sight of the landing area was that radio coverage would be continuous, and the lander would be in sight from the *Heinlein* at all times. The disadvantage was that they'd miss out on a lot of observing time. Without orbiting over different areas of the planet they wouldn't get the kind of mapping, weather and other data they were here to gather. At the higher altitude of synchronous orbit they'd also be exposed to more radiation, although that should be nothing the antirad drugs couldn't deal with. They'd elected the lower orbit, inclined to the equator. It was a compromise, of course. Some of the scientists had wanted a polar orbit to get complete coverage of the planet, but Drake overruled that, citing mission safety requirements; a polar orbit would put them out of contact with the landing party for too many hours at a stretch, even with a relay satellite.

"That is a moot point now," Klaar said. "They are in the orbit they're in. We'll call them in half an hour and figure out our next move. Meanwhile we can pull our gear out of the wreckage and see what else we can salvage. I have already begun that."

∞ ∞ ∞

Twenty minutes later they had their equipment laid out in several piles. There was the must-have gear that they'd take with them if they had to hike; the too-heavy or too-bulky gear which would be useful if they set up camp at the crash site; and the gear which had either been damaged in the crash or was otherwise useless. Tyrell had to rest several times during this process, as his headache came and went, but the intervals were getting shorter and further apart.

"*Centauri Station* this is Ulrika Klaar, over." The aircraft radio had survived, which was a good thing. The *Heinlein* certainly had instruments capable of picking up transmissions from their personal omnis, but they wouldn't be using it for that unless and until Tyrell and Klaar had gone a lot longer without checking in. She wasn't sure when *Chandra* would be able to report their predicament.

"*Centauri Station*, Klaar calling. Anyone there?"

"Are you sure the radio works?" asked Tyrell.

"Yes. Well, reasonably sure. They're just not up over the horizon yet. I don't know exactly when that will be." Klaar tried hail again. "*Centauri Station*, this is Ulrika Klaar, over?"

"*Ulrika, this is* Centauri. *Your signal is a bit weak. Go ahead.*"

"Good to hear from you. Get a fix on this signal and take a look, we had a forced landing. Over."

"Forced landing?" Tyrell snorted. "We crashed."

Klaar gave him a dirty look and shushed him.

"*Will do.* Chandra *said something about a bird strike. Are you both okay?*"

"We are a little bumped around, but yes. We won't be flying out again though."

"*Okay, Ulrika, we've got a fix and, yes, there you are in the scope. I see what you mean, doesn't look like there's much left of the plane.*"

"Should I wave?"

"*Image isn't that good, you're not more than a few pixels high. So how* are we going to get you out of there?"

"That is a good question," she said. "There is not really anywhere to land here. Is there somewhere nearby we can hike to where the other plane could pick us up?"

"*That might be a problem. The other plane was halfway through having floats attached. They didn't want to continue with that in case you needed a short field pickup, but if there's a clearer area or a lake, they'll finish that up. Glad to hear there are no broken bones or serious bleeding.*"

"As are we. So no ride home?"

"*Not immediately, but it could be ready to go by the time you get to where you're going.*"

"And just where are we going?"

"*Let me confer and get back to you.*"

"Don't be long, you will be below our horizon again soon."

"*Roger.*"

Tyrell said to Klaar: "Maybe we should just hike the rest of the way to the *Chandra*. Or back to *Krechet*, whichever is closer." Even though he was suggesting it, he wasn't particularly happy at the prospect.

"Are you in any shape to travel at all? Anyway, to the *Chandra* I think. We need to get there anyway and we're close to the halfway point."

"That figures," Tyrell said.

"*Ulrika, this is the* Heinlein.*"*

"Go ahead *Heinlein*, what do you have?"

"*Okay you're about halfway between* Chandra *and* Krechet.*"*

I told you so, Tyrell mouthed silently.

"*By air you're actually closer to* Krechet *but given the terrain it would be quicker to get to* Chandra. *The route takes you through places that could provide a landing strip for the other plane, if it's ready to go.*"

"Sounds good, how far are we talking about?"

"*That's the bad news, it's roughly a hundred and twenty kilometers. Are you guys up to that kind of hike?*"

Klaar look at Tyrell questioningly. "What do you think?"

He shrugged. "I've done fifty mile – eighty kilometer – hikes in my time. Say we can do fifty kilometers in a day," he looked at her questioningly. She nodded, she could do that. "Then that's three days, four days tops. EP01 should be ready long before that. Think of the exploration we can do on the way."

Klaar nodded. She keyed the microphone again. "That's affirmative *Heinlein*, north to *Chandra* it is. You will have to reconfigure the radio gear to talk to our omniphones, we can't take the aircraft radio with us."

"*Roger that, we've already got someone working on it. We'll download maps to your omnis.*"

"That would be very useful. Why did we not do that before?"

"*Why bother, the plane's nav system has it all.*"

"Ah, right."

"*Ulrika, we're about to go beyond your horizon. We're going to do an orbit change so we should be back around in eighty five minutes.*"

"I don't want to sit around that long. We're going to run out of daylight."

"*Then don't. Follow a bearing of three one seven, that looks like a fairly easy hike, mostly clear terrain. We'll be back in an hour and twenty five.*"

"Heading three one seven. Roger *Heinlein*, thank you."

The radio signal faded out less than a minute later.

"Are you sure you're up to traveling?" Klaar asked Tyrell. "If you've had a concussion that may not be the best idea."

He waved her off. "I'll be fine. The headache's mostly gone." They'd located the first-aid kit while organizing the gear. Fresh bandages, a broad-spectrum antibiotic, and a couple of painkillers later, Tyrell was indeed feeling better. He didn't know how long that would last though.

"Right, let's get this caravan moved out." Klaar grabbed up a bag and swung it over her shoulders. Tyrell picked up the other bag a little more slowly, favoring the injured arm and side. She shot him a look and raised an eyebrow.

"Just a twinge. Let's go."

Klaar looked at her omni, locked around her wrist. "Dammit, it isn't working properly."

"Banged up in the crash?"

"That must be it, but I thought these things were tougher than that. Don't they have a gazillion little nanocells that reconfigure themselves as needed?"

"Something like that. Maybe something messed up the software." Tyrell checked his own. "Mine seems okay." He turned left and right a little, watching the omni. "Okay, three- one-seven is that way." He pointed. "Let's go."

"Okay. You're the one with the compass, you might as well take the lead. And that way I'll notice if you keel over."

"Okay, enough with the wounded Fred jokes."

∞ ∞ ∞

They headed northwest, across and down the slope of the hillside where they'd made their forced landing. Down here where they had the time to look, the stones and potholes that had been hidden by vegetation from the air were obvious.

"Make a note, recommendation for future explorations—put a ground-imaging radar on the damn airplane." Tyrell recorded the comment on his omni but he was speaking loud enough for Klaar to hear.

"Good idea," she said.

"Actually that was part of the original design. We took it out to save weight for the crew reshuffle. I suppose we might have been able to transplant the one from the drone. On the other hand, we didn't have much choice on landing area."

"How about making the airplane a helicopter, or a quad?" Klaar asked. If they'd been able to hover and land vertically, the boulder-strewn field wouldn't have been a problem.

"You'd be in worse trouble if a bird broke the rotor, maybe less so in a quadcopter. But there'd be no wings, where would you put the solar panels?"

"The rotor blades? No, I guess that wouldn't work, connecting the power through the hub would be awkward. How about a roll up panel. Fly on batteries and unroll the panel to recharge when you land."

"That might work. We'll have to suggest it when we get back." Tyrell recorded a reminder in his omni.

"Do you think we will? Get back, I mean."

"Why wouldn't we? Yeah it's a three day hike but *Heinlein* will keep an eye on us."

"A three day hike across alien territory with who knows what in the way of dangerous animals, venomous insects, or terrain we can't cross."

Tyrell had been wondering about that himself, not to mention his uncertainty whether he was really fit enough to travel. His head throbbed with every jarring footstep. But this was not the time to bring that up. "No worries, there's no reason anything should attack us here any more that it would on Earth." Well, no reason besides the fact that most dangerous-to-human Earth life had been either driven extinct or had learned to avoid humans, adaptations that wouldn't have happened here.

"You're probably right. I don't think I'm going to sleep well tonight though."

"Maybe they'll be able to fly the other plane by then. If we can't find a suitable landing area they can at least drop supplies."

"I don't suppose they could drop a cabin with a bed and a hot shower."

Tyrell smiled at the thought. "Probably not, no. But you knew the job would be tough when you took it."

"I did. Don't mind me, I'm just complaining to keep busy. And to keep the bears away."

"Bears? What bears?"

"See? It's working," Klaar quipped. "No, seriously, on Earth this could be bear country. We would talk and make noise while hiking to alert bears to our presence, so we didn't startle them. Usually they stayed away. I don't know if there's anything like bears here, but the same principle applies."

Tyrell decided not to mention his earlier thought about the native life not having learned to avoid humans. It probably wouldn't make a difference either way if a bear—ursoid?—heard them or not. It would probably smell them, and either approach or leave as its curiosity dictated. Talking wouldn't make much difference. It would have been nice if the survival kit had included a rifle, or at least sidearms.

By now they had reached the bottom of the slope, and Tyrell paused while Klaar came up beside him.

"What now?" she asked.

He flicked on the compass in his omni again. The valley they were in ran east-west, sloping gently toward the west. The trees were thicker here, and though still sparse, with the trunks widely separated, their branches were close enough that there was no way they could have landed here. Their heading took them diagonally up the side of the next hill, the trees thinning out again.

"Up the hill," he pointed, "that a way."

They started up.

Even though the hill was not steep, climbing it was more of a strain than Tyrell had expected. The drag of his heavy pack and the pounding of his feet into the ground with each step made his head throb. He stopped and leaned against a tree trunk to catch his breath.

"Are you all right?" asked Klaar.

"Yeah, I'll be fine. Just need to catch my breath for a bit."

"We can rest here, or I'll take some of what's in your pack."

"No, you're already carrying enough. I can manage." Could he? A walking stick or staff might help. He looked around at the trees.

"I could probably use a hiking staff, let's see what we can find." His gaze swept the area looking for a suitable branch or sapling.

"Good idea, I wouldn't mind one too."

"To fight off bears?" Tyrell joked.

"Hah. No, if it comes to that, I will use it to hit you over the head and leave you for the bear while I escape."

"Nice." He strolled over to a tree that had a dead limb projecting at head height. "This looks like it might do," he said, reaching up to grab the branch with both hands. He pulled hard on it, and it bent a little but didn't break. He moved his grip further out on the branch for more leverage. "Ulrika, give me a hand here."

"Of course." Together they reached up and pulled on the branch, which creaked under their combined weight and the broke with a *crack*. They staggered to recover their balance as the branch came down.

"This will do." Tyrell began stripping the smaller branches and twigs from it.

"Okay. I don't want to hold us up, I'll keep an eye out for another one as we hike. Are you ready to continue?"

Tyrell took several experimental steps with his improvised staff. Being able to take some of the weight off his feet helped. His head still throbbed but it wasn't worth holding up the hike for, they had a lot of ground to cover. "Yes, this will work. Let's go."

∞ ∞ ∞

They stopped again an hour later. Tyrell unshouldered his pack and swung it to the ground, then sat down heavily beside it.

"Okay," he panted, "break time." The throbbing in his head was getting worse again.

"You should drink. Dehydration will only make you feel worse." Klaar set down her pack and squatted beside it. She checked the pockets then unzipped one and pulled out a water bottle from it. She loosened the cap and handed the bottle to him. "Here, take this."

"Thanks." He took a sip, then chugged nearly half the bottle. He hadn't realized how thirsty he was. "How much water do we have?" They'd inventoried it back at the plane but he couldn't remember, he'd been a little fuzzy.

"Four liters, less what you just drank. We'll need to find a water source by tomorrow."

"We'll ask the *Heinlein*. Speaking of which," Tyrell looked at his omniphone to check the time, "they should be in radio range in just a few minutes."

Klaar pulled out another water bottle and took a long drink. "How far do you think we've come?"

"Good question." He fiddled with his omni for a bit. "Damn, I forgot to set the origin when we left the plane. This thing has no idea where we are."

"I don't think that would have made much difference. We've been moving too slowly and irregularly, the accelerometers would have accumulated a lot of error."

"It's supposed to average out, but you may be right. On Earth I just always used GPS for hikes, I never bothered with the built-in inertial navigation."

"We never used it for exploring caves, either, we always brought along special purpose inertial navs."

"You're a caver?"

"Not any more. I did a lot in college, and my master's thesis was on the genetic changes in blind cave animals. I crawled around many caves doing field work."

"Huh. I had you figured as more the sun and surf beach type, not crawling around in dark damp holes."

"The North Sea hasn't warmed up *that* much," she said.

Before Tyrell could reply, his omni chimed.

"*Tyrell or Klaar, this is the* Heinlein *calling. Are you receiving?*"

"Affirmative *Heinlein*, this is Tyrell. Go ahead."

"*Ah, there you are. Okay we have a fix on your signal.*"

"How are we doing?"

"*You're only about three kilometers from the plane wreck. You might want to step up the pace a bit.*"

"Okay, we'll keep that in mind. *Heinlein*, what's ahead of us in the way of water sources? We've got perhaps a day's worth."

"*There should be small streams in the area you're in, we can't say for sure through the trees. Twenty-five kilometers ahead there's a small lake, and a river that you'll have to cross about forty kilometers from you.*"

"How wide is this river that we'll have to cross? You didn't say anything about it before."

"*It's small, it's really more of a wide creek than a river. Fifteen meters across, maybe. Shallow, too. When you get closer we can guide you to a likely crossing spot.*"

"Thanks *Heinlein*."

"*Okay, we're going to lose the signal soon. Anything else, how are you holding up?*"

"So far so good. Any word on the other plane?"

"*Still waiting on that. The weather at the landing site—*" The transmission faded out.

"Dang, lost them." Tyrell checked the time. "Okay, we can

talk again in about two hours. It will be getting dark by then." He heaved himself to his feet. "Let's push on."

"Think we'll make the lake by then?"

"Fifteen kilometers? That's a pretty good hiking pace." Tyrell considered. The rest and the water had helped considerably, his head no longer pounded. "Let's give it a shot."

"Okay. But don't overdo it, if you need to rest just say so."

"Yes, mother," he said. The words came out with a more sarcastic tone than he'd intended.

"Oh. I am sorry." Klaar took a step back. "I don't mean to nag."

"No, I'm sorry, I shouldn't have snapped. I really do appreciate your concern, I'm just frustrated with the whole situation." He looked at her and forced a smile. She smiled back, although a bit tentatively. *It's not her fault, dang it.* "Anyway, let's just get moving."

"After you," Klaar gave a half bow and swept out her arm in an openhanded gesture.

Chapter 20: Weather Forecast

Centauri Station, in orbit

"*Commodore Drake, sir?*" Drake heard a note of concern in the voice.

"Drake here, what is it?"

"This is Simms in meteorology. We've got what looks like it might be a major weather system building over the Western Ocean."

"What sort of weather system?"

"A tropical depression that's picking up a lot of moisture. The whole system is moving eastward at about twenty kph. There's already some gusting ahead of it."

"What's the significance?"

"Worst case it could build to a sizable storm that will come ashore somewhere between the *Krechet* and *Chandra* landing sites."

"Are we talking about a typhoon here?"

"I don't think so, unless it surprises us. We still don't have a good model of the ocean circulation here to make a reliable prediction. It could just start to rain itself out before coming ashore, although that's unlikely."

"How long?"

"About two days at the current speed. We'll have a better picture tomorrow."

"All right, keep an eye on it and keep me posted. Let me know if the situation changes for the worse." Not that there was much he could do about it. "And give the landing parties a heads up."

"Of course."

Chapter 21: A Night Out

Somewhere between Krechet and Chandrasekhar landing sites

The sun—Alpha Centauri B—was low in the western sky when Tyrell and Klaar saw the lake. It was about three kilometers off, down in a valley beyond a smaller hill than the one whose peak they'd just crested.

"There it is, I don't think we're going to make it before dark," said Tyrell.

"No. We should stop and set up camp while we still have some light." Alpha Centauri A would be bright, but there were enough scattered clouds that they couldn't rely on it.

"Agreed." He looked around. They were in a small clearing just past the crest of the hill, Twenty to thirty meters down a gentle slope the bare rock, possibly limestone, showed through the thin soil, forming a slightly tilted but flat surface about five meters wide and forming the lip of a drop off. Tree tops showed just beyond it.

"How about there?" He pointed at the rock shelf.

"That works," she nodded. "Nothing is going to approach from downhill and we can build a fire on the rocks without worrying about burning the forest down."

"A fire? Sure we can do that," Tyrell said as they started down to the ledge. "Grab what deadwood you can find, you're not burning my staff."

"I just wish we had marshmallows."

By the time they reached the rock ledge, Klaar had an armful of firewood. She dropped it at her feet and unshouldered her pack. "What do we need to do while it's still light?" she asked. In fact the light was fading quickly. Centauri B's light was more orange than the Sun's to start with, and it was dimming to deep red as it settled toward the horizon.

"Gather more firewood, set up shelter, check out the area for hostile wildlife."

"Such as?"

"Snakes, spiders, whatever other creepy crawlies there might be," Tyrell said. "Probably no bears though."

"Okay, do you want to set up camp while I gather more firewood?"

The idea sounded great to Tyrell, who had been pushing his limits for the last half-hour of the hike. He didn't want to let Klaar know though, she'd worry about him. He'd be fine after a night's rest. But "Sure. Just stay within sight, we don't want to get separated."

"Don't worry," she said, and headed back up to the trees.

Tyrell busied himself with digging their gear out of the backpacks. He had considered the survival packs an unnecessary waste of space and weight for the small plane, but it was part of the mission rules and the commander had insisted. Tyrell was now glad that he had.

He pulled a small package about the size of a soda can out of the backpack and read the label:

"Tent, survival, two-person. To deploy: place on ground, pull ring tab, stand clear."

There was a thumb ring at one end. Tyrell thought it made the whole package resemble a smoke grenade, but for the lack of a handle. The instructions helped that impression. He shrugged and set the package down.

Steadying it with his left hand, he pulled the triggering ring. The package spoke to him:

"Please step back. Deploying in three, two, one. Now."

Tyrell had been so amused at the thought that someone had bothered to put a voice chip in a tent that he'd forgotten to stand clear, and jumped back as the package suddenly extended a shaft a meter long and began unfolding itself like a compact umbrella. It went through a rapid sequence of unfoldings and unrollings, until at last it formed a geodesic half-cylinder a meter high with a base about two meters square. One end had a flap entrance. Tyrell stuck his head through the flap and a stripe running the length of the ceiling lit up with an orange glow. He looked around and saw a small rectangle at one end of the strip with the universal "on/off" symbol on it. He touched it and the light strip turned off. He shook his head, gently. Survival gear had come a long way since he'd been a Boy Scout.

He was almost disappointed at the low-tech sleeping pads, which also started out soda-can sized but had no voice chip and simply self-inflated when he rotated the end-cap to allow air in. The sleeping bags, of a filmy fabric that felt like silk but with smart pores that regulated the temperature, simply unfolded from their fist-sized stuff bags.

Klaar had already delivered another load of firewood and gone back for more when he exited the tent. With the tent set up, Tyrell dug out the small camp stove and pots, then dug through the food. It was all concentrated food that needed minimal preparation. He wondered about the stove and realized that it would be useful for boiling water, or for melting snow for drinking water under other circumstances. Thankfully they weren't anywhere near the snow line, and it was summer.

Klaar came back with another load. "How are we doing?"

"Good. Are you ready to eat?"

"I'm starving. What's for dinner?"

"Ration bars. Sorry, it's a survival kit. The tent is fancy, but not the food I'm afraid."

Klaar sighed. "I suppose that is to be expected. We can go without food for a lot longer than we can go without shelter if the weather is bad." She'd been arranging the firewood as she spoke, first sorting it into piles by size, then starting to build the basis for the fire.

Tyrell got up and stretched. He needed to pee. "I'll be back," he said, and started walking toward the trees.

"Where are you going?"

"To find a tree. Won't be long."

"What? *Oh*. Right."

When he got back, Klaar was getting the fire lit. The dried

deadwood caught easily, and soon they had a crackling blaze. By now Alpha Centauri B was below the horizon and the red glow of sunset was beginning to wane. The fire wasn't essential for survival—the bags and tent would keep them warm in anything less than arctic conditions, and the ration bars needed no cooking—but psychologically it helped immensely, Tyrell reflected. People had been using fire for a quarter million years or more, it was part of what made us human.

They sat in silence, chewing on their food bars and staring into the flames. Occasionally a piece of burning wood would split with a crack and send a shower of sparks skyward. Overhead the stars were beginning to come out.

"How far do you think we'll get tomorrow?" Klaar asked.

"Hard to say. We were slowing down at the end here, but if we head out at first light, after a night's rest, we should make pretty good time. It depends on the terrain." He unfolded the omni's big screen and opened the satellite photograph of the path ahead. "Once we get past the lake we've got another line of hills, but it looks like it's still lightly forested. We might be able to make the river by noon, early afternoon perhaps." He finished the last bite of his food bar (yummy peanut-butter flavor!) and washed it down with the remainder of the contents of his water bottle. He tossed the wrapper in the fire and watched as it flared up. The empty water bottle he stowed back in his pack, they could refill it when they got to the lake in the morning.

"Yes, we should head out at first light," Klaar said. "And you should get all the rest you can. That bump on the head you took gave you a concussion, you should have been resting the whole time, not hiking cross country."

"I know, but we had to get moving." Tyrell's head was still throbbing, but in fact he felt much better now for having eaten and rested. With any luck he be perfectly fine by morning. "Okay, let's turn in," he said, getting to his feet.

Klaar tossed the last of her food wrapper in the fire and stood up too, then turned to look at the small tent. "I'll have you know that I don't usually sleep with a guy on the first date."

"Trust me, all I'm going to be doing is sleeping. I'm beat." He started to crawl into the tent, then stopped, kneeling at the entrance. "Wait, what did you mean 'usually'?"

"None of your business," she said. The words were tempered by the grin on her face.

∞ ∞ ∞

Midway through the night they were both awakened by a raucous shrieking.

"What the hell is that?" Klaar asked, sitting up abruptly.

"I have no idea. Some kind of animal, obviously. Too high pitched to be anything big, though."

"Are you sure? Maybe Centauri animals have naturally high voices." She paused. "No, that doesn't make sense, it's simple physics based on the size of the resonating organ."

"Wow. How are you awake enough to think that through? I'm still trying to figure out what you meant by 'resonating organ'. Oh, vocal cords, throat length, whatever."

"Yeah, and it was the adrenaline. But the noise has stopped."

"Might have been a predator making a kill, or perhaps a couple of animals fighting over territory. It did sound a bit like a pair of tomcats fighting."

"Yes. It just startled me. Now I have to try to get back to sleep with all this adrenaline in my system."

"It'll wear off." Tyrell lay on his back staring up into the blackness. He could just make out the roof of the tent above him by the dim light from outside. Either the moon or Alpha Centauri A must be up. "Hey, want to hear a joke?"

"Sure, it'll take my mind off whatever that was."

"Okay. Sherlock Holmes and his buddy Doctor Watson—uh, you do know who Sherlock Holmes is?"

"Of course. The detective, yes? Everyone knows that."

"Oh, right. Anyway, Holmes and Watson decide to get away from London for a few days and go on a camping trip. They set up camp, eat dinner, and settle in for the night."

"The situation sounds familiar."

"Hush. Anyway, they're asleep when something wakes up Holmes in the middle of the night."

"A blood curdling scream?" asked Klaar.

"Who's telling this joke? Now be quiet."

"Sorry. Okay, I'll be good."

Tyrell continued his story. "Anyway, Holmes nudges Watson.

"'Watson, wake up!' he says.

"'What?' Watson says, blearily, 'What is it, Holmes?'

"'Look up above you, Watson, tell me what you see.'

"So Watson looks up. It's a beautiful clear night, the stars are shining bright, the moon is out. 'I see the stars, and the Moon, Holmes,' he says, wondering what the point is.

"Holmes says, 'Indeed, and what is the significance of that, Watson?'

"'The significance? Well, the number of stars reminds us how vast the universe is, and how insignificant we are by comparison.'

"'Anything else?' asks Holmes.

"'Let me think.' By now Watson figures this must be some kind of test, so he starts seriously pondering what he sees. 'Well, the moon is half full, waning as I recall, and it is about halfway up the eastern sky. That must make it about three o'clock in the morning.'

"Holmes is getting a little frustrated by this point. 'Very good Watson, but there is something more fundamental. What else?'

"This is too much for Watson. Some random thoughts come to mind—the lack of clouds means it will be a fine day tomorrow, the faint smell of smoke means there's a fire somewhere not far away, but he doesn't know what Holmes is asking for. 'Sorry Holmes, I don't see what you're getting at. The weather? The smoke?'

"'Damn it, man, you *see* but you do not *observe*. Somebody has stolen our tent!'"

Klaar collapsed in a peal of laughter. "Ha ha ha, that is priceless. I had not heard that one before."

Tyrell smiled. She had a nice laugh. "Glad you liked it. Now, nobody has stolen our tent, so get back to sleep. We've got a long day tomorrow."

"You're right. Goodnight." Klaar stretched out then rolled onto her side.

"Goodnight." Tyrell lay awake for a while longer, listening as her breathing shallowed in sleep. He was acutely aware of the young woman now sleeping beside him. Under other circumstances . . . but between the after-effects of the concussion, and the responsibility he felt for crashing the plane in the first place, he'd be happy with a good night's sleep. They had a major hike ahead of them, and who knew what dangers they might encounter. Eventually he too drifted off.

Chapter 22: Day After Crash

The campsite

The sky to the east was barely aglow when the two awoke and began striking camp. Klaar pulled out ration bars and water bottles from the packs as Tyrell began to roll up the sleeping bags and pads.

"I'd kill for some coffee now," Klaar said.

"Coffee? That would be wonderful. As would real food for breakfast instead of those bars." Tyrell stowed the rolled-up sleeping pads into the pack and examined the tent. "Any idea how this thing disassembles?"

"Hm? There should be instructions on the label."

"That was how to deploy it."

"Look again, it's probably context sensitive." Klaar said.

"Oh, sure." The technology had been around for a while, but Tyrell hadn't seen it in use much. He lifted the end of the tent.

Sure enough the label now read: "Tent, survival, two-person. To refold: Ensure tent is empty. Apply pressure at diagonally opposite corners. Keep fingers clear."

He picked up one corner of the tent, leaving the opposite corner on the ground. He pushed, and the frame bowed a bit then sprung back. He pushed again, this time holding the pressure. The voice sounded *"Tent will fold, please keep fingers clear. Folding in three, two, one, now."* The resistance against Tyrell's pushing on the tent corner suddenly went away, and the tent started to shrink, the framework folding at odd angles as he watched. It folded slower than it had unfolded, but still quickly enough to be hard to follow. In less than a minute it was back to a soda-can sized package. Idly Tyrell wondered what would have happened if his fingers *had* been in the way. He hoped it would have stopped folding, but he wondered just how smart the tent was.

The sky was brighter now, with a bright light to the east where Alpha Centauri B was just beginning to poke above the horizon.

Klaar said "I'm done eating. Here," she handed him a food bar and a water bottle, "eat your breakfast while I put the rest of the gear in the bags."

"Okay, thanks." Tyrell took the food bar and started to unwrap it. "'Bacon and egg flavor'? Really?"

"I think somebody has a cruel sense of humor. But mine wasn't as bad as I had expected."

"If you say so." He peeled the end of the wrapper off the end of the bar and cautiously took a small bite. The texture was exactly the same mealy texture as the peanut butter bar he'd eaten the night before, but the taste was indeed vaguely eggy and bacony. "You know, I think they make these things taste the way they do so that you don't pig out on them. One at a sitting is all anyone could handle."

Klaar laughed. "I think you must be right. Deviously clever, these survival planners." She finished packing the bags and stood up. "Ready to go?"

Tyrell put the last bite of bar into his mouth and the wrapper into his pocket. "Jus' a sec," he said, still chewing on the last bite of breakfast. He took a swing from the water bottle. "Ah. Sorry, yeah, now I'm ready to go." Klaar handed him his pack and he picked up his staff from the ground. The fire had burned itself out in the night and there was a small pile of charcoal and ashes on the bare stone where they'd built it. He was sure it was too cold to start up again, but his Boy Scout training wouldn't let him just leave it. They didn't have water to spare, but. . . .. "You go on, I'm going to make sure the fire's out." He waved Klaar ahead.

"What, how? Oh." She blushed and turned away to start down the hill.

He caught up with her a minute or two later.

"Is that something you learned in Boy Scouts?" she asked

him.

"You'd be surprised what I learned in Boy Scouts."

"I don't think I want to know."

∞ ∞ ∞

Landing Site One, aboard Chandrasekhar

Elizabeth Sawyer was reviewing data at one of the consoles in when the call came in. They weren't due for check in just yet.

"This is the *Chandra*, Sawyer speaking. What's up?"

"Chandra, *that tropical depression we mentioned yesterday is turning into a storm, it's building off the coast. The winds have picked up, so it will probably hit you late tomorrow, possibly sooner.*"

"Roger that, *Heinlein*. What do you recommend?"

"*You'll need to secure the lander, it probably wouldn't hurt to double the tie-downs. And finish up the lightning mast.*"

"Will it affect the *Krechet*?"

"*They'll get some rain but it looks like the storm track is to the north, they should be okay. I'm talking to them next.*"

"What about Fred and Ulrika?"

"*They were doing fine at last check-in. They're between you and* Krechet *so it's difficult to say how hard it will hit them. If they can keep up a good pace they might make it back before the storm hits. We'll be checking in with them in about a half-hour.*"

"Okay. What about *Krechet*'s plane? Will they be able to pick up Fred and Ulrika, or at least drop supplies?"

"*We'll check with* Krechet, *but it looks like they may be already getting some strong wind gusts. I'm not sure that's going to be an option by the time they get it ready to fly.*"

The lightly-built planes couldn't handle much in the way of a crosswind. It might actually be easier with floats if the wind was lengthwise on a lake, but then they'd have whitecaps to worry about. "Yeah, it's blowing pretty hard here too," Sawyer said. "How bad is it going to get? We can't return to orbit with part of the crew still at *Krechet* and Fred and Ulrika out in the wild."

"*That's your call; if Chandra is damaged then you're all stranded.*" That wasn't absolutely true, the *Anderson* could do a rescue so long as the fuel processor on the surface remained intact, and it was built low and tough. *"But it doesn't look like tornado weather, just heavy rain and high winds, some lightning. You'd better decide soon, you're going to get winds ahead of the storm that will exceed your launch parameters."*

"And we'd have to scramble to be ready to go in that time. Let me take it up with the team here, but we'll probably choose to ride it out."

"Okay, give us a call when you decide. If you are staying we recommend venting the hydrogen and methane tanks, you might want to keep the LOX for ballast."

"Sounds good. Anything else?"

"Not for now. I need to call Krechet *and give them the heads up on the storm."*

"Roger that. *Chandrasekhar* out."

∞ ∞ ∞

"It will take us six to eight hours to secure another set of tie-downs and get the lightning mast up," Darwin said after conferring with Patel. "It's going to take at least that long to ferry everyone from the *Krechet* if we decide to leave, and that's if they have everything packed and ready to go. How ready are we?"

"Hardly at all. We've got equipment and specimens to get properly stowed, we'd need a few hours to undo the tie-downs already in place and clear gear from the take-off area."

"If necessary we would omit that last step," Patel said. "So long as there is nothing which could explode or be thrown up against the ship, it doesn't matter what happens to the gear we are leaving behind."

"But what about Fred and Ulrika?"

"They're making good progress," Sawyer said. "They may be back. If not then they may have reached an area where *Krechet* can do a pick-up. Worst case—and only if we think *Chandra* is in danger—we'll have to leave them and hope that the fuel processor survives so that we or the *Anderson* can do a pick up after the storm passes.

"And if we do have to leave, don't forget that we'll need to offload equipment to allow for the weight of the *Krechet* team."

"That too. And I'm not ready to leave, there are still specimens I want to collect and examine. If this is a storm we can ride out, I say we stay here."

"Well, it's no hurricane, or we wouldn't have the choice. Any other considerations?" asked Darwin.

"What about flooding?" Patel said. "We are parked here in a river valley."

"Good point. Sawyer?"

"There's no evidence of recent significant flooding," she said. "With a hundred-year flood we might have to worry, but we're above the river banks and the river itself is down a half meter. This plain is well-drained, the valley through the mountains to the west is about three times wider than the stream bed; it's not a canyon. I'd almost be more concerned with storm surge pushing the tide upriver, but we're a good 15 kilometers from the ocean as the river flows."

"So we're good?"

"Yeah. We'll get some pooling just from the rain, but I can't imagine anything more serious than that. Like you said, with a hurricane I'd be worried, but if that's what was coming we wouldn't stick around. And I still have more geology to do."

"Okay. Anyone else got anything?" Darwin looked around the table at the team members. "No? Okay, then let's get things battened down for the storm."

Chapter 23: Continuing Adventures of Fred and Ulrika

About 90 km southeast of Chandrasekhar

"There's the lake!" Klaar called as she reached the top of the last low ridge. "Come on, let's go."

Tyrell, trailing a few meters behind, reached the crest a moment later. Before them in the broad valley between where they stood and the next line of low hills lay a long narrow lake. It looked like it might have been formed by some natural damming of a river, but the outlet of the lake was hidden from view by the curve of the hill they were on.

It was perhaps a kilometer wide and several kilometers long. The water was for the most part glassy smooth, but for a few ripples offshore. It was still early in the morning and there was little wind. He'd half expected to see a layer of mist above the water's surface, but the air must be too warm for that.

"Want to go for a swim?" Tyrell asked.

"I'm tempted, but it's not really hot enough. Anyway, we have no idea what might be in the water. I have no desire to be nibbled to death by space piranha."

Tyrell chuckled. "Good point. Okay, let's go, we still need to refill our water bottles."

The reached the shore about fifteen minutes later. There wasn't much of a beach, the hill sloped right down to the waterline and kept going, with just a strip of gravel where the ground was apparently too waterlogged for the land plants to grow, or perhaps worn by wave action, although now the lake was still calm.

"This is kind of awkward here to fill the bottles, I don't think I can reach out without falling in." Klaar said.

"I can grab hold of a bush and hold you," said Tyrell, "but let's just keep walking for now, maybe there's easier access ahead. We need to get around this lake anyway."

"Left or right?"

Tyrell consulted the aerial photograph on his omni. "Left, I think. We need to head more in that direction anyway."

"Okay." They started off, keeping parallel to the shoreline, following a game trail. The vegetation was thicker here than it had been earlier, with low scrubby bushes that made going a little harder.

"You know," said Tyrell as they hiked their way around the lake, "I was thinking about what you said about what life might be in the lake. There's probably nothing big; freshwater lakes tend not to have large predator species. Maybe there's not enough other life to support them."

"Ever hear of Nile crocodiles? Or hippopotamus?"

"In rivers, yeah, but this is a lake," Tyrell said.

"The water comes and goes somewhere. Anyway, that's on Earth. Who knows what aquatic life at Alpha Centauri is like?"

"Okay, fair enough."

"Besides, piranha aren't large," she said. "Nor are lampreys or toothpick fish."

"Right, point taken. Wait, toothpick fish?"

"You've never heard of them? Also called candiru, they live in the Amazon. You'd remember if you'd heard of them."

"Oh? Why?" Tyrell was genuinely puzzled, Klaar's tone of voice implied that toothpick fish were worse than piranha.

"Okay, you asked. A candiru, or toothpick fish, is a small fish that's about the size and shape of a toothpick. It's a parasite and lives in the muddy water near the river bottom."

"That small, it doesn't sound so dangerous."

"Wait for it. In the dark it detects its prey by the scent of urea and ammonia from the gills of prey fish. When it detects the water stream from an exhaling fish, it quickly swims into the open gill and anchors itself there with an array of backward-pointing barbs. There it bites a hole in an artery and drinks the blood. The host fish usually dies of the injuries."

"Okay, bad for the host fish, but we don't have gills."

"Here's where it gets nasty. If you're wading or swimming in the river and decide to pee, to the candiru the urine stream smells like gill outflow, only more so. It quickly swims up the stream and into the urethra."

Tyrell winced at the thought.

"Then the spines lodge into place and there's no way to get it out short of surgery. Even when the candiru is done eating, it can't back out because now it's too swollen. Apparently the native Indians, before access to emergency surgery, would choose castration rather than suffer the slow agonizing death that the lodged parasite caused. At least the men did, women didn't have that choice."

Tyrell fought the urge to curl up in a ball with his hands over his crotch. The mental image profoundly disturbed him. "I am really sorry I asked. Note to self, never pee in the Amazon."

"Or any river here until we know what's in it," Klaar added.

"So how do you know about this? You're not a marine biologist too, are you?"

"Some courses in it, but no, that's not how I learned about it. When I knew I was a candidate for the Centauri Expedition I read many different accounts by travellers and explorers in different Earth biomes, to get a feel for what to expect. I thought it might also help with the selection process, although a lot of the accounts were irrelevant in light of the technology available. Anyway, most of the accounts by Amazon explorers mentioned candiru. At first I thought they were making it up, that it was a native legend that got repeated because of the, uh, high squick factor, but apparently there are documented medical cases."

"'High squick factor.' Yeah, that about sums it up." Tyrell suppressed a shudder. "Can we talk about something else?"

"Sure, what do you want to talk about?"

"I don't know. What's a nice girl like you doing in a place like this?"

Klaar stopped and turned to look at him. "Seriously?"

Tyrell brought himself up abruptly. He'd almost walked into her when she stopped suddenly. He'd asked the question lightly, but as he thought about it he realized that he was curious. He didn't know much about Klaar's background. "Sure. Most people have no interest in any exploration that involves more effort than watching it on a three-vee screen. What brings you out here?"

"That's a good question." Klaar turned and started down the trail again, but kept talking. "I've always been the curious type, and three-vee shows never seem to get beyond the most obvious answers. Just as things get interesting they change the subject, never going into much detail. My interests are as broad as the next person's, but I also always want to keep asking the next question."

"That explains why you went into science, and even fieldwork. But why the Alpha Cee expedition?"

"Are you joking? The chance to see things that nobody else ever has before, the chance to learn things that nobody else knows?"

"The chance to die horribly on an alien planet four light years from home." Tyrell tried to put a light note on that, but it fell flat.

Klaar stopped and turned again. "We're not going to die horribly, we are going to walk until we get to the *Chandra* or we find a place where the plane can pick us up. What's wrong with you?"

"Sorry," he said, "that was a joke. That was supposed to be funny."

Klaar looked intently at his face, shifting her gaze from his left eye to his right. "No. You're worried, aren't you. Why?"

Was he? "I could have been killed in that plane crash. Worse, I could have got *you* killed. I don't know what was wrong with the prop, it should never have broken from a couple of lousy bird strikes, but I should have kept us out of that altogether. And who knows what we still might run into. This isn't a walk in the park, this is an unexplored planet. The wildlife here isn't afraid of humans, it has no idea what we are. Or we just slip on a rock and break a leg, or fall in the lake and drown, or—"

Klaar's method of shutting him up was as effective as it was unexpected. She threw her arms around his neck, drew him close, and kissed him, hard. It took a moment for Tyrell to stop resisting, he was that surprised, both at the kiss and her strength. Then he got into it, kissing her back, putting his arms around her and pulling her close. Then she broke it off, and he let her go.

"Wow," he said, catching his breath. "Obviously I'm not complaining, but what was that for?"

"To shut you up, you idiot. Of course we're going to get back. I had to snap you out of it." She took a step back, then another. The look of confusion on her face conflicted with her words.

"And that's all?" Tyrell wasn't sure how he felt, either.

"Well," her expression softened. "And perhaps a little bit for worrying about me." She smiled, then grew stern again. "But you're the injured one, I'm just fine. And we're going to get out of here. So snap out of it."

"I'm snapped, I'm snapped," he protested. "But we'll need to keep going, we can't stand around here all day talking." He smiled at her.

"Well, all right then," she huffed and folded her arms. "Let's go." With that she turned on her heel and started off down the trail at a brisk walk.

Tyrell stood there a moment, thinking about what had just happened, remembering the kiss, and wondering where things stood. Women were as alien as Alpha Centaurans, as far as he was concerned, but he wasn't complaining. He shrugged and continued down the trail after her.

A little while later they found a spot where the slope of the bank lessened, and there was a stretch of gravel beach that extended into the water at a shallow angle.

"Let's take a break here for a bit and refill the water bottles," Tyrell said, and set his backpack down.

While he attached the filtration system to the first water bottle, Klaar dug through the pack and pulled out the stove and a pan.

"Do we need to boil the water? The filters should take care of any microorganisms," Tyrell said.

"Emphasis on your word 'should'. I was also hoping I might find some coffee I might have missed earlier." She rifled through the backpack. "Aha!" She held up a clear plastic bag containing several small pouches, took one out, and peered at the label.

"Coffee?" asked Tyrell. He wouldn't mind some himself.

"It says 'breakfast beverage', whatever that means. Probably something almost completely unlike coffee, or tea, or even hot chocolate. It does, however, contain caffeine."

"Better than nothing, I suppose."

"That remains to be seen," she said. "Or tasted. Now, please fetch some water while I get this stove set up."

"Right." Tyrell walked to the water's edge, keeping an eye out for anything that might be lurking in the shallows. Fortunately the water was clear and the gravel beach meant it unlikely that anything would be hiding in a burrow. Still, he stayed out of the lake itself, tossing one end of the short plastic hose into the water and then pumping it through the filter and into the bottle.

He took the filled bottle back to Klaar, who poured the contents into the pot on the stove and handed the empty back to him. "Thank you, she said. "Your 'breakfast beverage' should be ready by the time you've got the bottles all filled." He went back to the water to do just that.

∞ ∞ ∞

As promised, the coffee, or whatever it was, was ready when Tyrell brought the filled bottles back and stowed the filter in his pack. He took the offered cup and Klaar held up hers.

"Cheers," she said, and took a sip.

Tyrell had just raised his cup to his own lips, and almost choked when he saw the face she made. Her eyes bugged, then her nose wrinkled and her brow furrowed. But she didn't spit it out.

"Revolting?" he asked, trying hard not to laugh.

"Not quite. All those drinks I mentioned? Coffee, tea, hot chocolate?"

He nodded. "Yes, what about them?"

"This tastes like somebody tried to mix all three, and badly."

Tyrell cautiously took a sip himself. It was hot, bitter, and with a faint aftertaste of both old chocolate and stale, burnt coffee. He took another sip to get rid of the aftertaste. In contrast the second sip wasn't quite so bad . . . until the aftertaste took hold again. "I think the idea is to make those breakfast ration bars taste good by comparison."

Klaar took another sip of her own drink, grimaced, and nodded. "As I said earlier, deviously clever these survival planners. I think I would like to strand them on a desert island with nothing to drink but this stuff." She took another drink and looked thoughtful for a moment. "Still," she said, "it is just marginally better than nothing."

They finished their breakfast beverages in relative silence, then cleared the aftertaste with plain water. After clean up and restowing the gear, they were ready to go again.

"So, we continue around the lake until we find the outflow?" Klaar asked.

"Yes, we'll cross as soon as we find a suitable place. After that we can either follow the stream to the coast and head north up the shore, or cut across country again if the terrain is suitable."

"Good. Let's go."

∞ ∞ ∞

They reached the end of the lake in less than an hour, Tyrell was feeling far better than he had yesterday. A low ridge extended roughly south-west to north-east, and it formed a natural dam at the end of the lake. A stream had cut a V-shaped gap in the ridge. Tyrell paused to examine the exposed rock. A vertical wedge of dark rock, probably basalt, split the roughly horizontal limestone layers, forming the center of the ridge. A few smaller veins paralleled it.

"Something interesting?" Klaar asked him.

"Magmatic dike," he said. "Some ancient crack in the limestone that underlies this area let molten rock force its way up into it. The heat and pressure probably hardened the limestone enough to be more resistant to erosion. Wouldn't surprise me if there's a laccolith beneath us which pushed up and caused the cracking in the first place. And me without my geologists hammer."

"No hammer? It was practically glued to your hand on our training field trip. Where is it?"

That was true enough. He never went on a field trip without it. He was surprised she had noticed, though. "I left it with my gear when I dropped off Elizabeth. This was just supposed to be a taxi run, I didn't expect to be making any other stops."

"Ah. I am sorry about that. Thor shouldn't be without his Mjölnir."

"Ha, I'm no Thor. I'm not even sore much anymore," he said. She giggled at that. "Anyway, not your fault, and no harm done. When the storm passes I can come back here and land on the lake with the floats." He turned to look downstream. "Let's find a place to cross, we should get going."

They came to a spot a few dozen meters later, where the stream widened and shallowed, leaving its bed littered with large rocks they used as stepping stones.

∞ ∞ ∞

"*Tyrell, this is* Centauri *Station.*"

"Go ahead *Centauri*," Tyrell answered.

"*What's your status? We show you as seventy-five kilometers south of the* Chandra, *nearing the coast.*"

"We're doing all right, *Centauri*."

"*Do you think you can make it to* Chandra *by tomorrow afternoon?*"

If he were uninjured, a seventy-five kilometer hike in that time wouldn't be, well, not easy, but not too hard. When Alpha Centauri A rose, there would be enough light to hike by if they wanted to push into the night. But that eighty klicks was as the crow—or whatever passed for crows here—flew, and he wasn't in his best shape. "That would be pushing it. What's the rush?"

"*There's a storm coming in from the ocean, it looks like a big one.*"

"So I guess we're going to get wet." Their pace would definitely slow if they hit rain, and the clouds would cut their light. "How bad is it going to be? Hurricane?"

"*Not that bad, but it would be nice to have everyone at the* Chandra *in case they have to launch."*

"What about the rest of the *Krechet* crew? And won't the weather exceed launch parameters before the storm hits?"

"Both valid points. Just trying to keep options open."

"Okay we'll keep that in mind. Is there any chance of the other plane doing a pickup from the lake we passed, or the coast ahead, if it still has its floats?"

"Negative, sorry. The winds are already getting too high on the coast to make it safe, and the waves are rising ahead of it. You're more sheltered being inland, but you'll be getting some gusts before long."

"Just thought I'd ask. Okay, we'll keep hiking."

"Also, when you get to the coast, you'll want to stay well clear of the beach. There'll be a surge ahead of the storm."

"Roger that. Any suggestions on heading north before that?"

"Sorry, no, the clouds are obscuring our view. We'll check the photomaps we already have, but without a good visual on you we won't be able to guide you."

"Okay." That figured. "We'll make sure we're on high ground when we stop for the night."

"Good idea. We're about to go out of range, anything else?"

"Thanks Centauri. We'll be fine. Talk to you later."

"Roger that. Centauri out."

Chapter 24: The Storm

South of Landing Site One

Klaar and Tyrell had paralleled the stream on its north side until they neared the beach. From the higher ground overlooking the ocean, they could almost feel the heavy pounding of the surf as the huge waves, choppier than usual, crashed down on the beach. Offshore the sky was dark and brooding, although it was still a good two hours until sunset. Windblown spray gusted up at them periodically.

"Let's get on the lee side of this hill, then hike north for another hour before setting up tent for the night." Tyrell had to raise his voice to be heard of the roar of the waves. "Sorry, no campfire tonight."

"And I was so looking forward to marshmallows," Klaar said.

"I thought we didn't have any."

"We don't. I can still look forward to them."

Tyrell doubted there were even any at the ship, and Ulrika probably knew it. He smiled and said: "That would be nice."

They hiked back over the hill and down the eastern side until they were out of the worst of the wind, then headed north again, staying below the ridgeline.

∞ ∞ ∞

Landing Site One - Chandrasekhar

The first rain had come at dusk, a sprinkling at first. Now it pelted down harder, the incessant drumming on the ship muted only slightly by the layers of insulation and equipment within the hull. Finley, somewhat bored, watched the view on the monitors;

the light amplification built into the cameras helped. Through the torrents he could barely see the river, let alone the hills surrounding the valley. Periodically a flash of lightning would momentarily dazzle the cameras, then he'd hear the *boom* of thunder.

"What's the speed of sound in the atmosphere here?" he asked, not addressing the question to anyone in particular.

"About the same as Earth," said Darwin, "about 350 meters per second. I can find you an exact number. Why?"

"Just timing the thunder. The lightning's three kilometers away then."

There was another flash, followed a few seconds later by the CRACK-BOOM of the thunderclap, and a prolonged rumbling roar.

"That was different," he said.

"What was?"

"The rumbling afterward. Probably just echoing off the hills." Finley cycled the monitor through the exterior cameras. Dark and rainy on all of them. He flipped the screen back to the river view in time to see a wave, about a foot high and the full width of the river, surge upstream. "What the hell?"

"What?"

"Look at this." Finley punched a control. Everything the cameras saw was continually recorded, they had plenty of data storage, and he rewound the image to a minute previous. He played it again. "Watch the river." On the screen, the wave surged upriver again. "What was that, a tidal bore?"

"I don't think so, we'd have seen one before. And it's the wrong time of day. Run it again?"

Finley touched the control. On the screen, the wave again advanced up river until it was lost in the falling rain.

"Do we have any other cameras on the river?"

"A distant view." Finley selected the camera. "There." The view was dim, showing mostly just the torrential rain and the wet ground, the river was indistinct in the distance.

"Back it up to the wave."

"Okay." Pause. "Here we go."

The dim image of the distant river changed subtly. It could have been an advancing wave but impossible to say for sure.

"Okay, yet another strange phenomenon. Go back to the other camera and we'll see if it happens again."

Finley flipped back to the original camera. The river looked different. "Does that river look different to you?"

"I'm not sure what you mean. You're the one who's been watching it."

"I'm not sure either. Hang on." He rewound the image to the time when the wave had passed. "That's a few minutes ago." He flipped the monitor to the live feed. "And that's now." The distance from the top of the riverbank to the water was noticeably less than a few minutes before. "Damn."

"The river is rising."

It was. In the few minutes since the wave had passed upstream, the river was already nearly a foot up its bank. Finley flipped the monitor back and forth between the recorded image and the live feed, then left the recorded image, paused at just after the wave passed, on the monitor and switched an adjacent monitor to the live feed. "It wasn't the wave, the water level is about the same right after that, but that's when it started rising. What the hell?"

"Was it rising before that?"

"Not so you'd notice. A little, sure with this rain, but not a foot in five minutes. Flash flood? Wouldn't the wave go the other way?"

Sawyer had been following the conversation. "Yeah," she said, "if there'd been a sudden surge of rain higher in the watershed we might get a flash flood. But Finley is right, the wave would go the other way. And it's been raining for hours. That wave came from downstream, not upstream."

"So what could—" Finley started to ask.

"Landslide!" Sawyer said.

"What?"

"That rumbling. If there was a landslide in the hills downstream it could have sent a wave upstream—"

"—and now it's damming the river." Finley said, catching on.

"What? Damming the river?" Patel had been reviewing something on his control console, but now they had his attention. If the river had no outflow from the valley they were in, it would continue to rise.

"Don't panic," said Sawyer.

"I am not panicking," Patel said, "but why shouldn't I?"

"The river will find a way around or over the blockage. It's likely to be loose material—sand, mud, small boulders—the river will start to wash it away," she explained.

They all turned to look at the two monitors. The water level visible on the live feed was higher now, just topping the banks in places.

"The question is, when?" asked Darwin. "This rain isn't going to let up for several more hours, and that river is getting higher. What are our options?"

"We need more information," Finley said. "If we know the rate of rainfall we can calculate how fast the river will rise. We have a rough idea of the total watershed."

"Emphasis on 'rough', and we don't know if the rain is constant across the whole basin, but it'll do for a first approximation. What else?"

"Somebody needs to take the boat downriver and check the slide area," Sawyer said, "to see how much it will rise before cresting it, and see how fast it's eroding."

"That's probably going to have to be you, you're the geologist."

"Yeah, I was afraid you were going to say that. All right." Sawyer turned to Finley "Can you handle the rainfall calculations?"

"Sure thing."

"Okay, I could use someone with me to help with the boat."

"Sure," Darwin said. "I'll come along."

Singh spoke up. "No, I will go. You guys need to stay here and evaluate our options if the water level is going to be a problem. I cannot help with that, but I can with the boat."

Darwin hesitated. She had a point. "All right."

"Good," she said. "I think the BIGs would make good rain

gear."

"Yep," Sawyer agreed. "Let's go suit up."

"Thanks people," said Darwin, "stay in touch and stay safe, that water's rough out there."

"You've got it."

Chapter 25: Singing in the Rain

South of Landing Site One

The rain came in torrents. Inside the tent it drummed on the roof, making conversation all but impossible. They had managed to get it up before the worst of the rain hit, thanks to its self-erecting design, but the showers had begun while they were still looking for a good spot to set up.

"I hope this tent is waterproof!" Klaar said.

"That shouldn't be a problem. I just hope it doesn't float away."

"*Heinlein* said it was going to be worse to the north. I wonder how the folks at the *Chandra* are managing."

"Heh. Probably watching something from the video library. I'm sure they're staying warm and dry."

"Maybe we should huddle together for warmth." Klaar pushed her sleeping bag closer to his.

"Are you cold?" asked Tyrell. They were both still a bit damp from earlier, but it didn't seem that bad to him.

"Stop being stupid."

"Huh? Oh. *Oh.*"

∞ ∞ ∞

On the river, near the Chandrasekhar

The rain came harder as Singh and Sawyer splashed through the puddles and mud down the river. It was already cresting its banks and nearly up to where the inflatable boat was beached by the time they got there.

"Any longer and we might have lost the boat," Singh said.

"It's really coming down."

The roar of the rain made normal speech impractical, they were communicating via headset.

"Yeah. That's going to make it tricky to navigate; we can't tell where the banks are." Sawyer began wrestling the boat toward where she thought the bank was.

Singh pointed downstream. "The vegetation helps, we steer between. But we have a shallow draft, it won't matter."

"You're right. Okay, climb in."

Singh clambered into the boat and sat on the deck while Sawyer leaned on the inflated side tube and pushed the boat forward over the rain-slick ground until she felt the water take its weight. She swung a leg onto the side and pushed off with the other, then climbed the rest of the way in as the boat glided out into the current. The flow grabbed it and they were already moving at a good clip by the time Sawyer got herself seated and switched on the motor. "This is going to be fun on the way back, with this current."

At the bow, Singh had the spotlights set up. The rain cut the range of the lights, but they still helped. Sawyer twisted the control on the motor and Singh sat back down with a bump as the boat surged forward into the darkness.

∞ ∞ ∞

Back on the *Chandra* Finley had finished his calculations. "It looks like we have an hour, hour and a half before the water starts lapping at the footpads."

"Okay. Ganesh, what depth of water can we take before it's a problem?"

"Ideally, none at all. But it won't hurt the landing gear. I would be more worried about a tree or something drifting downstream and hitting us, but by the time it is deep enough for that it will be up over the bottom of the heat shield. That is a concern. A little water won't hurt it but the shield was not meant to be submerged. We have about a half a meter clearance before that starts."

"Okay, so a minimum of three hours."

"Probably more like four or five," Finley said. "As the water rises it has more area of this floodplain to cover, so it will rise slower."

"Okay, that's good, but we can't count on it."

"Could we dam it off, use sandbags? We have plenty of large specimen bags."

"Enough? And what would we fill them with, there's no sand."

"Dirt, the soil here. We have shovels."

"That'd be tough going, I don't know that there's time."

"We could fill them with water."

"I'm not sure that would work, wouldn't they need to be heavier than water to keep from drifting away?"

"We don't have enough anyway," Patel said, looking up from a computer screen. "I just analyzed the numbers. We would need to stack them at least six high, and the perimeter is over thirty meters, that's over six hundred bags if the wall is only one layer thick. It has to be wider than it is high; we would need about four thousand bags. We don't have anywhere near enough. Plus, we would have to fill a bag every two seconds or less."

"That's for the whole ship, if we just surrounded the heat shield—"

"We'd still need to fill a bag every five seconds, and we still don't have enough. We need a different plan."

∞ ∞ ∞

"*Turn the boat!* Rocks ahead! Turn left!" Singh saw it first, a wall of soil, boulders and broken vegetation looming ahead of them as the river rushed toward it, raising waves around outlying boulders as the river curved to find a way around the blockage.

Sawyer steered the boat hard to port and threw the motor into reverse to slow them. "Jenn, get the lights, let's see what we've got."

Singh scrambled over to the spotlight at the bow, slipping on the rain slick deck. She caught herself on the gunnel and knelt down. With the pelting rain, water was pooling in the bottom of the boat. She took the handle of the spotlight and aimed it toward the pile of rubble ahead. They were about a hundred meters into where the broad plain had narrowed into the V-shaped valley through the hills. The rubble slope extended upward to her right, the broken trees and vegetation had fallen mostly with their roots in that direction. That was the slope which had collapsed. "It's a landslide all right. Nothing's going to get around that way." She swept the light back to the left. The mound of rock, mud and branches extended that way as far as they could see through the rain, about ten meters. Muddy water surged and splashed around them, and the mound was slick with runnels of mud and water as the rain beat down on it. "Let's check that way," she said, gesturing to the left with the light.

∞ ∞ ∞

Sawyer edged the boat back away from the debris. There were scattered boulders and trees lying out from the main pile, it wouldn't do to hit something. She moved the boat slowly parallel to the barrier. "There's a lot of soil mixed in with this, the rain and water should wear it down before long."

"What does 'before long' mean to a geologist?" Singh asked pointedly.

"Just a few years. Okay, I see your point." They followed the natural dam across the valley, the sprawl of dirt and rocks thankfully getting lower toward the water as they went. Singh played the light alternately over the muddy hill on their right and the path ahead, picking out any tree branches or large boulders in the water.

"Tree ahead, clear to the right." The crest of the landslide was about a meter above the water now, as best Singh could tell. It might rise again beyond that, they could only see a few meters in that direction from where they were. She turned the light forward again. Trees and bushes loomed before her, they'd reached the other side of the narrow valley. "Hold it, that's as far as we can go!"

"Okay, so the valley is choked. I'm going to have to get out and check the slide, see how wide it is and if it gets any higher."

"Get out? Surely that stuff is not stable."

"Probably not. Especially with the weight of this water behind it. If it collapses that would solve the problem."

"What about you?"

"Yeah, well, life's full of little trade-offs." She edged the boat into a small backwater between a downed tree and a boulder. "Okay Jenn, get back here and take the control."

Singh clambered back over the bench seat and sat down on the floor of the boat beside Sawyer. "Okay, I've got it."

"All right, hold it steady while I climb out. I'm not going far. The water's still rising so keep an eye on the shoreline."

"Okay. Be careful."

"Always." Sawyer took hold of a limb poking up from the downed tree and tugged on it. It held. Using that for balance she got up into a half crouch and stepped over the side of the boat, her foot squelching in the mud of the slope. She took a few experimental steps, then slipped and fell to one knee. "Damn it."

"Are you all right?" Singh called.

"Yeah, it's just a bit slick. With this kind of soil I'm not surprised it slid. I'll be fine." She dropped the rest of the way to her hands and knees and crawled up the low slope, using her hands to grab onto rocks or tree limbs that looked well enough anchored to hold. As she reached the crest, a meter or so above the water line, she stopped and carefully stood up.

"What does it look like?"

"Dark, I should have brought a light." She took a few steps in either direction. "Hard to say. It doesn't look like it gets any higher down the valley, but it does extend a ways."

"Here, have a light." Singh had retrieved a flashlight from the boat's kit. She turned it on and tossed it to Sawyer, who missed the catch. Sawyer's visor was fogging up with the cold and humidity. The light plopped into the mud about a meter away.

"Nice catch," Singh said.

"Thanks." Sawyer picked it up and smeared the mud around trying to wipe it off. Dang it! She pushed back her hood to better see what she was doing, ignoring the water streaming down on her head. Finally she just held the flashlight out in the rain for a few moments; the downpour cleaned it off quickly. She shone it over the ground, up and down the slope. Mud and broken vegetation as far as she could see, but in this downpour that was only a few meters. She couldn't see the far edge. She turned to look back at the river and Singh in the boat. "I'm going to see how far it extends." She turned again and slogged forward. Why couldn't they have landed in a nice dry desert?

She took a few steps up the muddy slope, then shivered and cursed as a hoodful of cold rainwater poured down the neck of her biosuit. She'd left the hood down so she could see, and now it kept filling with water and dumping down her back every time she bent over. *If this keeps up I'm going to drown. A fine end for a geologist four light years from home. I'm not even surfing.* She never had liked the damned suits.

She trudged further over the slick, soggy debris. In the worst case this could extend for a mile or more down the valley, in which case the landing field was on its way to becoming a lake. She hoped the crew back at the *Chandra* had a contingency plan figured out.

∞ ∞ ∞

"I hope Sawyer finds the blockage easy to clear," Darwin said. "We're running out of ideas."

They already considered and discarded wrapping the bottom of the ship in plastic sheeting to keep it dry. They didn't have anything big enough, although given more time than they had they might weld something together out of the supplies they had. Finley had suggested running the engines at idle to keep the water blown clear. Patel had blanched at the suggestion and categorically refused.

"What if we freeze it? Create an ice dam around the ship?"

"Freeze it how?"

"We've got a tank full of liquid oxygen, we ought to be able to rig something."

"There is only a small spigot valve to tap the tanks, which is adequate if we only need a couple of liters, but the flow rate is too low to freeze this quantity of water."

"What about just pumping it through the engines? That'd be

a high flow rate."

"That is almost as bad as just firing the engines," Patel said. "Also we would have to override all the sensors and software modules designed to prevent that sort of thing."

∞ ∞ ∞

Sawyer slipped again, scrambling for a handhold on a tree limb jutting out of the muck. She must be almost to the other side, surely. She paused to listen. Over the steady roar of the falling rain, was that a rumbling? The storm surge would have swept the ocean up the river, and the waves would be pounding hard, but the sound which Sawyer wasn't even certain she heard could as easily be distant thunder. But the slope seemed to be leveling.

A few meters further on and she was convinced she was on the back side. The ground sloped away at a steepening angle, and in the beam of her flashlight, Sawyer could just make through the rain a tree trunk. It looked to her more like the mud and debris and piled against the trunk rather than carrying it here, that was a good sign. The ocean was further away, wave action wouldn't be eroding this slope any time soon.

She'd better let the *Chandra* know.

∞ ∞ ∞

"Chandra *this is Sawyer*," came her voice over the radio.

Darwin keyed the microphone. "Go ahead, how does it look?"

"Could be better, could be worse. Looks like the water has about another meter or so to rise before it tops the dam formed by the slide."

Darwin, Finley and Patel looked at each other, grim. The water was already starting to lap at the lower footpad, another meter would put it over the heat shield, more than that and it would be splashing against the engine nozzles.

"And the good news?" Darwin asked.

"*Who said there was good news? But the dam isn't that thick, about fifteen to twenty meters, it's not like it fills the valley.*"

"We can't take another meter of water here. Half that and it'll be starting to splash the heat shield. Patel says that's not good."

"*Oh, crap. We'll have to cut a trench through the top of the dam then. This stuff is pretty loose and slick, once we get the water flowing through it the current should wear it down pretty quickly and the water will stop rising.*"

"Great, you've got two hours to dig a trench a meter deep and ten long. Did you bring a shovel?"

"*No, but I've got seismic charges back at the ship, that'll help. We're on our way back now.*"

"How many will you need?"

"*Probably more than I've got. They're for sending shock waves, not mining. If there's something else we can use for explosives, get that together too.*"

"Okay. See you soon." Darwin clicked off the mike and turned to the others. "Finley, do you know where the seismic charges are stowed?"

"Yeah, I'll get them." He got up to leave the cabin.

"Okay, and if you can think of anything else. . . .."

Finley paused at the hatch, turned, and shook his head. "I don't think anyone else had much call for explosives. I'll see what's down there."

"Maybe we can improvise," Darwin said as Finley left. "Ganesh, any ideas?"

"The ship itself has pyrotechnic components but they're all built in."

"What about the propellants?"

"LOX, methane and hydrogen. Sure, you could make a pretty big bang with those but I can't think of any way to transport them. Not the hydrogen, anyway, it would boil off. The LOX perhaps, we could use one of the nitrogen Dewars for that." The biology lab kept liquid nitrogen on hand to flash-freeze specimens. "I suppose in theory we could mix methane and liquid oxygen, it will form a kind of slush as the methane freezes, but I am thinking it would be too sensitive."

Darwin couldn't imagine that being stable. "I think it would detonate if you thought mean thoughts at it." He shook his head.

"LOX is a strong oxidizer, there must be something else we can react it with."

Finley had just come back into the cabin. "What's this about LOX?"

"Any ideas on improvised explosives?"

"LOX and charcoal will work. We can scrounge charcoal from the campfire . . . oh, it'll be waterlogged."

"Will that matter?" asked Darwin.

"I don't know, but I don't see how it will soak up the LOX if it's wet, it'll just freeze."

Patel spoke up. "The life support system uses charcoal canisters to scrub organics from the air. How much would you need?"

"The stuff is about the same strength as dynamite, from what I remember. I don't know, a few kilos?"

"Very well, the canisters are two kilograms each. Two are used, we can spare another. Six kilos?"

"Sounds perfect," said Darwin. He did some quick mental math. They'd need twice as much oxygen as carbon, and liquid oxygen was slightly denser than water. A bit over half of one of their 25 liter tanks, then. "Ganesh, you get the charcoal canisters. I'll get the nitrogen Dewar from biology. Then I'll need your help to tap the main LOX tank."

∞ ∞ ∞

In the fifteen minutes it took Sawyer and Singh to return in the boat, Darwin had shown Finley how to work the valves on the dewar fill and drain mechanism to squirt out the remaining liquid nitrogen – the same steps Finley would use with the oxygen – and with Patel's help, had filled the tank about two-thirds full with LOX. Probably violating all kinds of protocols, but since liquid nitrogen had a tendency to condense oxygen out of the air anyway, the Dewar was made of oxygen-safe parts.

∞ ∞ ∞

Ten minutes after that, Sawyer was headed back in the boat toward the landslide area. Finley was with her this time, to help her set the charges.

"Have you ever done this before?" Sawyer asked him.

"What, the LOX-charcoal explosives? Actually no, but I've read about it."

"Oh, great. Don't blow us up."

"That's why we're not mixing it until we get there. We'll dig a hole, dump in some charcoal, pour in some LOX, and then it's good to go."

"How sensitive is it?"

"Depends on the charcoal and what other organics are in it. This stuff is pretty pure, even the used canisters, compared to burnt wood. We should be okay."

"Will we be able to set it off?"

"Oh yeah, just hit it hard enough. If we spread the seismic charges out that should do it. We should wire them to all go off at once, though."

"That's what I was figuring on," Sawyer agreed.

"I just thought of something."

"What?"

"It's pouring with rain; the ground is soaking."

"Oh, you noticed that, did you?"

"No, I mean when I dump the charcoal in the hole, it's going to get wet. It's not going to soak up the LOX before the water freezes."

"Ah. Hang on." Sawyer patted at the pockets of her BIG and unzipped one. She reached into the pocket and pulled out a handful of transparent plastic specimen bags. "Here, put the charcoal in these, then put them in the holes."

"How do I mix the LOX in?"

"I dunno, leave the top of the bag open. You can figure it out while we dig the holes."

"Okay. We'll plant the seismic charges first, they're stable."

"Right. And it looks like we're here."

The water was now about half a meter from the top of the slide, which actually made things easier as they wrestled the heavy Dewar, now full of liquid oxygen, out of the boat and onto the mud and debris pile. Finley began unloading the other gear, the seismic charges, charcoal canisters and detonator wires, while Sawyer set up her geologist's coring drill.

"Okay, we've got twelve charges so we'll put them about a meter apart, then a half-kilo of charcoal midway between each? Will that work?"

"I can't be certain. But the ground is wet, that should conduct the shock pretty well."

"Crap, it would be nice to know for sure. Too bad we don't have any detonating cord. All right, the first pair of holes I'll put closer together. Maybe it'll help focus the blast."

"But I wouldn't worry too much; seismic explosives are designed to give a sharp hard pulse, makes the seismology easier." Sawyer started the coring drill. In the mix of muck and gravel it dug in quickly. She only needed to go down a meter. She pulled the drill out. "Okay, first hole's ready. You set the charge; I'll get the next hole."

Finley took one of the blue plastic-jacketed sticks and screwed a detonator onto the threaded end. He lowered it into the hole, which was already starting to fill with water and mud, leaving the wires trailing out. He pushed several handfuls of mud and gravel into the hole on top of the explosive. The loops of detonator wire he draped over a protruding tree branch to keep them from disappearing under the mud. By the time he'd finished, Sawyer was ready with the next bore hole.

They repeated the process across the width of the slide, until the last of the seismic charges was placed. As he went, Finley had been gathering grapefruit-sized boulders whenever he came across one.

"What are those for?" asked Sawyer.

"To cap the holes with the charcoal/LOX mixture. I don't want to just dump mud down on top, that might set it off, and I don't want the rain getting in either. After we pour in the LOX I'll just set one on top of the hole."

"Good thinking. Okay, I'll work my way back drilling those holes now."

While Sawyer was drilling the first of the holes for the charcoal Lox mix, Finley went back and wrestled the LOX canister to the other side of the landslide.

"Tell you what, I'll just cap these holes now and wait until you're done drilling before putting anything in them. No sense both of us being at risk."

"Just how sensitive is that stuff?"

"I wish I knew. Anyway, like I said, no sense both of us being at risk. Keep drilling, I need to fill these bags with charcoal."

"Okay."

As Sawyer moved back across the slide, drilling boreholes between where the wires to the seismic charges snaked out of the ground, Finley pried open the charcoal canisters and began scooping black granules into the plastic specimen bags, keeping everything sheltered from the rain as best he could with his body.

That done, he called over to Sawyer. "How is it going?"

"I'm just on the last hole now. Did you figure out how you're going to mix the LOX in?"

"Yeah, I swiped one of your drill tubes."

"Ah, clever. That should do it."

The coring drill that Sawyer had been using was designed to drill a considerable distance, too far to be practical with a one-piece drill bit. Just like its bigger cousins, sections of drill tube could be added at the top as the hole was dug deeper. There'd been spares of these with the drill, Sawyer wasn't going deep enough to need them, but they were perfect for what Finley needed.

He dropped a charcoal bag into the first hole, gently pushing it into place with the tube. Then he pushed the tube hard, twisting as he did so, to tear the top of the plastic bag. He hadn't sealed it, but this would make sure that the LOX could penetrate. Leaving the tube in place, he raised the Dewar—it was awkward and he struggled a bit to get the mouth of the nozzle lined up with the tube, then pushed the valve lever to pour what he estimated was liter of pale blue LOX down the tube. A cold fog flowed around the drill tube and up out of the hole around it. Finley set the container down and gently began withdrawing the tube from the hole. It was stuck. He tugged harder, highly conscious that the bottom end was now sitting on over a kilogram of shock sensitive high explosive. It didn't move. He bent down to peer into the hole, blowing the cloud of condensation away. The drill tube was covered in ice. *Of course!* The LOX had chilled the tube and the rain had frozen to it. Where it was touching the side of the hole, the mud would have frozen to it. *Great.*

"Sawyer, how many spare drill tubes do we have with us?"

"Two more. Why?"

"Damn. This one is frozen to the hole. I don't want to get violent with it now."

"Do you need to use the tube to pour the LOX?" If they pulled the drill tube out before pouring, they could make do with the remaining drill tube.

"I guess I don't have a choice. Okay, bring one up." Finley picked up the small boulder he was going to use to cap the hole and reached to put it on top of the drill tube. He was just about to set it down when he stopped himself. That shock would transmit to the bottom of the tube. It might not be enough to set off the explosive, but. . . .. He gently set the rock back down on the ground, took one of the unused specimen bags and slipped it over the end of the tube.

Sawyer was already at the next hole with another drill tube. "Look, it'll go faster if we both work. Give me the bags, I'll put the charcoal in, rip the bag, then go on to the next hole while you pour the LOX."

"But—"

"Never mind buts. The water's rising faster, it must be almost up to the heat shield back at the ship."

"Okay, but this stuff is sensitive. And depending on what other organic stuff is in the hole when I pour in the LOX, it could go off right then."

"Duly noted. Let's get moving." Sawyer dropped a bag into the hole, tamped it down with the pipe, gave it a twist for good measure, and withdrew it. "All yours," she said to Finley, and moved on to the next one. Finley knelt down beside the hole and reached for the valves on the oxygen Dewar.

∞ ∞ ∞

In the control room of the *Chandra*, Darwin, Patel and Singh watched one of the monitors. The screen showed the underside of the ship, a shot from a camera on one of the landing legs. The water pooled under the heat shield.

"I am starting to wonder if it is worth the risk to fire up the engines," Patel said.

Darwin looked at him. "Are you seri—" He was cut off by an ear-splitting *CRACK* followed by a rolling, booming echo. There had been no lightning flash.

"There go the explosives. I hope it worked."

As they watched the monitor, a wave raced across the water, again flowing up from downstream. Darwin keyed the microphone on the comms panel.

"Sawyer, this is *Chandra*. How does it look?"

There was no reply.

"Sawyer, Finley, this is *Chandra*. Come in."

Still nothing.

"What's wrong, could they have been caught in the explosion?" Singh asked.

Darwin looked worried, but shook his head. He keyed the mike again. "*Chandra* calling Sawyer or Finley. Answer me, dammit, what's going on?"

They all looked expectantly at the speaker. Darwin raised the microphone again, but before he could key it Sawyer's voice came through.

"*Chandra* this is Sawyer. Sorry about that, didn't hear you the first time. Our ears are still ringing."

"Are you all right?"

"Yeah, that was just a bit louder than we expected. I should have pulled the boat further back. We had to do some fancy motoring too once the channel opened up, we got quite the current."

"So it worked?"

"Like a charm. We cut a channel through the top of this dam nearly a meter deep, and the current is making it bigger even as we speak. We almost got sucked along it."

"So the water should start lowering?"

"That may take a bit yet, I don't think it's going out as fast as the rain and river's coming in, but it will slow down. That channel is eroding quickly, though, so the flow will increase. We should be good. And I think the rain is starting to let up."

"It's still coming down as hard as ever here. Okay, if there's nothing more you can do there, come on back. And thank you."

∞ ∞ ∞

Sawyer turned the boat upriver and looked up at the sky as she motored back toward the ship. As they came around the corner where the narrow valley broadened out into the plain, she could just see the lights from the ship through the rain. Yes, it was definitely starting to let up. They would be getting a lot of water down from the hills for hours yet, and the blockage, even with the channel they'd blasted, meant that there would be a small lake in the lower end of the valley for a while, but it looked like the immediate danger was past. She looked over at Finley, sitting in the bottom of the boat with something of a dazed expression.

"You okay?" she shouted over the rain.

"My ears are still ringing."

"Yep, that was a loud one all right."

"Loudest thing I've ever heard. That stuff is scary. But you know what really gets me?"

"What?"

"I was just thinking about that first hole." He held up his hand, his forefinger and thumb about two centimeters apart. "I came *this* close to kicking the damn drill tube to loosen it up before I remembered what was on the other end of it."

"Oh." Sawyer winced at the thought. "That would have been bad."

"Yeah." Finley shook his head, in disbelief or disgust at his own potentially-lethal stupidity. "By the way . . ."

"Yes?"

"You were wanting to survey that plateau to the north."

"Right, but we didn't have enough seismic charges . . . oh,

you're not suggesting—"

"Sure, why not? We have an almost unlimited LOX supply, and we can make charcoal."

Sawyer shook her head. It was a little crazy, but with suitable precautions it could work. "Okay. But let's wait until it's stopped raining."

As they motored the rest of the way back, the *Chandra* called again. "*We've been watching the monitors. The water level has peaked and may even be starting to drop. Great work!*"

Chapter 26: The Return

Campsite, south of Chandrasekhar

The glow of morning sunlight on the tent was becoming too bright to ignore. Tyrell didn't want to move. Ulrika lay beside him with her head on his shoulder, her arm across him. He opened his eyes, squinted at the glare, then kissed the top of Ulrika's blonde head.

"I was wondering when you'd wake up," she said, still snuggled against him.

"How long have you been awake?"

"A little while now. I didn't want to move. Last night was fun."

Tyrell grinned broadly at the memory. "That would be an understatement." He gave her a gentle squeeze. "It was more than fun."

She turned her head up to look at him, then gave him a quick kiss. "It was. But unfortunately we can't stay here all day, we have to get back." She rolled away from him and sat up.

"Slave driver," Tyrell said, but with a smile.

"Besides—" She was interrupted by the omni chirping. "—*Centauri Station* is about due to call in."

Tyrell sighed and thumbed his omni. "Tyrell here."

"*Rise and shine, sleepy heads. We see your tent is still up. What's your status?*"

"Almost ready to go." That was an exaggeration, but Ulrika had already stowed her sleeping back and was pulling her clothes on. "How are the others, did everyone survive the storm?"

"*Krechet is still standing, you guys did a good job on securing that landing leg, and fortunately the hole was on the upwind side. The*

Chandrasekhar *team got a bit wet, and the ship is still standing in a few centimeters of water, but it should be clear by the time you get back. The ship and crew are all fine."*

"Glad to hear it. I guess we're going to have a bit of a damp walk ahead of us."

"The weather's fine, but yes, the ground and vegetation will still be wet. The wave action is dying down, you should be okay once you get to the beach."

"Sounds good, *Centauri*. We'll talk to you next orbit."

"Roger that. Centauri *out."*

∞ ∞ ∞

By noon they had reached the river. The *Heinlein* had called it a "wide creek", but it had swollen from the night's rain and was definitely more of a river.

"Well, that's not going to work," Tyrell said as they reached the south bank. The river was close to twenty meters wide here, although aside from a low embankment, the surrounding area was flat enough that it might still be shallow.

"You don't want to try wading across?" Klaar said.

Tyrell looked at her. Was she hiding a smile? "Are you kidding, after what you said about toothpick fish? Maybe if the water was clear." Right now it was brown from silt after the storm.

"I was. The look on your face was worth it." She smiled.

Tyrell smiled back, he couldn't hold a grudge while looking at her face. "Fair enough. I guess we'll just keep following downstream until we find a place to cross. Worst case is that's the mouth of this stream, and it will shallow out at the beach."

He looked up and downstream as far as he could, but between the scattered trees and the banks, that wasn't very far. On the other hand. . . . "The river meanders, that's actually a good sign, it means it doesn't get very deep and the current won't be too bad."

"But doesn't the Mississippi meander too? Isn't it deep with a strong current?"

"It's not actually that deep. It is also very wide and drains a good fraction of the continent. Neither applies here."

"All right, then, downstream it is."

Five kilometers further, they came to a spot where the river did a tight turn. The inside of the curve was very shallow, even through the brown water they could see the far side shoaling gently. The near side, the outside of the turn, was flowing more swiftly and would be deeper. It had eroded a steep bank into the side of the hill they were standing on. That same erosion, perhaps coupled with the storm, had toppled a tree almost all the way across the river, angled down from the top of the bank where its roots were still partly embedded in the ground.

Tyrell and Klaar looked it over. It would be a bit of a clamber but it should hold them.

"What do you think, Ulrika? Up for a bit of tree climbing?"

She grabbed a wrist-thick root, gave a few tugs, then pulled herself up far enough to stand on another wide root. "Sure. What about you?"

"Yep. Want me to go first?"

"I'll go. You hold the roots in case the tree starts to twist."

To Tyrell the tree looked solid enough that it wasn't like to go anywhere soon, and if it was going to roll, it was heavy enough that he wasn't sure what he could do about it. "Okay," he said, and grabbed a root.

Klaar scrambled up to the trunk, started to crawl down it head first, then obviously though better of the idea and backed up to where she could turn around. "I may need you to spot where I put my feet," she said, "but I don't want to end up heads down at the end."

"Makes sense to me. Go ahead."

Tyrell watched as she backed down the rest of the tree, once or twice calling to suggest a better foothold, and she soon arrived in the uppermost—now lowermost—branches just short of the far bank.

"How does it look?" Tyrell called.

"Maybe ankle deep. I'll check." With that, before Tyrell had a chance to say anything else, she dropped into the river. It was indeed just ankle deep, and a few steps later she was standing on the far bank.

"Your turn. How stable is the tree?"

"It didn't move a centimeter. On my way."

He reached up for a higher root, then pulled and stepped up onto another. He was reaching to pull himself up to the trunk when he felt, or thought he felt, a small lurch. Uh oh.

"How am I looking?" he called down.

"Did the tree just move or did I imagine it?" Klaar called back.

"Must have been the wind," Tyrell said, and kept climbing.

"What wind?"

Tyrell ignored the question and kept crawling, looking back and up at where the roots stuck out of the bank. Were those dirt clumps there before? He looked down. He was only a couple of meters above the water, what was the worst that could happen?

The tree lurched again. *I need to stop asking myself that question*, Tyrell thought, *sometimes the universe shows you*. He quickened his scramble.

"I did not imagine that, the tree *did* move," Klaar called, a note of urgency in her voice. "There's no way I can hold it from here. Please hurry. But carefully."

Roger that, Tyrell thought. He reached the middle branches when the tree lurched again. *Okay, if it does fall, I do not want to be pinned under water by these branches*. He started side stepping along a branch, away from the direction of slippage.

That made the rest of the climb more difficult, the branches were thinner out away from the trunk. He had almost gone as far as he could when the tree lurched again, along with a resounding *crack!* as it broke free of the remaining roots.

"Fred!"

Tyrell jumped clear as the tree went down, landing with a splash in the river, going down to his hands and knees. He scrambled upright. The was just knee deep here, and he staggered to the bank. "I'm fine. But no more tree climbing or swimming for a while, all right?"

Klaar grabbed him and put her arms around him, then backed off a bit and examined his face.

"What?" he said.

"Just checking," she said, then kissed him. "Have you always been accident prone?"

"I, what?"

"Sorry, a joke." She hugged him again then stepped back. "Are you sure you're all right?"

"Never better."

"Oh, I doubt that. But we're on the right side of the river now, we should keep going."

∞ ∞ ∞

They came across the arboreal cephalopods later that day. They were nearing the mouth of the river they'd been following, and it had widened further. On either side were trees with a spreading root system that extended down into the water from part way up the trunk, something like a banyan tree. The leaves rustled, in spite of the fact that their seemed to be no wind.

"Stop," Klaar said in a lowered voice, holding her arm out in front of Tyrell. "Look up there," she pointed.

Tyrell looked. There was some kind of animal in the branches. Several animals, Tyrell realized as he looked around. Hairless and featherless, with wet skin, and differing colors, although mostly matching the surrounding foliage. Some kind of giant tree frog? Then he noticed the tentacles.

"Wow. It looks something like a squid but it only has eight legs, call it an octosquid?" Tyrell said, also keeping his voice lowered.

"That's taken, a species of *Mastigoteuthis*," Klaar said, grinning. "And technically they're arms, not legs."

"Spoilsport. All right then, tree octopus."

"That also is taken, but by a mythical species. The Pacific Northwestern Tree Octopus, *Octopus paxarbolis*"

"You're joking!"

"*Shush!* No, I am not, but the coiner of the name was. It was a hoax, about seventy years ago now, in the early days of the internet. That's about all I remember."

Tyrell shook his head. Ulrika's reservoir of zoological lore was amazing. "Fine. How about tree squid then?"

"Sure, that works at least as a common name. On this planet they're probably neither octopus nor squid, but a detailed examination might tell us which they're closer to. I'm intrigued by the tree climbing."

"Looks like they're eating some kind of berry." There was a vine growing in and around the banyan branches, covered with clumps small pale berries. "I thought cephalopods were carnivorous?"

"Indeed. But some carnivores eat other things. The berries may be high in protein, or sugars that ferment. We should take samples."

"Ferment?" Tyrell found the idea of drunken tree squids highly amusing. Not that these were acting particularly tipsy, although several were showing rippling color changes in their skin. "What's with the colors?"

"Possibly communication. The original adaptation was probably for camouflage, but some species on Earth appear to change colors as a way to 'talk', as it were. I wish we had time to study them further."

"Could they be intelligent?"

"That depends what you mean. Some squids and octopi on Earth are highly intelligent, considering that they're invertebrates. They're good at puzzle solving, but probably not as smart as chimps or dolphins, let alone humans. But these, well, they're alien. Who knows?"

"Huh. I was just struck by a resemblance to H. G. Wells's martians."

"I don't think these tree squids are going to be building walking tripods with heat rays in the near future."

"No, of course not," Tyrell brushed the thought aside. "We should get moving."

"Agreed, but first I'd like to get some pictures and video of these tree squids. Can I borrow your omni?" Since the hike was unexpected, she had left her camera and other gear behind just as Tyrell had his hammer.

"Sure," he said, and handed it to her. "Let's also get you some samples of those squidberries."

For the second time that day, and to his chagrin, Tyrell found himself climbing a tree—keeping well clear of the squids—and wading in the stream.

∞ ∞ ∞

The beach, south of Chandrasekhar landing site.

By mid-afternoon they had made it back to the beach and were following it north. The sea was still choppy but had calmed considerably since last night's storm. The beach was easily fifty meters wide at this point, although littered with storm debris above the high tide line. Right now the tide was out. Tyrell heard a whine somewhere behind him, which he at first dismissed as a flying insect, but it grew louder. Klaar was already turning to see what it was when his omni chirped.

"It's a plane!" Klaar said.

It was indeed. Tyrell thumbed his omni. "Is that you in the plane?"

Dmitri Tsibliev's voice came back "Da, *it is. I see you. Can I give you lift somewhere?*"

The EP01, rigged with floats along side its main wheels, buzzed passed them and waggled its wings, then banked to come back around.

"Dmitri! Happy to hear from you! Since you're offering, sure." Tyrell looked around at the beach. "Is there somewhere you can land?"

"*Water is a little rough, but beach is clear about a hundred meters ahead of you. See you there.*" With that, the little plane banked again as Dmitri lined it up for his approach.

They caught up with him a few minutes later. "So, how are we going to do this?" Tyrell asked. "You only have room for one passenger. Take Ulrika then come back for me."

"No!" she said. "You were the one injured, you should get checked out first."

"Please," said Dmitri, waving his hands. "Is *nyet problem.* We have plans for this."

"What plans?" This was news to Tyrell.

"We take out equipment to save weight. We reconfigure seats, one in front, two behind. It helps the balance."

Tyrell nodded, that was what had looked odd.

"Besides, Ulrika here is slender, she cannot mass more than what, fifty, fifty-five kilos? And you are looking skinnier too, Doctor Tyrell. The hike was good for you."

"Well, if you're sure." Tyrell said. He'd be happy to get back.

"*Da*, I am sure. Although you two will be a little crowded in back seat. Nice and cosy."

Tyrell and Klaar looked at each other. She smiled and lowered her gaze briefly.

"We'll be fine," they both said at the same time.

Dmitri raised an eyebrow. "So? Very good, let's get going."

The takeoff roll was a bit longer than usual, but true to Tsibliev's word, the flight back to the *Chandrasekhar* was *nyet problem*.

Part IV: Departure

Chapter 27: Leaving

USS Heinlein, *in orbit over Kakuloa*

Commodore Drake was conferenced in with captains Patel and Tsibliev, and his own second in command, Sawyer, on the planet's surface.

"*We're coming up against our timeline, people. Are you going to be ready to lift in two days?*" he said.

"Krechet landing party is all here at *Chandrasekhar*," Dmitri Tsibliev said. "I would like to make final trip back to *Krechet* to pick up any forgotten items, and to secure lander for long term parking, but *da*, we can do this."

"*Thank you. Patel, how is the Chandra looking?*"

"We need to run the final weight calculations and stow everything for launch. Propellants are available for loading and top up. It is desirable to clear the area by tomorrow for an engine test. It will be tight. What are the constraints on extending the launch window?"

"*The usual. Consumables, orbital positions, weather,*" Drake said. "*If we stay in-system more than another couple of weeks people are going to be getting hungry on the trip back, and I want a preliminary review of findings before we leave. We can't land again, but if there are additional observations we can make from orbit, or of the smaller bodies in the system, better to leave some time for that. You've got clear weather for the next few days. After that we're not sure. I'd rather have you up here by then.*"

"Understood, we will endeavor to comply."

"*Keep me apprised if there are delays. Sawyer, anything to add?*"

"I think most of the scientists would rather stay longer, but that will always be true. I'll get them rounded up and have them do triage on what specimens they want to take versus leave behind." Even if they didn't have the *Krechet* party to bring home, they'd probably amassed more samples than they originally had weight allowance for, let alone now. She knew that she and Tyrell had quite a collection of rock and mineral specimens between them.

"*Very good. All right, I will leave you folks to it. We have a bit of housekeeping to do up here to get ready for visitors.*" With the necessary abandonment of the *Krechet*, the voyage home would be a little more crowded.

∞ ∞ ∞

The science team did scream a bit at having to leave some of their specimens behind, a few even bargained to leave some of their personal gear behind if they could bring back the equivalent weight of samples. After reminding them that, in all probability, they'd never see again anything left behind, Sawyer went along with that.

The announcement had the unexpected side benefit of everyone working with a will to reduce any non-essential mass from the lander or its contents. It was almost comical.

"No, you cannot remove that panel, it is most essential," Patel said when they'd started getting a little too enthusiastic about stripping the interior of the ship.

"But it's just cosmetic, not structural. It covers up some wiring and plumbing. We can live without that for a few days."

"It is more like a few weeks, counting the trip back to Earth, and you are forgetting that will all be in microgravity. We don't want any foreign objects drifting into the 'wiring and plumbing', as you put it. The panel stays." That his voice was raised when he said that struck home, he was normally very mild mannered.

"How about we cover it with a sheet of plastic, or fabric cut from a BIG? We can seal the edges with duct tape to keep stuff from drifting in."

Patel relented. "Very well. But check with me on any panels you replace. Nothing structural, and nothing where a person might float into it either." He may also have said, under his breath, something about the interior of the *Chandra* looking like a gosh darn *Soyuz*, but nobody present would swear to it.

When they were done, Sawyer was happy to carry the remains of the BIGs out to the disposal pile.

The acceleration couches, except for the pilot-captain's command couch, were also disassembled and removed. The rest of the crew would be on sleeping pads taped to the deck. The eight-minute ride to orbit would be at three gees, easily tolerated. The liquid-fueled engines gave a much smoother ride than the old US Space Shuttle solid boosters allegedly had. In the unlikely event of something forcing a mid-flight abort, they were probably all dead anyway, a crash couch wouldn't help.

∞ ∞ ∞

Launch day eve

The previous evening, before dark, Patel had ordered everyone to a safe distance from the lander while he ran an engine test. It wouldn't be a full throttle test, the tie-downs weren't designed for that, nor did he want the exhaust to create too much disturbance to the nearby gear—especially including the refueling pod—until they were ready to lift off.

The sensors reported all systems were nominal. He started the pre-chill sequence, cold vapor from the fuel tanks flowing through the plumbing, pumps and valves to gradually cool them to operating temperature. A sensor light lit up yellow, one of the valves hadn't operated quite as quickly as expected. Patel toggled the *HOLD* control then pressed a button to manually cycle the valve a few times. The sensor changed back to green. He toggled it a few more times to be sure it stayed that way. It did. He made a note to visually check the valve just to be sure.

He released the hold and continued the sequence. At T-minus-thirty seconds he confirmed that the thrust limits were set to ten percent maximum. The tank pressures were nominal. A few seconds later he heard the whine of the turbo-pumps spinning up to operating speed. This was it, ignition sequence start. A muffled "whump" and then a growing roar came from below him as the first four engines lit, then a ripple of successive whumps masked by an increase in the roar as the other engines around the circumference of the ship fired up in rapid succession.

The console showed thrust at ten percent. He let it run for five seconds, then reached for the manual cut-off just as the computers also decided it was time to shut them down, and the roaring stopped. He heard the descending whine as the turbines slowed, and out the window all he could see was the clouds of steam from his exhaust. He and the computers began safing the system. It looked they were *GO* for tomorrow's launch.

∞ ∞ ∞

Centauri Station

Vukovich, the astrophysicist, would be monitoring the launch from orbit, on the *Heinlein*'s bridge. Drake sat strapped into his control couch watching the monitors. He rubbed his palms against his pants to get rid of the sweat. *If I'm nervous, I wonder how the folks on the Chandrasekhar are doing.* About seventy-five minutes to go. "Status?" he asked Vukovich.

"All systems are GO. I'll upload the final orbital elements at T-minus thirty minutes." They'd be out of visual range for that and for the launch; the relay satellite would handle the telemetry and communications. The timing allowed for the Station to be just catching up to *Chandrasekhar* when it reached orbit, so that they could do a final rendezvous and docking within one or two orbits after that.

"Thank you." Drake switched the comm to another channel. *Chandrasekhar*, Greg says systems are GO. Can you confirm?"

"*Affirmative,* Heinlein. *System lights are all green, propellant tanks are topping off, we are untied and hatches secure. Sawyer and Tsibliev are doing a final interior inspection to ensure everything is stowed properly, including the passengers. We're still on external air and will seal that as scheduled. We are GO.*" The life support system was still exchanging filtered air from outside to conserve the internal reserves. With nine people aboard a ship designed for five, even with design margins for ten, there was no point in pushing it.

∞ ∞ ∞

T-minus two minutes

"Everything still in the green, Greg?"

"Yes sir." Vukovich checked detailed screen. "Tank vent valves just closed and pressure is building up nominally. Life support is internal. Power is now internal."

"All right, read it off for me, would you." Launches hadn't been controlled by a roomful of people at consoles in a long time, one person could handle it now. But the functions of those consoles hadn't gone away, they had just been rolled up into different panels on a single screen.

Vukovich went through these panels one at time now, confirming to Drake that they'd been checked and everything looked nominal. "Okay. Propulsion is GO. FIDO is GO. Guidance, GO. EECOM, GO. Telcom, GO. Flight is GO, sir."

"Very good." He touched a key. "*Chandrasekhar*, you are GO for launch."

"Roger and thank you. See you soon."

∞ ∞ ∞

Chandrasekhar, T-minus thirty seconds.

Darwin lay on his pad on the control deck. A contoured pillow cradled his head, and Velcro straps across his chest and legs would keep him in place against any sideways force during launch, and against floating away in microgravity. *Here I am, first person to set foot on an extrasolar planet, and I'm riding in coach.* Even though he was amused rather than upset, he didn't voice the sentiment. Nobody would have any sympathy, least of all Elizabeth. She was strapped to the pad on his right. The only person with a proper couch was Ganesh Patel; as the pilot, he needed it. The weight trade-off for additional specimens was worth it, they'd had to leave enough behind as it was. *The things we do for science.*

Somewhere below there was a faint click of actuators closing and opening valves. Darwin heard the whine of turbines spooling up.

"Pre-chill complete, turbines are coming up to speed," Patel announced. "T-minus twenty seconds."

The whine rose in pitch then leveled out. There were more muffled clicks and thunks, and Patel announced "T-minus ten, ignition sequence start."

The engines started and their roar built in volume. This was the critical part. With nothing to hold the ship down while the engines came up to full power, there was a brief moment where the engines had enough power to balance the weight of the loaded vehicle but not enough to lift it off the ground at any speed. A wind gust then could be disastrous. Fortunately, the weather was calm and the engines were sequenced to let just a few of them come to full power first, to verify operation, then the rest would throttle up as fast as the design allowed. It would be fractions of a second, far too fast for human reflexes but a trivial exercise for the computers.

Darwin felt a hard shove from behind as the rocket lifted, growing in force as the propellant burned and the engines had less mass to push. They were away!

As best he could with what felt like the weight of two other people on top of him, he let out a cheer. Faintly, over the engine's roar, he heard others doing the same.

∞ ∞ ∞

Centauri Station

"How's their trajectory?" Drake asked Vukovich.

"Trajectory is nominal, but their engines are running a little harder to maintain it. They're still at 100%, they should have started to throttle back to maintain gee-loads."

"So they're burning fuel faster than expected. Cause?"

"We accounted for the extra mass and higher gravity. High crosswinds aloft would have meant tilting to compensate, the thrust vector would be off-nominal."

"Will they have enough delta-vee to make orbit?" Burning

extra fuel now might mean not enough later.

Vukovich checked the numbers, then the trajectory plot on another of his screens. "Make *an* orbit, yes, but they'll be too low for a good rendezvous. It looks like at least a day before the orbit decays."

"Only a day? Damn." Orbital rendezvous was a game of tweaking multiple variables. A lower orbit would mean *Chandrasekhar* would be pulling ahead of *Centauri Station*, but to get lower the Station had to lose energy, which meant either going higher, which was the opposite of what they wanted, or thrusting backwards, which would put them even further behind *Chandrasekhar* unless they did it at exactly the right relative positions in orbit. That could take more than a day.

"Do *we* have the delta-vee to catch them before that?" Drake said. There were contingency plans, Vukovich just had to persuade the computers to come up with the right one, if it existed.

"Maybe. Computer is running the details." He looked back at the FIDO and Propulsion screens. "Their engines are throttling back now, still on profile but they'll be fuel-starved at the end." Running the tanks dry was risky, if the pumps started to cavitate or the engines cut out asymmetrically, bad things could happen. "Four engines shutdown and the others have increased throttle. Looks like they're handling it." Either Patel or, more likely given the reaction time needed, the computers had figured out the risk and were taking steps to minimize it by changing the timing on the shutdown sequence.

"What about rendezvous?"

"*Centauri Station* can't make it. If we undock, either the *Heinlein* or *Anderson* could alone."

Drake didn't hesitate. He stabbed the comm button and broadcast station-wide. "All hands, emergency. Prepare for emergency undock sequence *now*. This is no drill. All hands, prepare for emergency undocking!" He released the button and said to Vukovich, "Greg, you stay here and keep doing what you're doing."

"Aye sir. Which ship is doing the pickup?"

Drake hadn't decided. The *Anderson* was probably better suited, it was designed as a lander so had a heat shield and more maneuverability, but it was still docked with its warp collar, which added a lot of mass. On the other hand, the *Heinlein*'s warp collar was part of the ship by design. *Anderson* was better suited without its collar, but *Heinlein* was better otherwise.

"Realistically, how quickly can *Anderson* undock and clear its warp collar?" It had taken *Chandrasekhar* a half-hour from closing the hatch to releasing its IPM, but they had been taking everything slowly and backing off half a kilometer before separation.

"Fifteen minutes from closing the hatch to clearing the collar, but that's not counting going through the checklists before that."

"Give me the numbers for first and second rendezvous opportunities using *Anderson*, but wait one." He toggled the station-wide channel again. "All hands, report ready."

"*Krysansky here. All assigned* Heinlein *personnel are strapped in, hatch is secure, still running the checklist.*"

"Anderson *here*," Geoff Tracey responded, "*We're missing Vukovich, remaining crew is secure, we're closing the hatch now.*"

"I have Vukovich. Continue prep and stand by."

"Roger that."

"Numbers?" Drake said, addressing Vukovich.

"First rendezvous window, *Anderson* leaves in—" he looked at a time on his screen "—twelve minutes. Next one is in twenty hours."

Damn it! That wasn't much wiggle room. "*Anderson*, status?"

"We'll all buttoned up, everything is green. What's happening?"

"Geoff, you have eight minutes to undock from station and get to a safe distance to separate from your IPM. Vukovich will upload your flight plan after that. You need to rendezvous with the *Chandra*."

"*Say again? Eight min...? Roger that, we're on it.*"

"Uh, Sir?" Vukovich said. "I said fifteen minutes."

"You also said first rendezvous opportunity was in twelve, more like eleven now. That number I believe. You did pad your first estimate, didn't you?"

Vukovich reddened. "Not by that much."

"They'll make it. Tracey is a damn good pilot. *Chandra* should be in orbit now. Check the numbers and get them to *Anderson*."

"Yes sir. They're in low orbit. They'll need to do a circularization burn in forty minutes, they can do that with maneuvering thrusters."

"Thank you," Drake said. "*Anderson*, status?"

"*Undocking now, Commodore.*" Drake watched as the appropriate indicators on his panel lit up, and faintly heard the clank of retracting docking latches. "*Stand by to take control of the IPM.*"

"Whenever you're ready, as long as it's within the next six-and-a-half minutes."

"*Wilco.*"

Drake touched the comm control again. "*Chandrasekhar* this is *Heinlein*."

"*This is* Chandrasekhar, *go ahead.*"

"We see you're a little low. The *Anderson* is on its way to pick you up."

"*Ah, thank you. Yes, I was beginning to wonder about that. We will just wait here for you then.*"

"Copy that. Vukovich will have some numbers for you shortly. Sit tight."

"*Roger.*"

Four minutes later, the Anderson called back in.

"Heinlein, *this is the* Anderson. *We are cleared from the warp collar and it's all yours on your mark.*"

"Nice work, Geoff. Mark."

"*Confirmed. So, what are we doing now?*"

"Dock with *Chandra* and boost them to a higher orbit, then we'll work out details for getting the station back together. You have the orbital elements?"

The was a brief pause before the reply as the *Anderson* crew checked the data. "*That's affirmative.*"

"Off you go then. You have a spaceship to catch."

"*Roger that,* Anderson *is listening out.*"

Chapter 28: Discussing the Findings

Aboard Centauri Station, in orbit

With the *Chandrasekhar* safely docked to the station, and its and the *Anderson*'s warp collars retrieved, Drake called Sawyer and Darwin into his cabin.

"All right, I've been hearing a lot of rumblings about anomalous results. I'm not sure I like what I think I'm hearing, but some of that may be exaggeration and speculation."

"Like what?"

"Apparently there's some thought that this planet didn't develop naturally. What I want to do is call everyone together and get it all on the table. I'd expect some weirdness in another star system, but I think this goes beyond that."

"Fair enough. When?"

"Let's give the teams a little while to re-settle and get their acts together. Shall we say 0800 tomorrow morning?"

"I can have the geology team ready by then. George?"

"Ditto for biology. Anyone else?"

"Yes, I want input from the Astrophysics team too. This will be an all hands meeting. Questions?"

There were none.

"All right, 0800. Go tell your teams, but also let me know the general gist informally before that."

∞ ∞ ∞

The crew were assembled in the inflated docking hub, the only volume suitable. The hoses and cables which had been left drifting during *Anderson*'s emergency undocking were now properly stowed or reconnected. But, after several weeks with half the crew on-planet, it still seemed downright crowed.

Drake called on Sawyer to present the geology team's findings.

"I'll give the planetological assessment first," she began, "and the geological follow through on the planet itself. Okay, background. We've got a twin star system, both stars about five billion years old, just a bit older than our Sun—"

"Can we skip ahead to the bits we don't know?" Of course that was Darwin. "We all got that briefing before we came out here. Even me."

At his last comment, Sawyer bit back what she'd been about to say, and instead said: "Okay, fair enough. First point, there's too much water on Kakuloa." That drew a round of laughter. She wondered what was so funny, then realized. "Aside from the flood, I mean. Okay, bear with me for a moment.

"First, even though more of the surface is ocean compared to Earth, on average the oceans are shallower, and the continents are thinner. That's troubling for a planet this old, but it means there's less water than on Earth. There's still more than there should be, though.

"Stable planetary orbits around A and B are within what we call the snow line, or the ice line, the distance from the star at which it's cool enough for water to freeze. That's good in that it means liquid water can exist. That's bad because it means when the planet is forming, it won't collect ice grains, and water molecules will tend not to condense with the protoplanet. That means the inner planets should be dry." She looked over at Vukovich, the astrophysicist. "Greg, how am I doing?"

"So far so good. There are some alternate theories, but what you've described is the current wisdom."

"Right, thanks."

"But what about Earth?" Klaar asked.

"That's where the problem arises in this system. In our Solar System, gravitational interactions with Jupiter pushed material from just beyond the snow line inwards, accounting for maybe half of Earth's water. After that, interactions between Jupiter and the other giant planets—Saturn, Uranus and Neptune—pushed Neptune from where it originally formed, closer to the Sun, out into the outer solar system. As it went it stirred up the Kuiper belt, sending a rain of comets into the inner solar system. Some of those crashed on Earth, filling up the ocean basins with yet more water. This all happened within the first hundred million years or so of the planets forming."

"So, couldn't that have happened here?" said Klaar.

"If it were an isolated star, yes, but it's a double. From just beyond Kakuloa's orbit out to well beyond both stars, orbits around one star get disrupted by the other. Anything much beyond the snow line gets thrown out to deep space."

"But there is a cometary belt here. We had a nasty reminder of that."

"The *Xīng Huā*, yes. But that's 70 AUs out, and the point is that there was never a Neptune, or any other gas giant, that formed and migrated out to disrupt their orbits. There should never have been a rain of comets on Kakuloa, or on Able, they should be dry planets."

"Wouldn't the other star be enough to cause that" Simms, the meteorologist, asked.

Sawyer glanced over at Vukovich. "Greg?"

"Not if it formed first," the astrophysicist said. "The possible exception is if A and B didn't form as a double but they captured each other later, after the planets formed." He quickly raised his hand to quell the obvious next questions. "The outermost planets of either star would have been lost, but the orbits of close-in planets might be stable. However, the problem with *that* is that both stars are, as best we can tell, the same age, so probably formed in the same nebula. The other problem is that both stars' planets' orbits, and the orbits of the stars around each other, are all more or less in the same plane. The odds on either of those happening by chance are, well, astronomical."

"So, how *did* Kakuloa get its water?"

"I have no idea," Vukovich said. "The explanation I'm going to go with for now is that the two stars captured each other after their planets formed. Any Jovian planets were lost in the capture. As for the odds, well, it's a big galaxy, things with astronomical odds against them still happen, and if it hadn't happened here, we wouldn't have bothered coming to look." He looked at Sawyer, who nodded.

"Thanks, Greg."

"That smells of the Anthropic Principal, that things are the way they are because we're here to observe them," Darwin said.

"I know," Sawyer said, "I'm holding my nose. But I'm really saying that we're here—in this particular system—to observe them because things are the way they are."

"Kind of odd that it's Sol's closest neighbors, though, isn't it?"

Vukovich spoke up again. "And then some. The Alpha Centauri system has a high relative motion to Sol, its orbit around the galaxy is apparently inclined to ours. In a few hundred thousand years it won't be anywhere near the solar system."

"So a coincidence in time as well as in space?"

"Yeah. Spooky, isn't it? Although we can't rule out that the system was originally orbiting coplanar with ours and was recently perturbed by some other gravitational influence."

"How recently," Sawyer asked.

"At a minimum, tens of thousands of years or we'd probably be seeing what perturbed it. No more than a two or three million or it would be somewhere else. But it's more probable it was in an inclined orbit to start with."

The biologists were not looking at all happy at this latest tidbit. Darwin muttered "Nothing is probable about this system."

Drake spoke again. "What about the geological anomalies?"

"Those are more related to inconsistencies in dating, isotope ratios, things of that nature," said Sawyer. She'd already gone over this with him, his question was for the benefit of the group. "Some of it could well be explained by different composition of the planetary nebula as compared to the Solar system. Let me just say that the crustal indications of tectonics and volcanism are more consistent with a much younger planet than the overall age of this system and the neutrino tomography results would suggest. As though the crust had been stirred up recently."

"What do you mean, recently? Same as Vukovich?"

"Not by a few orders of magnitude. Within the last hundred million years, we're still refining our dating markers. But this on a planet which should be close to five billion years old."

The biologists started whispering amongst themselves.

"Giant meteor impact?" Drake said.

"Well, sure, if there were a bunch of them, or a string like Shoemaker-Levy on Jupiter last century. But again we're left with the question of where that came from. And I would think the biologists wouldn't be happy about a potential planet-sterilizing event that recently."

"Okay, thank you. That sounds like as good a segue to the biology discussion as any. Darwin?"

"Thanks. Actually a planet-sterilizing event a hundred million years ago wouldn't surprise me."

"What? Then why are we seeing anything more complex than algae?"

"I'll get to that. First I want to show a few comparisons. Botanical first." He gestured to Singh. "Jennifer?"

Singh began discussing the cellular structure of the local flora. They had cell walls made of cellulose, and the chlorophyll —it was chlorophyll, or something remarkably close to it—was contained in chloroplasts within the cells. All very similar to plant life on Earth. Sawyer had heard much of it already, and had never really been particularly interested in botany, so began to tune out the presentation. It wrapped up with a series of images. The first showed plants that didn't look like any plant Sawyer—or Singh, for that matter—recognized, but whose microstructure was not especially unusual. The second series of images was a comparison of some local plants side by side with Earth plants, or sometimes fossils, which looked startlingly similar.

"Of course there are plenty of species and even whole genera that don't resemble anything we've found on Earth," Singh reminded them, "but it is all things that wouldn't particularly surprise us if we did find it, whether in some remote forest or in the fossil record. There's nothing really *alien*. Convergent evolution and universal fundamentals of biochemistry are certainly possibilities, but we would expect to see more variation than we do." She closed the final image she'd been showing. "Doctor Darwin?"

"Thanks," Darwin said. "Now I'll show you a few animals. Ulrika should really be doing this, but it started with this." He put a picture of the runny babbit up on the screen.

"This is the one that got me wondering," he said. "Let me show you some detailed comparisons." A picture of an Earth rabbit came up on the screen beside the Centauri babbit.

"Okay, gross morphology the same. Head, four legs, etc, etc. We all know how familiar the animals look in general, if not in detail. No six legged centaur-like creatures, no animals on wheels instead of legs, nothing really weird."

"What about the tree squids?" asked Tyrell.

"Okay, I'll grant that *those* are a bit odd, but they aren't a huge leap from what Earth cephalopods are capable of. There are already species of octopus that can crawl from one tidal pool to another. Climbing into a banyan tree is conceivable."

Klaar nodded and raised her voice to add: "We have also found some very strange-looking insects and arachnids, but they *are* insects and arachnids, as best we can tell. Nothing with a body plan we don't recognize, even if the details differ."

"But back to our furry friends," Darwin said. "Let's take a look at the skeletons." On the screen, the two animals were replaced by their skeletons. "Remarkably similar, aren't they? Now, amazing as it is that two animals on planets light years apart would both have evolved skeletons, made of bone, with remarkably similar microstructure and properties, it gets better."

Darwin touched a key and the skeletons on the screen disarticulated, all the bones separating from each other just a bit. The neck areas of both animals magnified. "See the neck vertebrae? Seven of them in the rabbit, seven in the babbit. That number seven goes for just about every mammal on Earth. It also goes for just about every mammal-like creature we examined here."

He touched another button. The neck area shrunk back to

normal size and the skulls expanded. "But wait, there's more. When paleontologists find a skull, one of the things they look at is the way the jawbone connects to the rest of the skull, the bones around what in us is the ear area, at the various foramen— holes—in the skull. They are what distinguish a mammal skull from a reptile from a dinosaur." At Darwin's touch, a series of labels appeared with lines pointing to features on both skulls. "If this skull," he pointed to the Centauran babbit's, "was found on Earth, any biologist or paleontologist would identify it as a mammal's. A previously undescribed species and even genus of mammal, but a mammal."

Darwin cleared the babbit/rabbit pictures from the screen and started a slide show showing pairs of animals, much as Singh had done with the plants. "Look, birds. Same feathers, same bones, same gizzard. A few minor differences, the birds here tend to have longer tails, but not all of them. Nothing inconsistent with having descended from *Archaeopteryx* or something like him, just like every bird on Earth." More pictures. "The same goes for the invertebrates. Those tree squids mentioned earlier, for example. Similar body plan to Earthly cephalopods. There's a cousin to the coelacanth swimming in the ocean, as well as plenty of fish. Oh, no species we particularly recognized, we only did limited sampling, but nothing that would seem out of place in Earth's oceans."

Darwin paused, then waved a hand and shrugged. "The list goes on. Unfortunately we lost the DNA sequencer, but we can say that the life here is more or less consistent with life on Earth. And I don't just mean any life on Earth, but *current* life. As best we can tell without the sequencer, the way life forms here compare with Earth life forms is consistent with the two having followed an almost identical evolutionary path for about the same length of time. That is highly improbable, to put it mildly."

"Well, the planet *is* about the same age as Earth, give or take a few hundred million years," said Tyrell.

"Yes, but lot can happen in a few hundred million years, and unless there are forces in play we don't understand yet, that doesn't explain billions of years of biological parallelism,"

Darwin said. "But there's something else."

"Oh?"

"Earth's history of complex multicellular lifeforms goes back more than half a billion years. From studying the fossil record, incomplete though it is, we've built up a pretty extensive catalog of species, genus, even entire phyla of plants and animals that went totally extinct at different stages of Earth's history."

"Like dinosaurs," Tyrell said.

"Like dinosaurs," Darwin allowed, "except for birds. But also ammonites, trilobites, gorgonopsids, and so on. Now, Sawyer mentioned a planet-sterilizing event of a hundred million years ago—"

"Could have been less," Sawyer broke in. "Could have been a bit more. Call it ninety plus or minus forty million for now."

"Okay, close enough for my point. The thing is, despite the fact that all the life that we've found here bears some resemblance to Earth life, none of it bears any resemblance to anything that went extinct on Earth *prior to* ninety million—give or take forty—years ago. For that matter, we haven't found anything that strongly resembles Earth life which *evolved* more recently than about fifty million years ago. It's like somebody, ninety million years ago, took a snapshot of Earth's lifeforms and set them up here, and they've evolved their own way since. Although by our biology estimates the number is more like sixty or seventy million years ago."

"Dinosaurs?" asked Tyrell.

"We haven't found any, not counting the birds, so maybe it was less than sixty-five million years ago."

"No, I mean," Tyrell paused, blushing slightly. "This is going to sound silly."

"You're wondering if intelligent dinosaurs could have done all this, right Fred?"

"Well, yes. I said it would sound silly."

Darwin started to shake his head, then stopped and said "Nope. Actually we'd already kicked that idea around. But there's never been any evidence on Earth of intelligent dinosaurs, and —"

"Absence of evidence—"

"—is not evidence of absence. Yes, you're right, maybe we just haven't looked in the right place yet. But then why aren't there dinosaurs here? And why let themselves get wiped out if they were capable of transplanting an entire ecosystem across four light years?"

"Sixty-five million years ago it could have been a lot more than four light years," said Vukovich. "That's about a quarter of a rotation around the galaxy, and at Alpha Centauri's current inclination it would have been well out of the galactic plane. Although we don't know if that's always been the case."

"Okay, now that's too weird. Does anything support the idea that Centauri's motion changed recently, so that it's in an inclined orbit now but wasn't always?"

"Yee..es," Vukovich said. "I'm not really happy with that hypothesis, because I'm not sure how you'd do that with a multiple star system without messing up the planet orbits, but I'm not going to rule it out without running the math." He paused as if thinking, then continued. "There *are* some simulations that suggest the few thousand nearby stars may have been clustered together about then, before diverging and converging as they orbit the galactic core. The galaxy isn't a rigid disk."

There was a low murmur of conversation as several of the crew made comments to each other. Darwin caught Sawyer making eye contact with Drake.

∞ ∞ ∞

Sawyer watched the Commodore intently as he ahem-ed for attention and then raised his voice.

"Suppose it were an act of God?" Drake said. The result was several seconds of dead silence, disturbed only by the whisper of fans in the life support system, as everyone turned their gazes to stare at him. Whatever she had been expecting him to say, this wasn't it.

"All right," he continued, "don't all look at me like I dropped a turd in the punchbowl. You *know* that will be what every religious fundamentalist on the planet will be saying when word of this gets out. Creation, intelligent design, God did it, Allah's will, and so on."

"You're right," Sawyer said. "Just what the planet needs, another excuse for religious fanaticism. We need to keep it quiet."

"Keep it quiet?" Darwin exclaimed. "How? I can see it now: 'Gee folks, how was your trip to Alpha Centauri? What are those life-bearing planets like?' 'Oh, that was a mistake, there's nothing there.' 'It took you a month to figure that out?'" He shook his head. "Yeah, that will go over well."

"Okay, we let it out a bit at a time," Sawyer said. "Just the objective facts, not our interpretations. It *could* be convergent evolution."

"It's worse than that," Drake said, resuming control of the conversation. "If it's not just incredible coincidence, and it wasn't intelligent dinosaurs, and it wasn't God, then *who was it?*" Again the meeting area in the hub grew quiet. Sawyer thought she heard somebody whisper "*holy shit.*"

"Think about it, people." Drake continued, although it was clear most of them were doing just that. "If what Sawyer is saying about water and everything else is correct, then these planets were deliberately modified. *Terraformed.* On a scale we can only dream of. Sixty-five or a hundred million years ago, somebody or some*thing* terraformed these planets and seeded them with life from Earth . . . or perhaps they seeded Earth too."

"But the fossil record—" Darwin began.

Drake raised his hand to forestall the argument. "Okay, perhaps not Earth. That's a side issue. The main point, the big stinking megatherium in the room, is this: Whoever did this had capabilities way beyond ours, and had them millions of years ago. Where are they now, and more to the point, do they know that *we're* here now?"

"Do you think that they—whoever or whatever they are—are a threat?"

"If they're still around—and frankly I hope they're long gone—I think that they could squash us like a bug without even noticing, perhaps unintentionally. 'Planet sterilizing event', that's what you said, right Sawyer? Now, since nobody seems to be around here at the moment, perhaps they *are* long gone. Or perhaps they are here but in ways unobservable by us. Ascended to a higher plane, uploaded their consciousness to nanomachine swarms, perfected invisibility, or whatever.

"However, even with the best of intentions, or no intentions at all, if they could control that kind of energy *then*, then they could be that much more powerful *now*. It's like a mouse sharing a bed with an elephant. The elephant isn't going to notice what the mouse does, but if the elephant twitches that mouse could be crushed. Okay, maybe that's not exactly how it goes, but you get the idea."

"So what are you suggesting?"

Drake gave a gentle shake of his head. "That's mostly above my pay grade, for which I am deeply thankful. But we won't be able to keep it quiet once we return to Earth. Our data will speak for itself, even if we try to hush up our conclusions. And yet Earth certainly doesn't need the kind of rampant speculation, hysteria, fanaticism, culture shock or whatever else we might get if this gets out in an uncontrolled fashion. It will need to be broken to the public slowly, let them get used to it a little bit at a time. Meanwhile I think the leaders of the world need to get their heads together and think about what this means for humanity as a whole."

Drake paused, letting that sink in, then continued. "'Planet sterilizing event.' You know, the man this ship is named after, Robert Anson Heinlein, once said something like 'the Earth is too small and fragile a basket for humanity to keep all its eggs in'. He was right—the Unholy War almost proved that—but he was thinking too small. The *solar system* is too small and fragile a basket. We've found a place, perhaps two, where we can set up another basket." That triggered another round of murmuring, and he held up a hand, palm out, to quell it. "Yes, assuming the original builders have abandoned the place. That seems to be a reasonable assumption; we haven't found anything smarter than the tree-squids."

Sawyer knew that the biologists insisted that they were closer to octopus than to squid, but the name tree-squid had stuck.

Drake continued: "We need to find more such baskets—and see if we can figure out just who the original builders were and what else they may have done. The interstellar exploration program must continue."

Damn right, Sawyer thought.

"It's either that or everybody is going to be so scared of what we might find out here that they'll all hide their collective heads up their asses and we'll never leave the Solar System again," Drake said.

We can't let that happen.

"Come on, let's go home and find out what it's going to be." Drake looked around at the assembled crew, as if preparing to dismiss them.

Now or never. "Sir?" Sawyer broke in before Drake could finish. "If I may suggest something?"

"Go ahead."

"I want to re-raise the point I made a few weeks ago, before the first landing."

Drake's eyes tightened. He had probably guessed what was coming, but he gave a slight nod. "Go ahead."

"We still have landers. We don't need three starships to carry everyone back to Earth, especially if some of them stay here." She heard a couple of indrawn breaths, people whom she hadn't already approached about this because she didn't think they'd be interested, but aside from a quick glance around she stayed focused, respectfully, on Franklin Drake.

"Sawyer, we discussed this before, after losing the *Xīng Huā*," Drake said. "I am not stranding anyone here."

"With respect, the situation has changed since then. You said yourself that they might pull their collective heads in and never leave the solar system again, but that we need to explore further."

Drake's frown softened slightly. That was good.

"If some of us are still out here, that would encourage them to maintain interstellar capability at least long enough to come out and bring us back."

"Us? You'd be willing to stay behind?" Drake asked, then added: "Not that I'm saying yes."

"Of course. I wouldn't have raised the point if I weren't willing to stay."

"Even if it means never returning to Earth? There's no guarantee that they will send a return expedition, let alone a timely one. New ships, or at the least refueling pods, would need to be built."

Sawyer had already considered that. At the most optimistic, the *Heinlein* could return with a refueling pod and drop it near the lander. The lander could return to space, link up with its Interstellar Propulsion Module—what everyone referred to as the warp donut—and return to Earth. The warp flight took a week. The problem was that as far as she knew, there were no fueling pods ready to go. The overall design was simple enough, but if parts hadn't already been ordered for the reactor and cryogenic pumps, it could be months or years. Sawyer hoped that spares ordered for the original mission were available, but she had no way of knowing that. There was no quick way to ask Earth. Radio signals took 4.3 years each way; hand-carrying a message by ship was 200 times faster. The best she could hope for, if they even let the *Heinlein* return here, was that she'd get a status update in four weeks. That was if the politicians could make up their mind in a day or two, which was improbable. On the other hand, she'd long ago accepted that any trip into space carried the possibility of not coming back.

"Yes, even if it meant never returning to Earth," she answered, "although I'm only speaking for myself. There's still a lot to learn out here, and I think it's worth the risk for a lot of reasons."

Drake turned his head to survey the faces of the assembled crew. Sawyer did the same. A lot of them were tired, and almost surely wanted to return home, but a few had shining eyes, their bodies tilted forward in anticipation.

"All right," Drake said, "let's put this on the table. I'm not convinced yet, but I'm willing to be. Let's see who here, and I'm not asking for a commitment now, or promising anything, just assessing the possibility, but who is willing to be marooned here. You're all intelligent, you know you will likely have to find native sources of food and endure other hardships before anyone returns for you. Sawyer, do you want to add anything before I call for a show of hands?"

"No. I'm not going to try to convince anyone to stay who doesn't already have his or her own reasons." Not again, anyway. She'd already talked with most of them.

"Good. I'm still not saying yes, but, show of hands, who is willing to stay?"

Sawyer raised her hand and looked around the hub at the others. Darwin raised his hand almost as quickly as she had, but she suspected that Drake would insist that Darwin return to Earth to explain the biological findings, even if he let others stay behind. Who else?

Klaar and Tyrell looked at each other questioningly. They both shrugged, and tentatively both raised their hands. Their overland hike after the plane crash had obviously been a bonding experience. Good.

Jennifer Singh said pointedly, "I am not planning to play Eve to anybody's Adam, but I am in." She raised her hand.

Sawyer wondered if Singh's comment had been aimed at anyone in particular. It didn't seem to be. Sawyer hoped it wouldn't come to that, but if so – she looked over at Krysansky, the expedition's primary medical doctor. He caught the look and glanced away, then half-raised his hand.

"Doctor, is your hand up or down?" Drake asked.

"A bit of both, Commodore. I would like to get back to Earth but I am willing to stay behind if a crew lands. A medical doctor might mean the difference between survival and death if the stay is prolonged. If my captain agrees, of course." He looked over at Tsibliev.

"*Da*, this makes sense."

"So noted, thank you both. Anyone else?"

Sawyer looked at the others. A few had already raised hands. Two more went up at the doctor's announcement. Nearly half of the crew. More than enough, perhaps too many. She'd have to trade off equipment and personnel for the landing, try to come up with an optimum.

∞ ∞ ∞

Drake surveyed the group. These were people who had volunteered for this mission knowing the dangers, people with an intense curiosity, so the show of hands didn't surprise him.

"All right," he said. "Let me think on it. If I agree to it, you won't all be staying. Some of you," Drake looked pointedly at Darwin, who shrugged, "will have to return to better explain our findings and to help lobby for the next mission. If I *do* make that decision, I will be on the hook for disobeying orders and potentially for misappropriation of government property. My mission was to bring you all, or as many as I could, home safely and *not* to abandon expensive hardware willy nilly. I will face an investigation, probably a court martial, even if everyone ends up agreeing that I made the right decision."

Given their surprising findings, it might not come to that, but it was better to assume that it would. The assembled crew were looking at him soberly now, some almost grim. "It will be easier for me to make that decision if you do the legwork. I'll give you twenty-four hours to put together a proposal."

He turned toward Sawyer. He wondered just how long she'd been thinking about this. She was too smart for it to be completely spur of the moment. No matter, the plan had merit. He was just glad he didn't have to order it. "Sawyer, I want the landing party roster, justifications, equipment lists, a mission plan, and so on. Based on that I'll make my decision to approve or deny the revision to the mission. Any questions?"

"Which lander would we use, *Chandra* or *Anderson*?"

Drake considered that. The *Chandrasekhar* would never be allowed to return to Earth itself; it had landed on another planet and paranoia about contamination was too high. It would instead land at the quarantine facility on the Moon, where it would no doubt remain as a historic museum piece: the first Earth ship to land on a planet of another star. Maybe when they were convinced that it was sterile they'd return it to an Earth museum, or break it up so museums in every country could have a piece. But if it stayed here, they'd be bringing the *Anderson* back, pristine and ready to go out again. The political implications, however, of returning with just the two American ships, even with a mixed nationality crew, would be awkward.

There was also the fact that the *Chandrasekhar* had been stripped to save weight for the return launch, and had still been nearly too heavy. There should be nothing that precluded it from doing another planetary landing, but the *Poul Anderson* would give a better safety margin. He wondered what choice Elizabeth would make if it were just up to her.

"Undecided," he finally said. "Write up the arguments pro and con each way and let me know which you'd prefer. I'll make the final decision, and you'll have time to transfer gear whichever way necessary. Any other questions?"

"How long after the landing would you remain in-system?"

"Long enough to get preliminary science reports back, it would be foolish not to do that. But there's a time constraint on our consumables. Put your recommendations and discussion in the mission plan." Drake looked around. "Anyone else? No? Very well, confer amongst yourselves and get that plan to me tomorrow. I'm available if anyone has further questions or concerns. Carry on." Drake twisted his body and pushed off to leave the briefing area.

∞ ∞ ∞

Sawyer watched him go, her heart pounding with a mix of anticipation and relief. She had been half-expecting him to reject the proposal outright. Had she been hoping he would? No, this was the right thing to do. She wanted to do it. It wouldn't be easy, though, she knew that. The easy part was over. One hurdle down, many more to go. The next twenty-four hours would be busy. And the twenty-four after that. And then the next twenty-four, until they'd landed on the planet. Then it would be twenty-six. . . ..

Chapter 29: Preparations

Centauri Station

They decided to land with the *USS Anderson*. Most of its original gear was still stowed. They would need the aircraft; of the two which had gone down to Kakuloa on *Chandra* and *Krechet*, one had been wrecked and the other left behind to save weight. The earlier drone surveys of Planet Able had turned up several possible landing areas. Some of the same constraints applied. They needed a large open area—this time one that might be used for agriculture if the stay was prolonged—and access to fresh water. The latitude constraints no longer applied in terms of returning to orbit, except that they'd want to keep that option open for when the next expedition fleet returned. They'd also want to avoid any extreme winters if it didn't return immediately.

∞ ∞ ∞

"Elizabeth," Franklin Drake intercepted her as she drifted across the docking hub. "A word if you would."

"Of course." She followed him to his cabin. "What's on your mind?"

"Too many things." He sighed. That was certainly true. "I've been looking at what we're keeping for the voyage back versus what we're leaving here. If there are any delays in a return expedition, you won't have enough food to last you more than a few months, even though we'll leave all we can. That's not a lot of margin for a delayed return mission. So what are you going to do for food when the concentrates run out?"

"We'll process protein and carbohydrates from the native life. We've adapted some lab gear to make a digester which will reduce everything to basic components; we shouldn't have to worry about protein compatibility."

"What are you basing that on? We haven't sampled the native life on Able."

"Not directly, but the drones did chemical sampling and we have pretty detailed spectrographic analysis of the vegetation. We're assuming the life is similar to Kakuloa's, that is, to Baker's."

His eyebrows raised. "Assuming?"

She quickly filled in. "We have good reason to assume that. Spectrographic analysis shows the vegetation quite similar to Baker's, and to Earth's for that matter. There's definitely chlorophyll down there. The drone results were consistent, and it's likely that even if Able wasn't seeded with Earth life by the Terraformers like Baker was, any large impacts would have splashed material that could easily travel from one planet to the other. There could be a lot of cross-contamination. We ran the numbers. An organism below the surface of a rock could easily survive the trip."

"It's still a risk."

"The biologists are confident. In fact at first they were downright disappointed there weren't more differences. We'll know if the local biochemistry is compatible within the first day or two. That's important—it affects what we think we know about the Terraformers. If we made a mistake . . . well, I don't think we did, and neither do the biologists. Not even George."

Drake stifled a smile at that. If Darwin was agreeing with her, it was a pretty safe bet. "Okay, but I'd hate to get back here and find you've all starved to death."

"Not half as much as we'd hate it, so get somebody's ass back here as soon as you can."

"That is my intention."

"And remember Mark Watney."

"Right." Drake got the reference, he had read *The Martian* as kid just as had most of the crew. "But you don't have any potatoes."

∞ ∞ ∞

"Sorry, George, I know you want to stay and yes, before you say anything, I know you could do good work here. But it's off the table, you have to come back to Earth."

"Damn it, Frank, you don't need me to argue the case for coming back here. You've got our reports. I'll record a speech if you like."

"That's only part of it," Drake said. "But like it or not, you're famous, or will be when we get back with the news. You're in a class with Neil Armstrong and Christopher Columbus; you're the first human to set foot on an extrasolar planet."

"Oh, right. There's another reason for me to not go back. We had enough of that when we got back from Mars, and we weren't even first." Darwin held up his hand. "Just joking. On the other hand, I was in that damn biosuit, who is to know that it was really me?"

"You mean aside from the name 'Darwin' in big letters on the suit's name tag?"

"Oh, yeah." He resigned himself to it. "Okay, I pretty much knew it was a lost cause when I asked, but I had to ask. I'll go back to Earth. I guess I'll work on my speeches on the return trip."

"Thank you. I'll recommend you for the next trip out."

"Frank, you and I both know that the chances of either of us getting another trip are slim. We're going to be embroiled in politics and public relations for years. Our experience won't count; the next missions will be a very different group of people."

Drake sighed. He'd suspected as much, but knowing that Darwin had reached the same conclusion made it that much more real. He didn't like it, but he didn't have to. Duty first.

∞ ∞ ∞

While they were prepping the ships for the trip from Alpha Centauri B to Alpha Centauri A, which would mean collapsing the docking hub and each ship making the one-minute warp jump separately. the landing plans came together rapidly. While this exact scenario hadn't been dreamed of, a lot of pre-mission planning had gone into contingencies which were not all that different, for example if a lander had been unable to take off again.

The *Anderson*'s Interstellar Propulsion Module would remain in orbit. The flight crew were modifying the software to make it controllable from the *Anderson* while on the ground. It would serve duty as a combination weather, navigation and communications satellite, in a synchronous orbit at the longitude of the landing site.

"Commodore, I have a suggestion, about the *Anderson*'s IPM." Greg Vukovich said.

"What about it?" asked Drake, looking up from his reader.

"I've been doing some calculations. If we rig a mesh across the diameter, fastened the right way, we can turn the whole thing into a dish antenna."

"Okay, and?"

"They'll be able to beam a signal to Earth, and to pick up one beamed here," the astrophysicist said. "It'll be faint, but there are stations on Earth that could pick up the signal and send back one strong enough to pick up here with a dish."

"So they have communications—with nearly a nine-year round trip time lag. I'm not sure I see the point."

"Well, when you put it that way...." But he persisted. "I still think it's important for them to send out regular signals. If something goes wrong—if we don't get back here—it will at least remind Earth that they're out here and keep them apprised of the situation. And vice versa."

"I sure as heck hope that someone comes back here before fifty-two months are up," Drake said. "That's when they'd get the first signal from Earth."

"Just think of it as a worst case backup for whatever data they generate."

"All right, draw up a plan showing me what you need in materials and manpower, and I'll think about it. What were you going to use for the mesh?"

"Just a couple of pounds of aluminum scavenged from the structure. We can program one of the fabbers to extrude it into fine wire and weave it together."

"Good." Drake thought for a moment. "How is this going to interfere with using the IPM as an observation and local communication satellite for the landing crew?"

"Well, for short times as it reorients itself they'll lose pictures and maybe comms. We could put the cameras and antennas on gimbals to eliminate that."

"Plan on that, everything helps. How fast is it going to burn through station-keeping fuel?"

"It won't. We're going to use a modified magnetic sail for that. It will push against the planet's magnetosphere." He paused for several seconds. "Although. . .."

"Yes? Although what?"

"If we could use the *Krechet*'s IPM too we could leave one oriented toward the Solar System and the other in synch with the landing site on the planet."

"How are we going to get it to Planet Able?" It was still in orbit around Kakuloa, and had no control systems to line it up and make the warp jump by itself. "Anyway, my orders are to at least destroy the warp drives on any IPMs we leave behind, and preferentially to deorbit otherwise destroy the IPMs. I'm already making an exception for this one." *As if I weren't going out on an even longer limb by leaving a team here,* Drake thought.

"What? But why?"

"So that the technology doesn't fall into the wrong hands. I never got a clear picture of who they were more worried about, other nations on Earth or some hypothetical intelligent aliens."

"That's a stupid directive. Ah, with all due respect. Anyone in a position to find the IPM has interstellar travel already."

"I raised that point myself. It didn't go over. I don't know if they're worried about Centauri inhabitants—"

"There aren't any."

"Maybe they're hiding. Look, I know there aren't any, and that destroying the things isn't really necessary, but the professional paranoids managed to come up with some crazy scenarios where they figure the risk doesn't outweigh the cost. Our orders are to destroy them."

"But—"

"No. I'm already stretching my orders as it is, albeit with good reason. And there's no easy way to get it there, and I want to leave for Able as soon as we're ready here. No, you will have to make do with the *Anderson*'s IPM."

Vukovich sighed. "All right, thank you. I'll get on it."

Chapter 30: Goodbyes

Centauri Station, orbiting Centauri A II

They had reassembled the station in orbit above planet Able. It hardly seemed worth it for the few days before they disassembled it yet again for the warp trip back to the Solar System, but it was the only practical way to quickly get from one ship to another.

∞ ∞ ∞

The *Anderson* was due to depart in just hours now. Sawyer's omni chirped. What now? "Sawyer here."

"Commander Sawyer, this is Drake, please report to my office."

Was he going to cancel at the last minute? Sawyer felt a knot in her guts. "Aye sir, be right there."

She made her way through the hub and into the *Heinlein*. She stopped at the Commodore's door and took a breath, steeling herself against what she thought was coming. "Sawyer reporting as ordered, Sir."

"Thank you. I know you're busy, so this won't take long, then you can get back to landing prep."

So he wasn't scrubbing the landing. Then what?

"Commander Sawyer, you are going to be in charge of the *Anderson* and the survival of your landing party until such time as there's a return mission, which I hope will be very soon."

"Uh, yes sir." *Where was this going?*

"That's way too much responsibility for a Commander. Therefore, I'm promoting you to Captain."

"What?"

"Well, acting Captain is all I can do for a field promotion, but I'll push to have that confirmed. I'm not sure how much weight my word will carry though. I'll announce it to the crew before you depart, assuming you accept?"

"Thank you, sir. Yes, sir." This was the opposite of what she'd been expecting, but in hindsight it made sense.

"Congratulations, then." He held out his hand for a symbolic handshake, which Sawyer took.

"Now, Captain, you have a ship and a landing to prepare for. I suggest you get back to work." The voice was stern, but followed by a smile. "And good luck, Elizabeth."

"Aye sir. Thank you." She turned to leave.

"Oh, and Elizabeth. . .." he called before she made it through the hatchway.

"Yes?"

"When you run into trouble down there, and I do mean when, not if, just ask yourself 'what would Mark Watney do?'".

She smiled. "He'd 'science the shit out of it.'", Her smile faded. "I think a better question would be, 'what would Shackleton do?'" She knew that Drake considered that early Antarctic explorer to be one of his heroes. When their ship had become frozen in the ice, Ernest Shackleton had kept his crew alive for more than a year and a half, and crossed over 700 miles of ocean in an open boat to effect a rescue, bringing them all back. No wonder the decision to let her and the landing party stay behind had been hard.

Drake nodded once. "Damned right. Keep your team alive, we'll be back here as soon as we can."

"Roger that." She turned back to the hatchway to make her way to the *Anderson*. *Her first command, good for all of one deorbit and landing.* And she did have work to do.

∞ ∞ ∞

Aboard the Anderson, *still docked to Centauri Station*

"Elizabeth, I know you're busy, but do you have a few minutes?" Darwin asked as he paused at the entrance from the docking hub.

She looked up from the console she had been working at, and glanced at the time on her omni. George's timing was terrible. "A very few, we need to get the *Anderson* locked down for undocking. What's on your mind?"

"Well, congratulations on your promotion. It also occurs to me that we might not see each other again. I suppose that's always been true, but 4.3 light years kind of puts a nail on it. And I'm going to miss you."

The thought hit her harder than she would have expected. For all their disagreements, there was still an attraction. *Must be pheromones*, she told herself. "Even if you're not on the next expedition, I'll be going back with it. We'll see each other again. You'll probably be gloating while I'm stuck in your damn quarantine lab." For all her brave words, she knew there was a chance she might not make it back. She was about to land on an unknown world, with no immediate way to return.

"Probably." Darwin sounded as unconvinced as she felt. "And speaking of the quarantine lab, I have something for you." He held out a small specimen box. "Something they gave me as a going away present. Right now you're more likely to find a use for it than me."

She opened it. "A *potato?*" Under any other circumstances, a girl would probably be offended. Now, though, Sawyer thought it was the most romantic gift she'd ever received. Damn it, she was *not* going to cry in front of George. Instead she put her arms around his neck and kissed him.

"You bastard," she said, her tone belying the words. "Now I'll miss you."

"You'll be too busy," he said. Sawyer thought he seemed a bit flustered, like he hadn't expected her reaction, or that he was feeling the same way. "Anyway, you're right, we'll likely see each other in a couple of months."

Perhaps. "On that note, I really do need to get back to work. Thank you, that was unexpected." Sawyer turned, somewhat reluctantly, back to her console.

"Sure," Darwin said, and he pushed off, grabbing the handle

by the hatchway and pausing for a moment. "Goodbye, Elizabeth."

He pushed off again, back toward the *Heinlein*.

Sawyer couldn't quite focus on her screen. She blinked a few times to clear her vision, and said to herself, aloud but softly, "goodbye George."

Chapter 31: Landing

In orbit, above Alpha Centauri A II

"Last chance to change your mind. After this you're stuck here."

"*We know. 'No way to return to orbit let alone Earth until a return mission arrives, if ever.' We're tired of hearing it. Give us a GO,*" Sawyer said over the comm.

"All right. *Anderson*, you are GO for deorbit burn. Good luck."

The *United States Starship Poul Anderson* had already backed off to a safe distance from the other two remaining ships. To the observers on the *Heinlein* and *Chandrasekhar*, the burn of the *Anderson*'s main engines came as a pale glow above the limb of the planet—the second out from Alpha Centauri A—and looking as Earth-like as Kakuloa had.

The *Anderson* receded quickly, slowing as the other two ships, docked together, continued in their orbit.

"There they go," said Darwin.

"Still wish you were going with them?" Drake asked him.

Darwin considered the question before responding. Part of him did wish he was aboard, descending for a landing on the second extrasolar planet humankind would explore. He looked up through the window at Alpha Centauri B, A's companion star, but the planet he'd landed on, Kakuloa, was lost in its glare.

"We did find some strange things there. I would still dearly love to compare and contrast whatever is down here—" he gestured at the planet below "—with Kakuloa's and Earth's biology."

If the Chinese *Xīng Huā* hadn't hit that comet fragment while in warp, destroying itself and their second fuel-synthesis module with it, then *Anderson* could have returned to space after its upcoming landing. He would have been able to explore that planet and still return to Earth. *Life's full of little trade-offs*, he thought.

"But," he continued, holding up a hand to forestall Drake's inevitable repetition of their ongoing argument, "I know I can't. You're right that I'm probably the best person to explain our findings so far, and the implications." He looked over at Drake and smiled. "Although I'm sure you just want me there to divert the first footstep hullabaloo from you."

"I never set foot on the planet. It's all you, George. But yes, you can explain it better than I can."

"That this place was terraformed, with life from Earth no less, about the time the dinosaurs died out? I can't explain that any better than you can."

"Perhaps, but you can justify those conclusions from the data we have better than me. I'm going to be busy urging everyone to keep exploring, to build new ships, and to rescue the crew we're casting away here."

"More like maroonees than castaways, but you're right."

∞ ∞ ∞

The *Anderson* landed without incident, and initial surveys confirmed what they'd determined from orbit via the probes. The air was breathable and the local biochemistry wouldn't kill them any time soon.

The *Heinlein* and *Chandrasekhar* would remain in orbit another two days while the landing crew attempted to resolve the question as to whether the local lifeforms could be related to Earth or Kakuloa forms, or whether they were clearly different. It would take considerably longer to determine if the planet itself had been terraformed.

∞ ∞ ∞

Aboard Heinlein, *above Alpha Centauri A II*

The ships had undocked and the inflatable hub, its job done, had been discarded. There was a general buzz of activity to secure everything for the trip back. Darwin was already feeling a little cramped, between the jettison of the central docking hub and the extra crew. The landing party was a mixed blessing, there were fewer crew making the return voyage, but they were also short one starship. Two, counting the *Krechet* still on Kakuloa's surface.

His omni chirped. "Darwin here."

"*There's a message for you from Dr. Singh on the planet.*"

"Go ahead."

"*She says, 'We have found several species of monocotyledonous plants, their hollow stems have leaf-bearing nodes. Their flowers are spikelets. We haven't been able to catch a local furry creature yet to count the vertebrae, but we have definitely found grasses.'*"

"Huh. We didn't see any grasses on Kakuloa. Maybe we weren't looking in the right place, or it never established itself."

"So, yet more evidence that life here is Earth related?" asked Drake. None of the preliminary tests so far had shown anything different.

"Yes. Very much so."

"That's good enough for me," Drake said. "Let's go home."

Chapter 32: Home Again

Entering the Solar System

The trip back was relatively uneventful. With the confidence they now had in the warp drives, and the fact that there were now just two ships to coordinate, the times in warp were longer and closer together than they'd been on the trip out.

In a week they were entering the outer Solar System, cautiously and from below the plane of the ecliptic to minimize the chances of a repeat of the *Xīng Huā* accident. If it was one.

When they reached about the distance of Neptune, the two ships paused to more carefully calibrate their position. The Solar system was a lot more crowded than the Alpha Centauri system, whose two suns had cleared a lot of it out. The *Heinlein* also began broadcasting news of their return, along with some of the less startling data they had collected. The Terraformer hypothesis could wait.

The news that only two of the original five ships had returned stirred up considerable consternation, and Drake gave a brief synopsis of the situation, along with his assurance that he'd give full details and data dumps after they landed on the Moon.

"We're going to be in quarantine for at least a month, it will give us something to talk about," he said.

∞ ∞ ∞

Quarantine Facility, Luna

The *Heinlein* and *Chandrasekhar* settled onto the landing pads at the Interstellar Quarantine Facility on the Moon. The crews would be essentially prisoners there for the next month, and their samples would remain there indefinitely. But there was lab space for them to work, and with less than half the expected number of crew returning, plenty of living space too.

Drake made sure the crews were settled in while the medics checked them over. Then he sought out the base security office. He wanted a secure circuit away from anyone else in the facility who might overhear.

∞ ∞ ∞

"You've been a little restrained with the data you downloaded," the officer said. "Keeping secrets?"

"Actually yes. We had some disturbing surprises in the Centauri system. Bottom line is that we're probably not alone, it looks like those planets were deliberately engineered."

"What? Engineered? Do you mean *terraformed*? By who?"

"That we have no idea. There were no signs that we saw, other than the planet and the life on it. But that's not what I came to talk about right now."

"Oh? There's something else?"

"Two things, actually. First, since I exceeded my orders by leaving the *Anderson* and half the crew at Alpha Centauri, I should probably turn myself in to await court martial."

The security officer shrugged. "Fair enough, consider yourself confined to base," he said, and grinned. Nobody was going anywhere for a while anyway. "Besides, if the place *was* terraformed, it sounds like you did the right thing. They all volunteered, right?"

"Of course!"

"Then any court martial will probably exonerate you. So what's the second thing? You mentioned two."

Drake paused, then said: "We have reason to suspect that the *Xīng Huá* wasn't really destroyed in a collision. The data didn't add up. If it wasn't, they probably hightailed it back here and have been reverse-engineering the warp drive. Any signs of that?"

"No, but space is big. If they weren't in near-Earth orbit we might not notice them. For all we know they could be fifty kilometers from here on the Moon. If we weren't looking for them we might not notice."

"You might want to start looking."

"Indeed." The security officer ran a hand through his hair and let out a low whistle. "It would explain a few anomalies, and some of the orders that Chinese companies have been placing, or refusing."

"We'll have to bring them into line. What we found is just too big and, frankly, too scary for Earth not to face with a united front."

"Yeah, but good luck with that."

"I guess it depends what we find at the next star we go out to."

"Let's just hope we don't find the Chinese there first."

Epilog

Near Epsilon Eridani, 10.5 light years from Earth

The Chinese *Dragon*, or *Longzi*, class starships *Xinglong Huā* and *Tianlong Huā* came out of warp well above the plane of Epsilon Eridani's ecliptic. The star had two asteroid belts, as well as a cometary belt twice as large as Sol's Kuiper belt, so it was prudent to take the last steps of the approach carefully. Captain Lee didn't want a repeat of what he'd only faked at Alpha Centauri.

From Earth, telescopic observation had given strong evidence of planets, and hints that one might be life-bearing, but the crowded system made it difficult to be certain from ten light years away. The Chinese mission would find out. The odds were long. Epsilon Eridani was less than a billion years old, and in Earth's history, life had barely gotten started by that point. But *something* showed a hint of blue and a surprising oxygen line in its spectrum.

The *Xinglong* and *Tianlong* moved deeper into the system, observing everything. There it was, well within the inner asteroid belt, at a distance from the star that would put it between Venus and Earth if were orbiting Sol. Since Epsilon Eridani was slightly dimmer than Sol, this put it within the not-too-hot, not-too-cold Goldilocks zone.

The blue planet had a single large moon, and as they approached the planet, telescopic observation showed clouds and continents. It looked startlingly Earth-like, although perhaps with more land and less ocean, it would be dryer, like a larger, partially terraformed Mars. It had sizable ice-caps at the poles.

The ships settled into low orbit around the planet, then sent down a remote drone for close inspection and sampling. The crew watched the monitors as the drone ejected its heat shield and came to flying speed, soaring away under its own power.

"Look there, a group of flying creatures."

"Bring the drone closer," ordered Lee. "Let us get a look."

"They are avoiding the drone, but look," Wu froze a frame and enlarged it. "Two wings, two legs, a beak—"

"—and feathers. Are those *birds*?"

The drone pilot was still watching the live feed, now flying it low over the broad open plain they had targeted as a landing area. A herd of large animals grazed there, disturbingly familiar looking animals, with shaggy hair or fur. "I do not know about birds, but those," he pointed to the screen, "could be cousins to elephants."

∞

END BOOK I

The story continues in Book II, *Alpha Centauri: Sawyer's World*
Available late May 2017

Glossary

Alcubierre[*]: Miguel Alcubierre derived a series of equations consistent with Relativity which describe warping of space in a way which permits Faster-Than-Light travel. Several others have built on Alcubierre's work, showing lower-energy ways to achieve a warp bubble (q.v.)

ANT scan[*]: Anti-Neutrino Tomography scan. Analogous to a CAT (computerized axial tomography) scan in current medical use, except on a planetary scale and using anti-neutrinos instead of x-rays. Neutrino tomogrophy in real life is a budding field in the geosciences, but it uses solar neutrinos or those emitted from natural nuclear decay deep within the Earth. Neutrino detectors have also been considered for identifying nuclear reactors which may be generating weapons-grade fissionables.

EECOM[*]: Electrical, Environmental, and Consumables Management (EECOM) Monitors electrical power sources (batteries, fuel cells), and electrical distribution systems; cabin pressure control systems; and vehicle lighting systems. atmospheric pressure control and revitalization (O2/N2/CO2 management) systems, the cabin cooling systems (air, water, and refrigerant loop), and the supply/waste water system.

EECOM's critical function is to maintain the systems, such as atmosphere and thermal control, that keep the crew alive. (From Apollo/Shuttle terminology)

FIDO[*]: Flight Dynamics Operations. Responsible for the flight path of the space vehicle, both atmospheric and orbital. The

FDO monitors vehicle performance during the powered flight phase and assesses abort modes, calculates orbital maneuvers and resulting trajectories, and monitors vehicle flight profile and energy levels during re-entry. (From Apollo/Shuttle terminology.)

Finazzi instability*: In 2009, Stefano Finazzi, Stefano Liberati, and Carlos Barceló applied a quantum analysis to the Alcubierre warp metric and deduced that quantum fluctuations could destabilize the warp. The term "Finazzi instability" is mine, from the first-listed author.

Interstellar Quarantine Facility: A base on the moon to receive returning planetary and interstellar missions to prevent any contamination of Earth by extraterrestrial organisms. Something like Michael Crichton *The Andromeda Strain*'s "Wildfire" facility but on the moon, and with more accommodation for returning humans. Based loosely on the Lunar Receiving Laboratory of the Apollo era.

omni: Short for omniphone - compares to today's smartphones as smartphones compare to walky-talkies. (Search for "Nokia Morph" on YouTube for a nearly-there concept video.)

omniphone: See omni.

parsec*: A distance of approximately 3.26 light-years.

SSTO*: Single Stage To Orbit. A concept (with a variety of possible implementations) for highly reusable spacecraft which can launch from a planet (Earth) to orbit, and return to a safe landing, using a single stage (thus requiring as little as just refueling to launch again). As of this writing, no practical SSTOs have been build (it is just within the limit of technical feasibility) although several examples (Atlas, the Shuttle External Tank with 6 Shuttle Main Engines) come close. See the work of, in particular, Phil Bono and later, Gary Hudson. More recently Elon Musk's SpaceX and Jeff Bezos's Blue Origin are getting closer with their reusable launch vehicles, but aren't there yet.

Terraforming*: The hypothetical practice of engineering a planet, possibly including giving it a biosphere, to be more Earth-like. This could range from thickening Mars's atmosphere to (at a much more technologically advanced scale) changing the crust of a planet and/or modifying its rotation rate to make it long-term stable (as would need to be done, for example, to terraform Venus).

Unholy War: A nuclear war which took place in the early part of the 21st century, involving primarily the smaller nuclear powers, purportedly for religious reasons.

Warp bubble*: The thin shell of highly curved space that surrounds a ship in FTL flight. Based on Van Den Broek's lower-energy configuration of an Alcubierre warp metric.

* Items marked with an asterisk are non-fictional, at least in a theoretical or hypothetical sense, in 2016. The others may or may not be in the future.

Acknowledgments

Several of the scenes here, in particular the early landing phase, were inspired by commentary and illustrations in Duncan Lunan's book *Man and the Stars* (Souvenir Press, 1974), with illustrations by Ed Buckley. In particular, the use of aerospike SSTO landing vehicles. See Philip Bono and Kenneth Gatland's *Frontiers of Space* (1970) for more on the concept, although my landers were more inspired by Gary Hudson's Phoenix-C and Phoenix-E from Pacific-American Launch Systems circa 1980.

I received valuable feedback on early drafts of this book from a number of fellow writers, including Lou, Danielle, Miranda, RGW, and Jill. Of course any omissions, errors, boring bits, or other screw-ups are entirely my fault. Well, and the computer's, of course.

Thanks to my kids, Selena, Robert and Arthur for tolerating their father's idiosyncrasies during the too-long writing of this novel, and to the many readers of my earlier T-Space works who nagged me to get this finished (hi Jason).

My son Robert, currently working toward a degree in paleontology, provided useful insights into which flora and fauna may have arisen before the KT extinction and survived, and those that evolved far too late to be ancestral to any extraterrestrial T-space denizens.

And while I discovered them late in the writing of this novel, Dr. Martin Beech's non-fiction books *Terraforming: The Creating of Habitable Worlds*, and *Alpha Centauri: Unveiling the Secrets of Our Nearest Stellar Neighbor*, both from Springer (2009 and 2015 respectively), made for fascinating reading with useful insights.

Preview: *Alpha Centauri: Sawyer's World*

The following excerpt is from the upcoming *Alpha Centauri: Sawyer's World,* set immediately after the events of this book. It is still a work in progress, so some details may change.

Chapter 1: Landing

USS Anderson, above Planet Able

Aboard the *Anderson,* Captain Sawyer throttled back the engines to idle as they began their drop through the atmosphere. The black sky out the window lightened to a deep indigo blue as the air grew thicker, then brightened with pink and orange streaks as the energy of the ship's near-orbital speed heated it to plasma.

Sawyer felt herself pushed into her seat with the increasing gee force. She scanned the instruments and reported back to the Heinlein. "On descent track, everything looks nominal."

"Roger that. You are GO for landing."

"Like we have a choice?" Sawyer replied, amused. They didn't have the fuel to abort now. "Roger GO."

The orange glow faded as they descended through the stratosphere, the ship shuddering at odd intervals as the upper winds buffeted them. Sawyer felt as much as heard the turbo-pumps spool up as the engines began increase their throttle, readying to apply braking thrust for landing as they backed towards the ground.

"I've got visual on the landing zone," Finley, flying copilot, said. "Looks like we're tracking a kilometer east, we've got some winds."

"Okay." Sawyer tweaked the throttles and adjusted the attitude to bring them back to track. They were headed for the edge of a broad plain—no river valleys after what had almost happened to the *Chandra*—and were worried enough about herds of large animals that they didn't want to land in the middle of it.

∞ ∞ ∞

Sensors in the *Anderson's* landing gear lit a panel light as soon as one of them touched the ground.

"Contact light," called Finley."

"Okay, engines off, pumps off, auxiliary to detent."

"Check."

Sawyer keyed her microphone. "*Heinlein*, Sawyer here. The *Anderson* has landed."

"Good to hear from you."

"Touchdown was real smooth. A little bit of crosswind at altitude but nothing to worry about."

"Roger that. Very good, Anderson." The voice from *Heinlein* became more serious. *"Obviously there's no immediate return option, but you still need to follow protocol."*

"No worries, *Heinlein*. The biologists are already checking the atmosphere. They're about ready to deploy a canary—odd name for a white mouse—shortly. We'll be in BIGs—" biological isolation garments "—for the next forty eight hours. Check that, fifty-two hours, we'll have longer days here."

"Roger that, Anderson. Give us a status update when you have something or in two hours, whichever is first."

Sawyer checked the mission clock and keyed in a reminder. "You've got it, *Heinlein*. *Anderson* is listening out." Sawyer clicked off the microphone and turned to the rest of the crew.

"All right, people. I want preliminary atmosphere readings, chemical and biological, in a half-hour. If it all checks out, Ulrika Klaar and Roger Dejois," the zoologist and the ecologist, all both had broad ranges of experience, "will suit up in BIGs for initial survey. Let's see how much we can give them in two hours."

Chapter Two

Anderson landing site

"All right," Sawyer said, after the initial team had returned, "our top two priorities are: One, researching the planet and its life in general, to determine if, as seems likely, this planet was also terraformed. If so, then also anything we can about the Terraformers. Two, making sure we can survive here indefinitely, and setting up whatever we need to do that. I'd give that latter our highest priority but researching this planet feeds directly into that. Everyone with me so far?"

There were general nods and mumbles of agreement.

"Okay. Dr. Singh, you're the botanist, I want you to do a survey with an eye to both plants that we can eat and of those, which could be easily cultivated."

"Cultivated?" Naomi Maclaren, the engineer, interrupted, "You think we'll be here long enough that we have to become farmers?"

"Would you rather have it the other way? What if we're still here come winter with no food left? Better to be prepared."

"Plants are a lot more likely to contain toxins than animals," Jennifer Singh said. "Most mammals and birds on Earth are edible. If life here is descended from that, the way life on Kakuloa seems to be, shouldn't we focus on finding food animals?"

"We'll do both, of course. If life here *isn't* Earth-descended then plants may be a better option." Sawyer was reasonably sure that even in the worst case, they could rig up some kind of fermenters and digesters to process plant material down to basic sugars, oils and amino acids, but they were already sure from spectrographic analysis and the data returned by the drones that the vegetation was biochemically almost identical to Earth's, and to Kakuloa's.

"Right," said Jennifer.

"Dr. Klaar, start on an animal survey to similar ends. Including bugs, if it comes to that." Sawyer ignored the wrinkled noses of a couple of team members.

"Sure. I also want to check for any venomous or stinging animals or insects."

"Good point. Folks, assume any animal is poisonous—"

"Venomous!" Ulrika Klaar said.

Sawyer glared at her. She knew the difference. "—poisonous or venomous until further notice. Don't eat it, and don't let it bite you." She looked around the cabin.

"Okay," she continued. "so much for food. Next, shelter. We've got a roll of solar film we can use for power. We do want the aircraft running and we'll want to keep some film in reserve, but we can set up enough to run instruments and communications. At some point soon I'd like to move the cooking to regular fire. We can shelter in the ship for now, but we're going to want more space before long. We have tents like we used for additional working space on Kakuloa, but we might want something more secure if we're sleeping there. Also, I'd rather not wear out the ship's plumbing." She looked around. "Finley."

"Yes?"

"You have extensive field experience, you're in charge of setting up a field latrine. Check with the biologists about concerns that any of our intestinal bacteria don't set off a plague that kills everything else on the planet. And no," she said, holding up a hand, "I know that's extremely unlikely."

"Anyone else with camping experience, help Finley or investigate what we can use to set up shelters other than the ship. Coordinate with me. The rest of you—think about everything you've ever read about surviving in the wilderness, any wilderness, fact or fiction. If you've read *Swiss Family Robinson*, or *Mysterious Island*, or *Tunnel In the Sky*, then write down everything you remember about survival techniques. If it's something we have in the ship's database or library, that's great, make a note." Sawyer was sure that all that and more was in the ships computers, the required storage would be tiny, and survival manuals of all kinds would be a logical inclusion. What she *really* wanted was the team to focus on what might important to survival if they weren't picked up within a few months. Best to plan ahead. Sawyer thought for a moment. What else? "Finley?"

"Yes?"

"When you're done with the latrines and are ready to start your geology surveys, think about potentially useful mineral deposits. We can probably come up with some plastics for the fabber from organic matter, and maybe some ceramics that will work, but our supply of metals is limited."

"Right. Tyrell can get started on that from the orbital survey data, that should point us at interesting places to look."

"Good. But let's focus on what's nearby. We don't want to have to mount a major expedition to find a bit of copper, and I'm sure Tyrell doesn't want to face another hundred-mile hike if the plane crashes."

Tyrell blushed, and then said "Well, maybe if Ulrika was along." She and Tyrell had faced just such a hike when a double bird strike had broken their prop back on Kakuloa. Tyrell had been the pilot.

"Okay. That's all I have for the moment. Anyone else? Questions? Comments? Rude remarks?"

∞ ∞ ∞

"This is your lucky day, Dejois," said Finley. "I'm going to show you how to dig a latrine."

"*Très drôle.* You know there was a reason I never joined the Scouts or the Armed Forces. I have an allergy to digging latrines."

"Oh, come on, at this stage it's just a trench. It's covering them up later that's the fun part."

"Strange sense of fun. But where are we going to dig? The landing area is a pretty thin layer of soil over solid rock. I don't want to be hiking a mile or two just to go to the bathroom."

"Heh, you haven't seen how I dig. Here, hold this." Finley handed a bulky piece of equipment to Dejois, then opened another storage locker and began pulling out metal tubes.

"Okay, this is the drill, *n'est-ce pas*? What are you going to do, just drill a bunch of adjacent holes?"

"'We', what are we going to do. And no, we only need a few

holes. Now we need one of the charcoal filter canisters. There should be a used one."

"From the life support system?"

"Yeah. I'll also need something to carry liquid oxygen. A Dewar if the biology lab has one, or just any kind of well-insulated bucket or container. It won't need to stay cold very long."

"Charcoal and LOX? You're going to dig a latrine with *explosives?*"

"A time-honored tradition in the military. The seismic charges would be easier but I want to hold onto those. The little bit of LOX left in the fuel tanks will evaporate in a couple of weeks anyway, so we might as well get some use out of it."

"Very well then. You're getting to quite like that stuff, aren't you."

"It's the only reason we're not stranded on Kakuloa, after that landslide caused our landing area to flood. And you just sitting in orbit twiddling your thumbs."

"Hey, we did warn you the storm was coming. There wasn't much else we could do."

"No worries, I know that."

They'd moved through the ship as they talked, collecting the gear they needed.

"Okay. I'll get Sawyer to help me tap off some LOX, you take the gear out to the site I've picked." Finley gestured towards a clear area about seventy-five meters from the ship, away from any vegetation but some short stubby growth.

"That's a bit exposed, isn't it?"

"You shy? No, don't worry, after the pit is dug we'll put up a privacy screen."

"Oh, of course."

Twenty minutes later Finley was leaning into the drill, digging out another borehole in the line he'd scratched for the latrine.

They finished drilling out the blast holes and began placing the charges.

"Okay, watch this stuff. After the LOX and charcoal are mixed it's sensitive. Be gentle with it."

"Like a mother with a baby," Dejois said. "Are you sure we're not too close to the ship? I would hate for a rock to hit it, we may yet need it to get out of here."

Finley looked up, surprised. He looked down at the drill holes then back to the ship. Was it far enough? He shook his head. "We should be good, I doubt we'll get debris more than a third of the way there. Halfway, tops." At least, he hoped not. "What was that about needing it to get out of here? You don't think they'd send another lander?"

"The quickest way to retrieve us would be to load up the *Heinlein* with another propellant synthesis unit and send it back here, then land that and we refuel, *non?*. If the *Anderson* is damaged that wouldn't do us any good."

"That's a good point. I was just assuming we were stuck until they sent another lander. Stupid of me." He looked at how he'd laid out the charges. If the ones furthest from the ship detonated a few milliseconds before the nearer ones, then the later ones to blow would have solid rock on one side and fractured rock on the other, and the blast would tend to push the fractured rock away from the ship. But this charcoal and LOX explosive was improvised, not calibrated the way their seismic charges and detonators were.

"Let's change this around a little bit. We'll just run the det cord to the far side blast holes. The shock-wave will detonate the nearside explosives."

"Are you certain of that?"

Finley thought back on the emergency demolition they'd done to dig a trench in the landslide which had blocked the river valley downstream of the Chandra's landing site. The rising water in the torrential rain had threatened to flood out the Chandra's engines and clog the injectors with silt. They'd used a mix of seismic charges and charcoal there, but it had worked fine, cutting a nice channel across the dam to let the water begin draining. But yes, they had relied on the shock-waves from the seismic charges to detonate the charcoal.

"Yes," he said, "it'll work. No problem."

They unreeled the detonator wires to a good safe distance—in fact back almost to the Anderson. Finley checked in with Sawyer.

"Is everybody clear of the area?"

"Yes, everyone's accounted for, go for it."

Finley cupped his hands and yelled at the empty field. "Warning, blasting! Warning!" There was no response, nor had she expected any. This was just a standard precaution.

He gripped the detonator and thumbed off the safety switch. "Fire in the hole! In three! Two! One!" Finley pressed the fire button. He felt the shock through the ground almost at the same time the plume of rock and dirt geysered into the air, and a split second later he heard the *BANG!* of the detonation. He watched as the dust and rock soared up and then started to settle out, mostly away from the ship. Then his gaze caught one rock that had climbed almost straight up and was just reaching apogee, and if anything was curving back towards them. Oh, crap! Finley watched, horrified, as it turned lazily while plummeting towards them. It would fall short, good. The rock slammed into the ground forty meters from the ship and then bounced, leaping back up at about a forty degree angle, still towards the ship. There wasn't anything Finley or anyone else could do as they watched the boulder hit the ground and bounce again, like a slow motion train wreck, heading towards the *Anderson*. Finally, after what seemed like hours, it stopped bouncing and rolled to a stop less than a meter from one of the landing pads. Finley exhaled a held breath. "And that," he said, referring to the small boulder near the foot of the lander, "is what we geologists call an erratic."

"'Halfway, tops' I think you said?" Dejois looked at him with a raised eyebrow.

Finley looked out to where the dust was settling out around the pit. "You saw it. It hit the ground no more than halfway from here to there. It took a bad bounce. I didn't say anything about bounces."

Sawyer, who had been observing all this from nearby, said: "Finley, no more bad bounces, okay? Or I'll bounce you."

"Uh, right," Finley replied, chagrined. He turned back to Dejois. "Let's go check out the pit. If we're lucky most of the debris blew out of the hole and we just need to do a bit of cleanup."

It had. There was still loose rubble in the bottom of the trench they'd blasted, but a half-hour with a shovel cleaned most of that out. They used some of the larger boulders to build a low wall around the pit. To the west was a small stand of trees. They'd rig up some kind of privacy screen on poles, and cut and trim some trunks or thick branches to serve as a seat. Excavating the trench had been the easy part, now came the hard work.

∞ ∞ ∞

The story continues in Alpha Centauri: Sawyer's World *coming in May 2017.*

About the Author

ALASTAIR MAYER was born in London, England, and moved to Canada with his family as a young boy. He describes his interest in space flight and science fiction as genetic: his father, Douglas W.F. Mayer, had been an early member of the British Interplanetary Society as well as a science fiction fan (who in fact published some of Arthur C. Clarke's first tales in *Amateur Science Stories*).

After attending school in Canada, Alastair became involved in both the L5 Society (now the National Space Society) and computers, publishing articles in *Byte*, *Final Frontier*, and other magazines, as well as becoming an accomplished scuba diver and a private pilot. In 1989 he moved to Colorado, where he still lives, and where he works for a satellite network company.

His short stories have been published in several anthologies and his work has appeared often enough in *Analog Science Fiction* magazine to gain him entry to the "Analog MAFIA" (Members Appear Frequently In *Analog*). Many of his short works can be found in e-book format on Amazon, Barnes & Noble, Smashwords, and other e-book vendor sites.

Alpha Centauri: First Landing is his third novel, the first of a two-part prequel to *The Chara Talisman* and the other T-Space stories. He is currently working on both *Alpha Centauri: Sawyer's World* and *The Eridani Convergence*, a sequel to *The Chara Talisman* and *The Reticuli Deception*.

Visit his web site at *www.alastairmayer.org*.

Other books by Alastair Mayer

Mabash Books trade paper editions are available from Amazon or order through your favorite bookseller:

The T-Space™ series:

- *Alpha Centauri: First Landing*   ISBN 978-153913229-5
- *Alpha Centauri: Sawyer's World* (forthcoming in 2017)
- *The Chara Talisman*   ISBN 978-061556623-8
- *The Reticuli Deception*   ISBN 978-061571102-7
- *The Eridani Convergence*   (forthcoming in 2017)

Ebook editions are available for most e-readers through Amazon, B&N, Apple, Smashwords and others:

The T-Space™ series:

Novels

- *The Chara Talisman*
- *The Reticuli Deception*
- *(others available simultaneously with print editions)*

Short novels and stories

- *Stone Age* (contained in The Chara Talisman)

Jason Curtis adventures:
- *Into the Fire*
- *Renee (and the Space Raiders)*

Other stories:

- *Snowball* (also appears in Footprints, Hadley Rille Books)
- *Poetic Justice* (also appears in Space Horrors, Flying Pen Press)

Collections:

- *Starfire & Snowball*,   including:
    Into the Fire
    Snowball
    Renee
    The Gremlin Gambit

Printed in Great Britain
by Amazon